FIVE YEARS LATER

GRACE E SUMMERS

If you didn't have tears,
you wouldn't have a heart.

...Matthew

Chapter 1: October

It's been five years, and I still can't remember what happened. It's only a matter of minutes that are missing, if that. The memory is there, hiding somewhere in my subconscious. There are days I want to remember and then there are days I'm grateful I don't. Gloria, my therapist, tells me I'll remember those few minutes when I can handle it. How is that possible when I can't cope with what I do remember? Why can't I just live my life without the past being my shadow and haunting me? Why am I sixteen again?

"Dad, what…what happened?"
When I came to after the blackout, it was like I had awoken from the deepest sleep of my life. My head was in a fog.
"It's going to be okay."
Still disoriented, I had no idea what Dad meant when he said that. Was I late for school? Had I dropped something and broken it? I didn't even know what day it was or why I was in the kitchen. The fog in my head cleared within seconds. That's when I found out what had happened. Mom was lying on the floor with a knife in her chest. It scared me so much, I screamed and cried at the same time.
Dad grabbed my arms to steady me, being the wobbly mess I was. *"Carlen, listen to me. The police are on their way. When they get here, don't say a word."*
Like I could speak coherently staring at my mother's lifeless body.
Dad yelled at me for the first time in my life. *"Carlen, did you hear me?"*
It scared me even more, if that was possible. My wide eyes went to his. I don't know how I even spoke. *"Um, okay, Dad. I won't say anything."*
Sirens blared like they were coming from every

1

street in the neighborhood. Unlike me, Dad was calm and in control. He quickly walked me out of the kitchen.

"They're coming. Now, remember what I told you. Don't say a word. Let me talk to the police and tell them what happened."

By the time we were in the living room and Dad sat me on the couch, the sirens were silent. Within seconds, someone pounded on the door.

"Carlen?"

Gloria's voice pulls me out of the memory and back to the present. Our chairs face each other with our knees only feet apart. Sometimes I don't feel anything when I remember the day someone murdered my mother, but this isn't one of them.

I look at Gloria and hope she didn't notice I slipped back to that day. "I'm sorry. What was that?"

She always smiles so sweetly. "I asked if you are still having those nightmares. You haven't mentioned them lately."

It takes a moment to answer. Thinking about my past sucks the energy out of me, so I'm drained. "Sometimes," I finally tell her just to be saying something. To break the silence. Also, to stay in the moment and not go back in time. "Guess you can't escape your past, can you?" My tone comes across between sarcastic and comical, but Gloria knows I'm not laughing.

"No." She smiles with understanding and shakes her head. "Unfortunately, you can't. What happened to your mother was horrible."

"Yeah, it was," I mumble and look away. In the silence, I slip back into that moment. A terrified sixteen-year-old sitting on the couch while her dad tells the police someone broke into their home and stabbed her mother. As the memory intensifies, raw emotions flare up. The ones I don't want to feel, because I can't handle them.

"And I'm sure the person never being caught adds to the trauma."

Enough, I scream in my head. My eyes dart to Gloria, begging her not to say anything else about that day.

"I know it's hard, but coming here and talking about it can help you cope. It will get easier in time."

Therapy mumbo-jumbo. What does Gloria know about

2

coping with what I've been through? From the pictures on her desk, she's had a good life. A beautiful family, hugging and smiling. Grandkids. A home at the beach. And with the degrees hanging on her wall, she's productive in life, unlike me, who will never go anywhere because I'm stuck in my past. Why am I even here? Why do I keep coming back? I've been in counseling for six months, and my life is still in the ditch.

"Carlen, are you okay?"

"Sometimes I think…" I wave my hand like a maestro and sing, "This is my life. The depression. Being antisocial. Having panic attacks. It's who I am. A prisoner of my past, and there's no key to unlock this cage I'm in."

Gloria sits back, rests her elbows on the arms of the chair and exhales, giving me her disappointed glare. "Carlen, that's a choice, not your destiny."

Here we go again. I roll my eyes and look out the office window at the view of the mountains. The leaves have changed to a burnt orange, a fiery red, and lemon yellow. The fall colors are beautiful. Weird how something is only eye-catching when it dies.

"Carlen? What's going through your mind?"

I lean my head back and exhale. "I'm only twenty-one and tired of fighting my way to survive in a world I don't understand, because I'm screwed up." The emotions buried deep inside of me want to surface, but I won't let them. They control me enough as it is. "No one is ever going to love me. I'm damaged goods. I have nothing to account for my miserable life except a high school diploma. I didn't go to college because…" I laugh at myself. "Me, go to college? Now *that's* funny."

Gloria toys with her long necklace. "Let's pretend you want to go to college. What would you study? What would you like to do with your life?"

"Well…" Suddenly, I'm smiling at a silly notion. "There is something I would *love* to do. Remember me telling you how much fun I had decorating my room when I moved in with Stacy?"

Gloria smiles and nods. "Yes, I do. We spent a whole session talking about it."

"If I could…" I pause and let my imagination run wild. "My dream is to have my own business and decorate homes for people. I'd have a logo on my car and business cards."

"Oh, Carlen." She smiles wider, adjusting her glasses. "That's a wonderful vision. What's stopping you from going after that dream?"

Her question steals my smile. "Money, for starters. And having my own business seems like a mountain too high for me to climb."

"There's that negative thinking," she singsongs. "A negative mind frame never leads to anything positive. We've talked about this."

Gloria scolds me like Grandma Dupre would if she were here. And she reminds me of her in many ways. Not because she's a grandma as well, but it's her old fashion mannerisms.

The timer on her desk chimes.

"Already? Lord have mercy, where does the time go?" Gloria reaches behind her on the desk and silences it. "I know we have to stop, but are you going to be okay?"

"Yep." I get to my feet and button my coat. "I've got to be at work in an hour, so that'll keep me busy and my mind occupied."

"Okay, then." Gloria heads to the door and opens it for me. "Same time next week?"

"Unless I win the lottery." I laugh and walk out of her office.

~ ~ ~

An older couple shuffles my way. Per company policy, I smile and greet them. "Hello. Can I help you with something?"

The woman raises her shaky hand. "Can you tell us where the restrooms are?"

"Of course." I point to my left. "Go down three rows and turn right. They're at the end of that aisle."

She pats the arm of the older gentleman with her. "Let's hurry, Ralph, or I ain't gonna make it."

He motions with his hand. "After you, dear."

"Lord, all I need is to have an accident here in the store," she mumbles and scurries away.

I continue on and pass the lumber aisle, taking in the smell of cut wood.

Matthew darts out of the hardware aisle, always hyper and happy. "Hey, Carlen. Working hard?"

"Me?" I frown, still walking. "Always."

"Assistance needed in the appliances," Shannon announces in my handheld pager.

"On my way," I respond and pick up my pace.

A cute man waits at my desk. He really is cute with jet-black hair combed back, a spiky five o'clock shadow, and muscular arms I'd like to squeeze. *Down Carlen.* My negativity is quick to warn me this adorable-looking man is too perfect for me.

"Hi. Can I help you with something?"

When he turns my way and those warm brown eyes meet mine, my heart can't keep a straight rhythm.

A soft smile quickly appears. "Yes. My fridge is about to go out on me, and I need to buy a new one."

Holy cow. He has the most gentle and coaxing voice. I could listen to him talk all day. And I'm probably staring like some boy-crazy teenager.

"Are you looking for anything in particular?"

"Something nice that will last a long time."

"Would you like for me to show you what we have?"

"Yes, please."

"Follow me." I hold my breath and lead the way.

Mr. Handsome walking next to me causes goosebumps to run up my arms. That's never happened before. My hands, inside my orange apron, become sweaty. Something is going on in my stomach, and it's not hunger cravings.

"You guys deliver, right?"

"We sure do." I point to the row of refrigerators and come to a stop. "Here are the upscale models. We have three-door with bottom freezer. Side-by-side. We have them in white, black, almond, and stainless steel." I side-eye the perfect man next to me. "Anything catch your fancy?"

He scratches his jaw while looking at them. "Yeah, that stainless steel. The third one."

"Let's go look at it." Once there, I open the doors but can't remember my sales pitch. Thankfully, he's focused on the refrigerator.

"Wow, I like this. A lot." After giving it a full glance-over and pulling out the crisper drawers, he looks at me. "It's probably more than I should spend, but I might have to buy it. I swore my next one would have an ice maker on the door." His eyes go to my chest and then back to mine. "Carlen? That's a pretty name."

I instinctually cover my name written on my work apron, and I'm probably blushing, because my cheeks feel warm. "Thanks. Dad named me after my grandma." What a lame comment. Like he cares.

He closes the doors on the fridge. "Have you been working here long?"

"Almost two years."

"Really?" He squints one eye. "Can't believe I haven't seen you in here before."

I shrug and try not to sound girlish. "Well, I've been here."

"You have a Southern accent. Where are you from?"

"Charlotte."

He raises his eyebrows. "Oh, the Queen City," he sings with vigor.

"That's the one," I sing back.

"Do you like it here?"

"How can you not love the North Carolina mountains?"

"Is that what lured you to Hendersonville?"

We're not talking about refrigerators. Is he flirting with me? If he is, I don't mind.

"No. Just looking to start a new life away from the big city."

"Did you find it?"

"Um…" I rock my head back and forth. "Guess you can say that."

"*Brad.*" A feisty girl marches toward him, giving him the look of death. When she comes to a stop in front of us, she crosses her arms. "I've been looking *everywhere* for you. We need to go."

He raises his hands in defense, no longer smiling. "Chill. I was just looking at the refrigerators."

Her eyes dart to mine, and she looks me over. "Yeah, I can see that."

Mr. Handsome has a girlfriend? My stomach feels like it's been kicked by a horse. I was foolish to think he was interested in me when he has a tall, sexy girlfriend in skinny jeans with beautiful auburn hair.

"You can look at refrigerators another day." Before he can say anything, Ms. Feisty takes his wrist and drags him up the aisle like a child who wandered away from his mother.

This is why I'm negative, Gloria. I was fool enough to believe this guy liked me.

My phone vibrates.

I reach for it in the pocket of my work apron.

It's a message from Stacy. *Hey, won't be home tonight. You have the apartment all to yourself.*

6

My roommate has a new boyfriend. I should be happy for her, but I don't want to be home alone after having a therapy session, especially one that makes me think about Mom. But I wish her a good time.

Have fun.

Pulled into a gloomy moment, I stroll along the kitchen aisle and look at the cabinets and countertops. My thoughts drift to what I told Gloria. If I won the lottery, I would start my own business and decorate homes. Like a puzzle, I would put a kitchen or living room together, piece by piece until I had an amazing picture. But I'll never win the lottery or have my own business.

"It's not negativity, Gloria," I mumble under my breath and trail my fingertips across a granite counter. "It's called…being realistic."

~ ~ ~

After work, my night consists of a sandwich for supper and a movie for entertainment. Story of my life. Gloria tells me I should get out of the apartment and make friends. Antisocial me? Have friends? Yeah, right. I surf the channels and start on my sandwich, eating and punching the button. I stop at a movie. It's a cheesy comedy, but it has my attention, so I lower the remote. If it makes me laugh, it's a winner.

Thirty minutes later, I'm slouched out on the couch and laughing at the main character. Poor girl has worse luck than I do, but she's able to laugh it off.

My phone pings.

I read Matthew's message.

Want some company? I'm bored.

Sure, come on over.

Since Matthew lives in the same apartment complex, he'll be over in a few minutes. I pause the movie and head to the kitchen for a snack. Ice cream is tempting, but it's a cold night. I ran out of my favorite cookies, but there's a bag of popcorn.

The doorbell rings.

I take the bowl of popcorn, head to the living room and open the door. "Just so you know, it's boring here too."

He grins, always so positive. "Then we can be bored together."

I nod for him to enter. "Finish watching this movie with me."

"I accept your invitation." He enters. "What's the movie about?"

After shutting the door, I head to the couch. "Comedy. This girl gets dumped, and her best friend dares her to date someone who turns out to be the ex-boyfriend's cousin."

"Boring." He sits on the couch next to me. After resting his feet on the coffee table, he reaches into the bowl and grabs a handful of popcorn. "Can we *please* watch something else?"

"Here." I offer him the remote.

"Now, for a real movie."

Matthew surfs the channels and stops at a murder mystery. It's sure to trigger my past. I can't watch movies like this, but I don't know how to tell him to keep scrolling. Matthew doesn't know about my mom's murder. It takes ten minutes to work up the courage to ask him to turn it, but in that time, I'm not triggered. In fact, it's got my attention. Perhaps because I know who the killer is.

"It's the husband," I whisper, my eyes on the dark shadow that appears in the hallway.

"No, it's the neighbor."

Matthew and I are sucked into the movie. The lights are off, creating a spooky ambiance with the fast, high-pitched musical score turning climactic, about to reveal the killer opening the door.

Staring wide-eyed, goosebumps travel up my arms and across my neck. I swallow hard, anticipating the killer. It zooms in to his black boots and then pans up his legs.

Matthew turns to me in one swift move and roars, "Boo!"

I spread eagle and scream, kicking the bowl off the coffee table.

Matthew doubles over from laughing so hard.

"I *hate* when you do that." After grabbing the first thing I can get my hands on, the couch pillow, I pound his shoulder.

While holding up his arms, defending himself, Matthew continues to laugh. "Stop so we can see who it was."

How dare I miss the moment. When I look at the television, the detectives have the killer handcuffed. "See, I told you it was the husband."

"No way. I thought for sure it was the neighbor."

I tuck the pillow back in its place against the arm of the couch. "Come on, Matthew. It's never the one they want you to think it is."

"True." He reaches for the bowl and picks up the popcorn kernels. "Thanks for letting me come over and watch it."

I yawn. "No problem."

Matthew sets the bowl on the coffee table. "Guess that's my cue to go home."

"Yeah, I think it's my bedtime."

Instead of getting up to leave, he stares at me. "Can I ask you something?"

I press the button on the remote to turn the television off. "Depends on what it is."

"We've been friends for four months, but I don't know anything about you."

"What do you want to know?"

He jerks his head to shift the long bangs away from his eyes. "You never talk about your friends or family. I know more about your roommate than I do you, and I work with you."

"Is there a question in there somewhere?"

He playfully nudges my elbow. "Seriously. What's your story?"

"Well…" I take in a deep breath, pondering a short version of my life. Something to hopefully douse his curiosity. "I met Stacy about five years ago. She drove to Charlotte to meet her online boyfriend who happened to be my neighbor. We got to know each other. They eventually broke up, but we stayed friends. Sometimes she would come to Charlotte and visit, and sometimes I would drive to Hendersonville. When I graduated high school, she offered to let me rent a room from her, so I moved here."

"What about your family?"

Because I really like Matthew and trust him, I'll share that with him. "In a nutshell…I'm an only child. My mother died when I was sixteen. My dad still lives in the house I grew up in. The only grandparents I had died when I was young. I have a few aunts and uncles, but that's it."

"No ex-boyfriends?"

His question sends me back in time. Terry and I were high school sweethearts. He was tall and skinny and always wore a hoodie because he had big ears. I still don't know why he broke up with me. As for my recent ex-boyfriend, I don't want to think about Andy. It still hurts.

"I have two ex-boyfriends. Why?"

Sitting sideways on the couch, he rests his elbow on the back and leans his head into his palm. "Just wondering. I figured someone broke your heart, and that's why you're not dating anyone."

"Who would want to date someone like me?" I reach for a lock of hair and toy with it. "Guys go for girls who wear makeup and dress pretty."

Matthew pops my arm. "Why do you put yourself down? You *are* pretty. Okay, so you're a simple-kind-of-girl. There's nothing wrong with that."

If he only knew how broken I was inside. But that's why we're such good friends. We seem to like and accept each other without knowing each other. I never share who the real Carlen is, fearing people will walk away from me. It took a long time to confide in Stacy. She's the only person who really knows me…and my secrets. Some of them, anyway. And it's time to change the subject to Matthew. "How come you're not dating anyone?"

"Too shy to ask someone out."

"I think that new girl likes you. Maybe you should ask her out."

"Who?"

"Shannon."

He shakes his head. "She's not my type. Too hyper for me."

"Life sucks. There was this *really* cute guy who wanted to look at refrigerators. I mean, he…was…gorgeous. And I swear he was flirting with me. Then his girlfriend shows up."

"What an asshole."

"Yeah, but he was a handsome asshole." A yawn slips out.

Matthew taps my knee. "On that note, I'm outta here."

We get to our feet at the same time and amble to the door. "Are you working tomorrow?"

I open the door for him and yawn again. "No, I'm off."

"Then I guess I won't see you at the store tomorrow."

"Nope. Don't work too hard."

"They don't pay me enough to do that." He chuckles and walks out. "See you later."

"Bye."

I close the door, lock up, and call it a night.

Chapter 2: Triggers

Sometimes it's hard to call him, fearing the past is going to suck me in. I stare at my phone, working up the courage. The anxiety already has my heart going faster than it should. Regardless, I swipe Dad's number.

"Carlen, hey, sweetie. I was just thinking about you. How's my girl doing?"

His voice immediately washes away the anxiety, and all is right in my world. "Good. I've got to get ready for work but had you on my mind and wanted to see how you're doing."

"Oh, you know me. When I'm not out in the yard doing something, I'm watching westerns. It's been cold this week, so I haven't been able to do anything outside. I'm sure it's colder in the mountains."

"It is, but I've gotten used to the winters here. And it's really pretty when it snows."

"The weatherman said we might get a big one this year."

I laugh at the thought of Charlotte getting a big snow. "What, a whole inch?"

"I miss that laughter."

"And I miss my dad."

"Why don't you come and see him?"

Listening to his voice, it would be easy to hang up, get in my car and drive to Charlotte right now. It's the memories of what happened in that house that keep me planted on the stool.

"Carlen, I know it's hard to come here, but don't let the past keep you away."

"I'm trying not to."

"Then come and see me."

"Are you off Thursday? I could come then."

"As a matter of fact, I am."

"Then maybe I should take a drive to Charlotte."

"I think you should."

Stacy sprints into the kitchen, still in her pajamas and her hair in a messy ponytail. "Have you seen my phone?"

I hold up my finger, gesturing her to give me a minute. "Dad, um, I hate to cut this short, but I need to go so I can get ready for work. I'll see you Thursday."

"I can't wait. Want me to cook your favorite since it's cold?"

"You know the answer to that," I sing, eager for his homemade chili.

"Love you, Carlen."

"I love you too. Bye." Now, to Stacy in her panicked moment. "Where did you leave it?"

She searches the kitchen counter. "If I knew, I wouldn't be asking you, silly."

"Want me to call you?"

"It won't do any good. The battery was almost dead." She ruffles through everything on the island bar in front of me. "I thought I had it on the charger, but I guess not."

"Where was the last time you remember having it?"

"If I didn't put it on the charger…" She bites her lip, and her eyes shift as she ponders. "I remember I had it last night talking to Dillon, so I know it's in the apartment."

Mentally, I replay last night. "Did you check the laundry room?"

She points at me with her eyes wide and her mouth open. "You know what? I bet that's where I left it." Like a cat after a mouse, she dashes out of the kitchen. A few seconds later, she screams, "Found it."

My phone chirps. It's a message from Matthew.

My car won't start. Can I ride with you to work?

Sure. Give me twenty minutes.

Thanks. I'll meet you at your car.

Stacy enters the kitchen and plugs her phone into the charger. "I need to tell you something." Her eyes cut to mine. "The last thing I want to do is say something to upset you."

Great. The tone of dread. I take my cereal bowl to the sink. "What is it?"

"When me and Dillon were at the mall yesterday, I saw Andy. He asked about you."

The mention of my former boyfriend slices at my heart. Why do I still have feelings for him after he shredded it?

I hold up my hand for her to stop. "Don't wanna hear

anything about him. I might not be the prettiest flower in the garden, but I'm not stupid enough to take him back."

Stacy reaches into the fridge. "Good for you." She pours a glass of orange juice and returns the container to the fridge. "But that's not the reason I'm telling you. He hinted he was thinking about calling you, which means that's what he's going to do."

"Why do men have to be assholes and cheat on you, and when you catch them…" I raise my hands and wiggle my fingers and sing in a high-pitched tone, "…they're suddenly the sweetest man you ever met?"

With a comical smirk, she brings the glass to her lips. "Because men can't think past their sexual desires, that's why."

"There was this guy in the store last week. The kind that makes you want to drool. I swear he was flirting with me." That face is still a beautiful image I can't erase, even though he turned out to be a jerk.

Stacy sets her empty glass in the sink, looks at me, then laughs. "You saw a guy you like? Oh, do tell."

I wash her glass, the last dirty dish, then take the towel from the wire rack to dry my hands. "He wanted to look at refrigerators. His hot girlfriend shows up out of nowhere and drags him away like a kid."

"Ouch. If you ask me…" Stacy picks up her phone and scrolls through it. "I think you and Matthew make a cute couple."

"Me and Matthew? You're funny." I laugh at the notion and get my lunch cooler ready to fill. "We're just friends. That's it."

"Maybe he's not a hottie, but he's a sweet guy. And you two sure get along."

"Haven't you ever had a male friend that…" I open the cabinet and take out the snack basket, then dig through it. Don't tell me I'm out of cheese crackers.

"That what?"

"You know, had a guy who only wanted to be friends?"

"Not unless it's with benefits. Don't tell me you and Matthew are—"

"No. Don't *even* go there." I find a pack of crackers and drop it in my lunch cooler. Then I reach for a bottle of water and glance her way, grinning. "What about you and Dillon?"

She stops scrolling and looks at me, then squints. "Let's just say, he wants it, but he hasn't gotten a homerun yet."

"He's always got his hands on you."

"Oh, Dillon is very affectionate."

I open the freezer but forget what I'm looking for because *he* pops into my head. Andy was affectionate too. When he held me, I felt safe, and I miss that. Please tell me he's not going to haunt me all day. Don't I have enough bad memories without him tagging along? Oh, a frozen meal. I grab one and stuff it in my cooler.

Stacy's phone rings. "Speaking of the affectionate guy who wants sex." She sits on a stool, puts the phone to her ear and whispers seductively, "Hello, baby. Miss me?"

I smile and roll my eyes. Someone is in love. Once my lunch is packed, I head to my room to get dressed. While brushing my hair, those stupid memories of Andy flip through my head like a photo album. What if he calls me? There's one way to keep that from happening. I pull up his number and block him before I walk out of the apartment.

Matthew leans against my car while glued to his phone.

"You didn't have to stand out in the cold." I thumb my fob to unlock the doors. "You could've come to the apartment and waited."

He gets in the passengers seat. "Figured it was just as easy to wait here."

After buckling up, I start the car and head to work. While Matthew is in his own world, playing games on his phone, my thoughts drift to Andy. The good memories surface, and I let them. I pass the Sweet Frog on Main Street where we had our first date. It was a hot summer's afternoon, so we decided on some frozen yogurt. It seemed to be our place after that. We would sit on one of the benches that line the street and talk while devouring the cool treat.

The light turns red, so I come to a stop and watch pedestrians stroll along the sidewalk. Andy liked to people-watch, so he said. What he enjoyed was looking at women. Stupid me was blinded, thinking he only had eyes for me. "Matthew, can I ask you a guy question?"

"Um, that depends. How embarrassing is it?"

"It's not embarrassing." I pop his arm as he continues to play on his phone. "Hey, it's important. Pay attention."

"I'm listening. What is it?"

"Why do men cheat?"

He lowers his phone and looks at me. "Whoa, that's a loaded question."

The light turns green, so I mosey on my way. "What's the mysterious answer?"

He scowls, offended. "How would I know?"

"True." I smile at him. "You're so sweet and honest."

"Is this about your ex?"

I turn back to the traffic. "Yeah. Stacy told me she ran into him. He hinted he might call me."

"Do you want him to?"

"Hell no. He's an asshole. Why would I want him back?"

"You're still thinking about him."

"More like, thinking about what he did." I change lanes and press the gas to get away from the traffic. "The day we broke up, I ended up not working over and decided to go to his house and surprise him. The surprise was on me. When I walked in, I caught him on the couch with a girl."

"You mean like...doing the deed?"

My eyes dart to Matthew. "You mean...screwing her? Yeah, that's exactly what I saw." I turn back to the traffic and mumble, "I still can't get the image out of my head."

"Now I see why the guy was a secret."

"It's not that he's a secret. It's just, it still hurts to talk about him. That's why you saw me crying in my car the day we met."

After seeing Andy screwing someone on his couch, I drove home, somewhat numb. For the longest time, I questioned if what I had seen was real and almost drove back. When I got to my apartment complex, as soon as I killed the engine, it hit me. I had never cried so hard in my life. Matthew, a stranger at the time, parked beside me and noticed. He tapped on my window to see if I was alright. There's a blurry moment when I don't remember him getting into my car to sit with me. Although I didn't tell him what had happened, we talked.

Matthew was having a bad day as well. He had lost his job. I told him we were hiring and would put in a good word for him. After my crying spell, we ended up going out for burgers. Matthew has been my best friend since that day. I don't know what I would have done if he hadn't parked beside me, because seeing Andy with another girl almost broke me.

"So that's why you were crying?"

"Yep. I just caught my boyfriend with another girl."

Matthew raises his fists and grunts, mocking a fight. "Want me to beat him up for you?"

I laugh. Then I laugh more. Matthew fighting? He's not the type. He's too gentle and sweet. "Nah, that was four months ago. I'm over what happened."

Maybe, but it still hurts.

~ ~ ~

After being on my feet all day, it's going to be a lazy night with leftovers. I look in the fridge at my options. The three-day-old pizza is beyond edible, so I throw it in the trash. Stacy's meatloaf was delicious, but it doesn't tempt me. A turkey sandwich does. My stomach agrees, so I grab the loose meat container and mayonnaise and set them on the kitchen counter.

Stacy, holding her stomach, shuffles into the kitchen and grabs the Tylenol bottle from a cabinet. "I got my period this morning. The cramps are always killer the first day." She moans in pain, filling a glass, and then takes the caplets.

"Guys have no idea how lucky they are not to have to go through the things we do."

She catches her breath after chugging the water and sets the glass in the sink. "They wouldn't survive what we have to go through. How was your day?"

"Busy with the holidays around the corner." I lay out two slices of bread on a plate. "You and Dillon going out tonight?"

"Yeah, we're going to the Shine. Come go with us. We can sit at the bar and have drinks before we eat." She nudges my arm. "Maybe you can meet a nice guy."

"You know I don't drink." I reach for a small tomato on the window sill. "And you know my evenings consist of a movie and chilling on the couch." I open the drawer and grab a knife. Instead of slicing the tomato, I stare at the shiny blade, somewhat mesmerized. Then I blink, only to see Mom lying on the kitchen floor with a knife in her chest. I blink faster and wheeze, trying to make the memory go away.

"Carlen, what is it?"

Unable to move or speak, I wheeze harder.

"Look at me and not the knife." Stacy grabs my wrist with one hand and carefully takes the knife from my grip with the other and tosses it on the counter. "Look at me," she commands loudly and shakes my forearms.

I manage to look at her, although I can't speak from the rapid, deep wheezing.

"It's okay," she tells me softly, but firmly. "Focus on my voice and where you're at. You're not that teenager. It's only a bad memory."

Thankfully, Stacy knows what's wrong. It's not the first time I've freaked out looking at a knife.

She grips my forearms harder. "Carlen. Come on. You can do this."

Still wheezing like someone having an asthma attack, I look into her brown eyes and tell her what I can't say verbally. *Help me.*

"The leaves are really pretty, aren't they? I bet the view from Jump Off Rock is breathtaking. Remember the first time you saw snowcaps?"

With her distracting me, the wheezing simmers, which allows my body to calm. My mouth is dry. I lick my lips and catch my breath.

"That's it." Stacy rubs my shoulders and smiles. "You've got this."

I'm able to breathe in deep and release it.

"Are you okay?"

I nod, still a bit shaken. "Better."

"Good." Stacy blocks my view and slices the tomato for me. "Sure you don't want to go with us tonight?"

"Not after what just happened."

Once Stacy has my tomato sliced, I finish making my sandwich while she washes the knife and returns it to the drawer.

"I'm going to have to hook you up with someone, or you're going to end up an old maid."

"Don't even think about it. I'd rather be an old maid than have someone who cheats on me."

"Not every man cheats."

"Maybe, but I'm not ready to test the waters again." I reach for the bag of chips. Mr. Handsome pops into my head. Admittedly, I would have tested the waters with him. What a jerk.

Stacy's phone rings, and she answers it lightning fast. "Hello, baby. Give me fifteen minutes, and I'll meet you in the parking lot."

I pour barbecue-flavored potato chips next to my sandwich.

Stacy side-eyes me. "I'm trying to get Carlen to go with us."

"No," I mouth in passing and head to the fridge to get a soda.

"That's what I told her."

I take my plate and give Stacy an I-said-no glare and leave the kitchen. Once I'm settled in my spot on the couch, I surf the channels until a movie catches my eye. While eating my sandwich, I take in the plot. A young couple are on vacation at a remote cabin. Both have a secret they plan to tell. Although it seems slow and cliché, it continues to keep my interest. As they paddle in the canoe, someone on the bank watches them with binoculars.

"Dillon just pulled into the complex. I'm heading out." Stacy struts through the living room in a tight black dress and her hair in a high ponytail. "See you later."

"You guys have fun."

Once I finish eating, I stretch out on the couch. During a boring scene, my mind drifts to that day, even though doing so could trigger another flashback. Why can't I remember what happened? We came home from the store. Mom put the groceries away. My next memory is seeing her on the floor. Why am I trying to remember? I left home to forget.

The movie isn't going anywhere.

I sigh, bored and restless.

Wonder what Matthew is doing?

Wish he were here.

I send him a text. *If you're not doing anything, come over and hang out.*

Once the message is sent, I take my plate and soda can to the kitchen. An instant chill hits me when I enter. Not like the air is cold, but like I'm not alone. Mom is here, in my kitchen. My pace slows, the scaredy-cat that I am. Perhaps coming in here after what happened earlier wasn't a good idea. If I'm triggered again, Stacy isn't here to help me. Spooked, I drop the plate and soda can in the sink and run out before the past grabs me. As soon as I return to the living room, the chill is gone.

My phone beeps.

I read Matthew's message.

On my way.

With Matthew here, it will keep me distracted.

Someone knocks.

"That was fast." I leave the couch. When I open the door, I grin and tease my best friend. "Did your sister catapult you over here?"

"No, I was getting something out of my car when you messaged me." He eyes me, walking inside. "Is something wrong?"

I shut the door. "Why do you think something's wrong?"

"Because I know you." Matthew takes off his coat, tosses it on the couch, and sits in his usual spot.

"It's nothing." I curl up on the couch and cover my legs with a blanket. "If you're hungry or thirsty, you know where the kitchen is."

Matthew still eyes me. "He called you, didn't he?"

"Who?"

"That ex-boyfriend."

"Oh, no." I shake my head and wave him off. "The jerk's been blocked."

"Then what is it?"

"Nothing, really. Let's watch a movie."

"Is that offer for food still good?"

"You know it is."

"Got any popcorn?"

I give him a pouty face and moan. "Yeah, but do you mind making it?"

"Nope." Matthew gets to his feet, his long jeans gathered at his shoes. "While I'm doing that, find a good movie."

"A romance or chick flick?" Watching him grimace like he's going to throw up makes me laugh. "You know I'm kidding."

Matthew rolls his eyes and heads to the kitchen. What would I do without him?

~ ~ ~

Gloria sits in the chair across from me, our knees only feet apart. Her warm eyes study me, always giving me her full attention. "Is there anything you would like to talk about today?"

"Yeah, um…" I wring my hands and swallow the lump in my throat, dreading this session. "It happened again."

There's no expression of shock or surprise on her face as she reaches for her legal pad off her desk. "What happened?"

"A trigger."

"Tell me what happened." She thumbs her ink pen and makes notes.

Let's hope talking about it doesn't put me in a bad place.

"I took a knife out of the drawer to cut a tomato." I wave my hand and sing, "Just like that, I'm sixteen again and looking at the knife in Mom's chest, not the one in my hand."

"Had anything happened before that?" She stops writing and looks at me. "Did you have a nightmare? Were you talking about that day with someone?"

"No. One minute I'm making a sandwich, the next minute I'm freaking out at a knife. Why? It's been five years since her murder and then six months ago I suddenly can't handle looking at a knife."

Gloria places her hand flat on her legal pad and exhales. "Sometimes our minds block out traumatic things that happen to us. Especially at a young age. When we're older and can handle it, the memory often surfaces."

"What if I don't want it to surface?"

She raises an eyebrow. "How else are you going to cope with what happened?"

"Why can't I cope without having to go back in time and relive something horrible?"

"I wish it were that easy." Gloria shifts in her chair and crosses her legs, gently tugging the skirt over her knee. "If you've blocked something out, it's because you couldn't handle it at the time. The repressed memory will eventually surface."

"There's no reason it needs to surface. I'm struggling as it is and don't need to relive something I can't handle. I thought we're supposed to focus on the future and not the past."

"That depends. If someone's past isn't causing him or her to stumble in life, then perhaps there's no need to deal with it. However, if someone struggles to function and cope in life, then perhaps there needs to be closure."

"So, my past is why I struggle with depression and have panic attacks?"

She smiles and challenges me. "You don't think there's a connection?"

I, in turn, challenge her. "How do you know I wasn't born this way? Maybe I have a medical condition, and that's why I have issues."

"That could be possible, but from my experience, I do believe it's from the trauma you experienced."

I mumble under my breath, "Either way, it feels like I'm screwed."

"Carlen, one of your goals when you came here was to find out why seeing a knife triggers you after all of these years. Maybe if you work through that, the past will rest, and then you can move on with your life as you mentioned."

With no words to respond or challenge her with, I take a mental break. It's silent other than the clock ticking.

"What are you thinking?"

Nothing and everything at the same time, but there is something I need to talk about before the session ends. I sit up. "Dad wants me to come and visit, so I'm driving to Charlotte tomorrow."

"That's wonderful. I know you miss him."

I lower my chin to my chest and squint. "And you know how my anxiety is when I go there. My stomach is already in knots, thinking about being in that kitchen."

"That's understandable. We can work on ways to help you cope and manage the anxiety. Are you writing and journaling your thoughts like I suggested?"

"You know when I do that it's like reliving my past. And I don't mean Mom's murder."

Gloria reaches for a glass of water next to her. "You've never talked about her death, other than the details of what happened. May I ask…how did you cope with it?"

That's not something I want to confess, but maybe it would ease my guilt if I told her. After all, this office has been a safe place for telling my most private thoughts. And Gloria won't judge me.

"This is going to sound horrible, but…" I look at my hands and twirl a ring on my thumb. "I didn't have to cope with her death. I'm not sad Mom's dead." That sounded so cold. I quickly look at Gloria. "Don't get me wrong, I hate what happened to her. It was horrible. Even *she* didn't deserve that, but I've never shed a tear over her and don't plan to." Even though I'm not sad, guilt pokes at me. After all, she was my mother.

Gloria finishes her sip of water and graciously places the glass on the table next to her chair. "You are certainly entitled to how you feel, but keep in mind, as you heal, you might find you feel differently."

I laugh facetiously at the idea I'll ever feel different about Mom. "Are you saying there's going to come a day when I cry over her, knowing what she did to me?"

Gloria smiles, not offended by my curt tone. She shakes her head. "No. I'm saying as you work through this process, you might find you see things from a different perspective. One that isn't blurred."

If Gloria thinks I will ever shed a tear for Mom, then she's the one who needs a therapist.

I take in a deep breath and white-knuckle the arms of the chair. The more I ponder her comment, the harder I breathe. "There is *nothing* blurred about the way my mother looked at me with evil eyes and said the hateful things she did. The only memories she left me with still haunt me. Not leave me crying for her."

In my moment of spewing emotions like a busted water hose, Gloria hasn't moved, and I don't think she's even blinked. "Carlen, I'm so sorry your mother treated you the way she did and said the things she did to you. You were an innocent child who did nothing wrong."

"A child believes her mother. The things mine said to me…" I look away, unable to repeat them.

"Carlen, they weren't true. That's *not* who you are. Don't carry on where she left off and continue to play those old messages."

My teary eyes dart to her. "You don't think I've tried? I'd do *anything* to get her out of my head. Some days I forget she's dead, because I still hear her. It's like having a wound that won't heal."

"That's because you were harmed as a child. You didn't have the ability to protect yourself. And I'm sorry your father didn't—"

"Don't say it." That's where I stop her. No one is going to bad-mouth my dad, because no one knows what he went through either. "Dad tried. He really did. But he was afraid of her too."

Gloria doesn't say anything, although her eyes tell me she wants to counter.

"Look, I know he should've…intervened in some way, but he's passive. That's no excuse, but you didn't live in that house, so please don't…" I can't finish my sentence. There are no words to say that will make anyone understand what Dad and I went through.

"Are you okay?"

"Gloria, I um…" I pause, struggling to talk about this, because I don't want to.

"Take a few minutes if you need to."

And I do, staring out the window, collecting my thoughts and simmering others. "When I saw Mom lying on the kitchen floor, I knew she was dead. No matter how much I hated her, you would think if I were human, I would have cried and broken down over her death. But I didn't. I felt free from her." I turn back to Gloria and shake my head. "But I'm not free. Even in death, she's haunting me."

"Carlen, she's not haunting you. It's old messages you're replaying. You *can* be free of her." She eyes me. "Remember when you described your past like being in a cage and held prisoner?"

I nod.

"You do know that *you* have the key." Gloria points her pen at me. "*You* can open that cage any time you want."

"You know what's weird?"

"What?"

"If I woke up one morning and that cage was mysteriously open, I don't think I would walk out of it. Even though I want to be free, it feels safer to be in the cage. How screwed up is that?"

"It's not screwed up. That's very powerful, what you said. But don't you want to overcome that fear and be free so you can live your life?"

It's one of Gloria's questions I can't answer. Logically, yes, I want to be free and live my life, but it scares me so much I would rather hide in my cage.

Chapter 3: Charlotte

Minutes into my trip, the view of the colorful fall mountains is incredible. The red, yellow, and orange leaves paint an amazing picture. At least the two-hour drive is off to a relaxing start before I run into a wall of anxiety and flashbacks. But I can do this. Spending time with Dad is worth being in that house for a few hours.

Bluetooth alerts me of an incoming call. After punching the touchscreen to accept, I sing, "Hey, Dad. I'm on my way. Can't wait to see you."

"Me neither. I couldn't sleep last night. I sure miss my little girl, although she's not so little anymore. You know you're my world, Carlen."

My eyes mist over. "Dad. You're going to make me cry."

It's silent. If I had to guess, Dad is also teary-eyed.

"Since you're driving, I won't keep you. Be safe."

"I will. See you around nine."

"I'll be waiting for you."

"Love you."

"Love you too."

The miles accumulate. The morning traffic thickens, but I'm still making good time.

My phone beeps. It's a text from Stacy. *Hope things go well. Call me if you need me.*

When I stop, I'll send her a reply. Stacy knows these trips are hard for me, even though I love spending time with Dad.

Ten minutes after nine, I turn onto Ridgeway Drive and swallow the lump in my throat. My heart races as though to warn me danger is near. My sweaty hands grip the steering wheel. Coming here is never easy, but I'll be fine once I see my dad. As a distraction, I focus on the houses to see what's new or different. Most of the people have lived their whole lives in this community.

One more street.

I turn the heat off, already in an anxiety-induced sweat.

Take a deep breath. It will be fine.

When I see the two-story half-stucco, half-stone house on the right, I slow down and turn into the driveway. I come to a stop next to Dad's truck and kill the engine. Mentally, I prepare myself, because there are two things we do not talk about—Mom or the day she was murdered.

"Here goes."

After getting out, I mosey to the front of the house. When I turn the corner and see Dad standing on the porch, it makes my eyes water from the love exploding inside of me. I run to him and throw my arms around his waist. "I've missed you so much." I hold him tighter, drawing in the positive energy and love.

He gives me a bear hug. "And I've missed you. Let's go in where it's warm."

I lean him back and take a good look at him. "Dad, your hair," I squeal and take a tendril. Look how long it is. You can put it in a ponytail."

He laughs and walks me to the front door. "Now that would be a sight to see."

We head inside. I take my coat off and hang it on one of the wall hooks. The living room is nice and toasty with a fire burning. The embers crackle in rhythm.

Dad has the curtains pulled back, letting the sun penetrate the living room. Something Mom never allowed. When she was alive, this room was always dark, but now it's inviting. I smile at the newspaper sprawled out on the coffee table. Something else Mom never allowed. She didn't understand why Dad couldn't read the newspaper in one sitting and then throw it away. Everything was all about her. Dad's a slow reader, so now he can enjoy the newspaper without being rushed.

When I glance at the couch, I smile even harder at the pillows not sitting at attention against the arms. That means Dad used them when he was stretched out on the couch. He can finally live in his house the way he wants and not have to worry about Mom's perfectionistic ways.

A basket of clean towels folded and waiting to go upstairs on Dad's next trip brings back a memory. I stare at the basket and rub my arm where Mom slapped me several times.

"Carlen, I told you they have to be folded perfect. Fold every one of those towels again, and do it right this time."

25

She's here. Dead or not, Mom is in this room.

"Are you hungry?"

Dad's voice startles me, but I don't want him to know she's in my head. I force the biggest smile. "Um, not really. But if you are, I'll make you some breakfast."

Dad takes off his checkered-flannel coat and hangs it next to mine, then he kicks off his boots. "I was thinking of having some coffee and toast. Sure you don't want anything?"

Food is suddenly tempting. "Yeah. Come on, and I'll fix it."

When I head toward the kitchen, in passing, Dad takes my hand and stops me.

I turn to him. "What's wrong?"

"You don't have to go in there. I can fix it, and we can eat in here."

I stand tall and hold my head high to let him know I'm alright. And looking into his eyes, I am. "Don't worry. I can handle going in there. It's not like I haven't gone in there before."

Dad raises his eyebrows. "Are you sure?"

"Trust me. If I didn't think I could handle it, I wouldn't go in there," I tell him honestly.

"If you're sure."

In the kitchen, Dad sits at the table while I start the coffee. He seems relaxed with his legs outstretched and one arm on the table, watching me. For now, it's only the two of us. No haunting voices or vibes she's here. Although, I make sure not to look at the floor where Mom was lying with a knife in her chest. Speaking of, I need to avoid that drawer.

While the bread toasts, I search the fridge. "Grape jelly or honey?"

"Whatever you're having."

Once everything is prepared, I sit at the table with Dad. He tells me about the new neighbors at the end of the street. Then he tells me about Patty, his next-door neighbor. Her husband died two years ago. Dad helps her out with the yard, and she brings him some of her home cooking.

"Still want chili for lunch?"

I add sugar to my coffee and then a little milk. "Of course I do."

"After we finish, I'll start on it."

"Let me know if you want any help." I sip my coffee and watch Dad spread jelly on his toast. It's still weird seeing him with a mustache and goatee, and now it's his long hair. I smile at the thought of him rebelling against Mom. What I wouldn't give for her to see him right now. Mom forced Dad to wear a buzz cut, only because she knew how much he hated it. She controlled everything he did. What he wore. What he ate. Even what time he went to bed. It took a few years for Dad to be who he is. To be free from her rules and control. He found the key to his cage and is enjoying life. Maybe one day I will find my key.

He bites into his toast and looks at me, then stops chewing. "What is it? Do I have food on my mustache?"

"No. I can't get over how long your hair is. I love it."

He finishes chewing. "You don't think it's too long for an old man, do you?"

"Not at all," I tell him sincerely.

He chuckles and reaches for his coffee. "I don't look like some bum or hobo?"

"No. It suits you. You even look younger. I'm so glad you're wearing it the way you want to." That's all I can say without mentioning *her*.

"Well, I'm glad you like it, but I was planning on getting it cut."

"Dad." I eye him.

He holds his hand up. "Don't worry. I'm not getting a buzz cut, only a trim."

I exhale with relief. "Good. I like it long. You look...hip."

Dad chuckles. "Hip?"

"Okay, how about...cool?"

"I can go for that."

I love how we can laugh in the kitchen. That never happened when Mom was alive. I do hate what happened to her, but I won't feel guilty for not missing her. She's what I call the cage I can't escape. Yet.

Breakfast is over, but we continue to talk and catch up.

I rest my arms on the table and eye him. "Dad, how are you doing? Not just in general, but how are you?"

He lowers his mug and gently pats his lips, hesitating as though I asked him an embarrassing question. "Doing okay, I reckon."

Dad has never complained in his life, so if something is wrong, he won't tell me. He had diabetes for two years before I found an empty pill bottle in the trash.

I reach over the table and place my hand on his. "Dad, are you taking your medicine like you're supposed to?"

He sits back in the chair and gives me his don't-ask squinty eye. "Carlen, you don't have to worry. I'm fine."

"Dad?"

He smiles, and it makes me smile. "I'm fine. Really."

"How am I supposed to know? It's not like you'll tell me if something is wrong." I scold him with my daughterly love. "You should sell this house and move to Hendersonville. That way I can keep my eye on you," I tease, although I'm very serious.

Dad chuckles and leans closer. "Why don't *you* move back to Charlotte if you want to keep an eye on your old man?"

"Why do you still live in this house? I couldn't *wait* to move out of here." As much as I want to say more, it would cross a line on a subject we don't talk about. But there is still a way to say what's on my mind. "This house is so big. Wouldn't you like something smaller where the upkeep is less work?"

He reaches for his mug. "This is home, Carlen. You grew up in this house." He sips his coffee and adds, "If I moved, I wouldn't have memories of you in a new place."

"Ah," I coo and sit up straight, smiling wider than ever. "That's so sweet."

Hearing Dad say that makes me worry less about him. If his memories here are good ones, unlike mine, then he should live here. Me? It's all I can do to come here for a few hours and visit. There's no way I could ever spend the night in this house. It's creepy just thinking about it.

Dad stands. "Can I interest you in watching a little television with me before I start the chili?"

"Absolutely." I gather the dishes and carry them to the sink.

"Need some help with that?"

"No. You go ahead. I'll be there in a minute." I run water in the sink.

Dad kisses my cheek and leaves the kitchen.

While washing the dishes, a cool breeze makes me shiver. Like someone opened the window and cold air blew in. She's here. I stop washing the coffee mug, but my heart is in turbo speed, ready to burst through my chest. I'm scared to look behind me, fearing she is standing there.

"That water isn't hot enough. I told you it has to be hot, or it won't kill the germs. The next time I have to tell you, young lady, I'll make you rinse the

dishes with the water as hot as it'll get. Maybe that'll teach you to listen to me."

If I were still that little girl, I would be shivering from her tone. As an adult, I'm fuming with anger. Out of rebellion, I slap the handle on the faucet to cold water and continue to wash the dishes. If I don't calm down and ignore her, she's going to control this visit.

After the dishes are finished, I wipe the counter and return things to the fridge. When I turn, I blink at a dark shadow I swear I watch zoom across the kitchen and disburse. It happens so fast, maybe my mind is playing games with me, and I didn't see anything. But it doesn't explain the lingering presence someone is here. The weird thing is, it doesn't feel like Mom. If it's not her, then who could it be? Mom never let anyone in the house. Ever. The only person I can think of is the guy who killed Mom.

The shadow was the killer?

I run out of the kitchen but slow my pace and erratic breathing before entering the living room so Dad doesn't see me spooked. He's laid back in his recliner and watches his favorite show. I sit on the end of the couch closest to him and bring my legs underneath me. "I should've known you'd pick *The Rifleman*," I groan, teasing him.

He grins and sings, "It's a good show."

Westerns are not my thing, but I love how Dad enjoys them. He'll narrate what's going to happen, because he's seen all the shows a million times. He'll tell me all about the characters and what kind of guns they use. He didn't get to watch what he wanted when Mom was alive, so I let him watch whatever makes him happy.

A commercial comes on.

"Bathroom break. Be right back." Dad leaves the recliner.

I lean against the arm of the couch and casually scan the living room. When I look at the picture of Mom on the fireplace mantel, I cringe at it. It's the only one of her in the house. Dad said she was eighteen. You can't tell, but she was pregnant with me.

Drawn in, I leave the couch and walk up to the fireplace, staring hard at the picture. Without thinking, I take the frame and hold it with both hands and try to read into her eyes. It's the only time I've looked at Mom and they not scare me. Admittedly, she was beautiful with long wavy hair, flawless skin, and lush model lips. She even had a warm and friendly smile. One I never saw. Why couldn't this sweet-looking lady love me?

Why did you have to be so mean? You were supposed to love me, not—

"Carlen?" Dad stands next to me.

"Why do you have a picture of her?" My eyes dart to him, wanting an answer.

"We agreed not to talk about her," he reminds me in a dry tone, and his glare telling me to let it go.

"No, I *never* agreed to it. You pretty much told me that was the way it was going to be."

"It's for the best." Dad takes the picture from me and returns it to its spot.

For the first time in five years, we are talking about her, so I take advantage of the moment and ask the question he's never answered. "Why did you marry her if she was so mean to you?"

He's not going to say anything bad about Mom. He never has. While I admire his good heart, it comes across as protecting her, and that angers me.

"Carlen, we don't need to talk about the past."

I huff, frustrated. "Why won't you tell me?"

"Let's not go there." He returns to the recliner and leans back.

"What if I have questions I want answered?" I march toward him, determined to have this conversation. "Questions I need answered if I want to put the past behind me. Don't I deserve to know them?"

"You know everything you need to know." His wide eyes warn me not to continue with the subject.

And for five years, I've done as he's asked and been silent. It wasn't like I wanted to talk about her either, but now I'm having nightmares and want them to go away.

"Dad, can we talk for two minutes, and then we'll never mention her again?"

"No. Let it be."

"Why not? There are things I want to know." Maybe my sad and desperate eyes will change his mind. After all, I am a daddy's girl. "Please talk to me. Tell me why you married her if she was so abusive to you."

He turns back to the television, although I'm not convinced he's watching it. Perhaps if I give him a moment, he'll answer, so I sit on the couch and wait.

Just when it seems our talk isn't going to happen, Dad mutes the television but doesn't look at me. "Are you sure you want to know, because you might not like what you hear?"

Oh my gosh. He's going to tell me. My heart pounds with anticipation like the greatest secret in the world is about to be revealed. I curl up, ready to hear anything he will tell me. "Yes. I need to know."

Still staring, he takes in a deep breath, and his body relaxes into the recliner. "When your mother was fifteen, you know her parents were killed in a car accident. Her grandparents took her in, which meant she had to move to Charlotte. Polkton is a really small farming town. She was scared of the big city. It didn't help that the kids picked on her. I caught her crying under a tree one day after school and talked to her. Marion reminded me of a kitten caught in a rainstorm with nowhere to go. She missed her folks and wanted to go home. She said her grandparents were not attentive. Maybe because they were dealing with the loss of her mother. I just know she was sad and alone."

This is the most Dad has ever told me about their past. Captivated, I sit on the edge of the couch and listen.

"After that day, we spent a lot of time together and became close." Without moving, his eyes dart to mine. "Are you sure you want to hear this?"

I nod with eagerness. "Yes."

"Once we got close and she opened up, she was this sweet country girl. Although she still didn't make friends, she was happy. Or so I thought. I fell in love with her smile. She said I was the reason for it. Then our senior year, she tells me she's pregnant. Back in those days, that brought disgrace on your family. When I told my folks, they suggested I do the right thing and marry her. So, I did. Your mother moved in with us. My parents helped us since we were still in high school. Everything was fine at first. Marion did get a bit moody and bossy, but your grandma told me it was her hormones. She told me I should be patient and understanding, so I was. After high school, I got a job as a supervisor at a factory. We were able to get our own place. That's when a different Marion came out. There were times I thought about leaving her, but your grandad told me to do right by my choices and make the marriage work."

How could Grandad make him stay with Mom? Surely my grandparents saw how she treated him.

"When you were about three years old, I came home from work, and Marion was in one of her moods. I couldn't take it anymore and told her I was leaving. Marion threw things at me while I packed my bags and told me what a horrible husband and father I was. Somehow, you slept through it. Before I walked out, I kissed you goodbye and told you I'd be back to see you. I would have taken you, but I wasn't sure where I was going. I just wanted out of there. Marion followed me out the door and told me if I left she would leave town, and I'd never see you again. I didn't even make it to my car. Marion meant what she said, so I went back."

It's the first time Dad has shared what life was like with her, and I feel guilty. "I'm sorry you had to put up with her because of me."

His head falls back into the recliner, and he sighs. "Let's not talk about bad memories, okay?"

"After what she's done, why do you still have a picture of her on the mantel?"

"Carlen." He massages his temple like he's fighting a headache and mumbles, "Can we *please* not talk about your mother?"

I pound my thighs and tell him in anger, "She doesn't deserve a place in this house. And I haven't said anything about that picture being there until now. Why honor her memory, Dad? I hate looking at that picture."

"The reason I have that picture there is because I need to remember the girl I fell in love with. That was a time when we were happy. But if it bothers you that much, I'll put it in her closet."

I love him even more, if that's possible, for loving someone who didn't love us.

"No. It's fine. Leave it there."

Dad lowers his hand from his temple and looks at me with tired eyes. "Are you sure?"

"After what you told me, I'm okay with it." I grin and flash my teeth. "See how talking helps?"

Dad raises an eyebrow. "Are we finished with that subject?"

Maybe not for good, but for now.

"Yes. We're done talking about her."

"Good. Now, on to more important things. I should start the chili." He leaves the recliner and offers me the remote. "See if there's something you want to watch."

I take the remote. "Thanks for talking to me."

Dad kisses the top of my head. "Just trying to protect my girl."

I smile, watching him leave the room. He's the best dad in the world. I get comfortable and surf the channels but reflect over

32

everything Dad told me. Having answers help me understand, but one still remains. What was that dark shadow I saw in the kitchen?

Chapter 4: Mom's Closet

"Carlen, the chili is ready."

"Coming." I turn the television off and leave the living room, lured by the aroma of spices. When I enter the kitchen, I inhale deeply. "It sure smells good."

"Hope it turned out good."

"It always does." I take two bowls from the cabinet and offer one to him.

Dad spoons the chili. "Tell me when."

Since the bowls are big, I stop him when it's half full. "That's good."

"Be careful. It's hot." He reaches for his bowl and fills it.

With the delicious meal in my hands, I head to the table. My stomach growls with anticipation. I'm about to satisfy it as soon as I crumble my crackers.

Dad takes his seat across from me and stirs his chili. "Guess I know what I'm having for supper."

"It's even better reheated." My crackers are mixed in. I spoon my first bite. The second it hits my tongue, I fan my open mouth and pant.

Dad laughs at me. "I told you it's hot."

I grab my glass of water, still fanning my mouth. "I know, but I had to have that first bite."

As we enjoy our lunch, a shiver causes the hair on my arms to stand. She's here. I tense up, waiting to hear that cold voice scold us for something.

"Carlen?" The way he calls my name with concern, he knows.

"It's okay, really. Just had a moment. It's gone." I smile and raise my next spoonful. "Dad, you nailed it again. The chili is perfect."

Mom never complimented him, so I make sure to do it every chance I get. Not only because he deserves it, but I love seeing him blush.

"Thank you." He puts a cracker in his mouth. "What would you like to do after lunch?"

Whatever my dad enjoys. I ponder ideas. One comes to mind. "Want to play Uno?"

He raises an eyebrow while holding a spoonful of chili in front of his mouth. "Are you kidding? I'd love to."

I point to my upper lip. "You've got some on your mustache."

He reaches for a napkin and wipes his mouth.

We enjoy the chili and talk about work and the holidays. Although I sense Mom is here, the more I stay focused on the present, it seems to block her. Before my chili has a chance to cool, I have devoured it. My belly is full, and my insides are warmed. Now I have to fight off a food coma.

"Want seconds?"

I shake my head and rub my stomach. "No. I'm too full."

Dad stands and gathers the dishes.

"No, don't. I'll do them since you cooked."

He corrals them to his side of the table. "I'm going to put them in the dishwasher. If you want, you can take out the trash for me."

"Okay." I leave the table and remove the bag from the trash can. Once I tie it, I head out the back door.

"Hi, Carlen." Patty's voice echoes from her backyard.

I march down the back steps and yell, "Hey."

She heads toward me wearing her garden gloves, a straw hat, and black rubber boots. "How have you been?"

"Good." I lift the trash can lid and toss the bag in it. "Working in your flower beds?"

"Yeah. I'm trying to get my fall bulbs planted. We've already had a few nights of frost, so I need to get them in the ground." She comes to a stop in front of me, winded from her rushed walk. "I'm sure Paul is tickled to death to see you."

"Not as much as I am to see him," I tell her with a big grin.

She adjusts her hat to block the sun from her eyes. "I haven't seen him outside lately. Is he doing okay?"

"He's fine. He said it's been too cold to do anything outside."

"Okay. I was just checking. Tell him I'm making dumplings next week, and I'll bring him some."

"That's really nice of you."

She wipes her cheek with the back of her wrist, leaving a trail of dirt. "Hey, Paul's been a lifesaver since John died, so bringing him a home-cooked meal once in a while is my way of thanking him."

A cool breeze sideswipes me, and I cross my arms. "Do you want to come in for a visit?"

"I would love to, but I need to finish up. Maybe next time." She walks backwards and waves. "It was good to see you. Maybe I'll see you for the holidays."

"I'll be here."

Another cold breeze hits me, tossing my hair in my face. I march up the steps and head inside. Dad is at the table, getting the cards ready. "Patty said to tell you she's going to bring dumplings over next week."

"I thought I heard her out there. Why didn't you invite her in?"

I sit at the table and watch him deal out the first round of cards. "I did, but you know her. She's busy with her flowers."

We sort through our cards.

"You can go first," Dad offers.

Once I have my cards sorted by color, I lay a yellow five on the table. Dad places a green five over it, and the game is on. For a while, I'm winning and then Dad takes the lead. There's nothing like seeing him smile and having fun.

"Paul, put those damn cards away. You're not doing that in my kitchen."

"Marion, supper isn't for hours. We have time to play a few rounds."

"If you don't put those cards away, I'll grab a skillet and let it do my talking."

My jaw clenches, angered at all the times we couldn't play cards in the kitchen.

"Carlen? Are you okay?"

I can't let him see me upset. My focus turns back to the game. "Yeah. Just trying to figure out what to put down." With three cards left, I place a blue seven on the deck.

Dad lays a red seven and proudly announces, "Uno."

That means he has one card left. If he can match the card I lay down, he wins. The green six calls out to me, so I place it on the deck.

Dad lays a green four on top of it and raises his hands in celebration. "I'm out. I win."

"Ah, and I was so close." I toss my cards on the table, and he adds them to the deck and shuffles them. My mouth is dry. "I need something to drink." I leave the table and head to the fridge. "Do you want something?"

"Nah. I'm good."

I fetch the pitcher of lemonade from the fridge and set it on the counter. When I reach into the cabinet for a glass, it slips out of my hand and falls to the floor. I reach down to pick it up, but instead, I'm reaching for the knife in Mom's chest. Her head is to the side, but she turns to me and opens her eyes wide. I scream in horror and step back with my clenched hands against my chest. Although the image is gone as fast as it appeared, it's still disturbing.

Dad holds my forearms. "Carlen, it's okay. It didn't break."

"She, she looked right at me."

"Who?"

"Mom. I saw her lying on the floor."

Without saying anything, he escorts me out of the kitchen. And just like that frightened sixteen-year-old, he sits me on the couch.

My hands still tremble. My heart is still racing. I look up at him and plead, "Dad, I'm not a kid anymore. Please. Let's talk about that day. I *need* this." I don't dare tell him it's because I'm having flashbacks when I see a knife.

He sits on the couch and faces me while taking my hand. "Carlen, it's not going to do either of us any good to bring up what happened. And I can't have you going home and having nightmares because we talked about it."

Dad doesn't understand. I'm having nightmares because we're *not* talking about it.

For five years I've wanted to ask him a question, and it's time I do. "Is that because you know who killed Mom?"

"Carlen." His hand goes up lightning fast. "I told you after the funeral was over, we're not going to talk about that day ever again."

With the tension between us rising, I debate whether or not to push the subject. Something tells me if I don't, there will never be another chance, so I challenge him. "What if they catch the guy? We'll have to talk about it then."

"If they haven't caught him by now, they probably never will. Too much time has passed. So, until they do, *if* they do, there's no reason for us to mention it."

"What if I need to talk about it?"

37

Dad gently places his hand on my knee. "You've been through enough. Talking about it isn't going to change anything, so why put yourself through that?"

Disappointed, enough that my eyes water, I look away but don't say anything. Maybe if I tell Dad I'm having nightmares, he'll understand and talk to me about that day. But then he will worry about me, and I don't want that.

"Sweetie." He pats my knee. "Don't go around stuck in the past."

"Dad, if I didn't think I could handle it, do you honestly think I'd ask you to talk about it?" In his hesitation, I add, "Gloria says I might be ready."

He raises his eyebrows and taps my nose. "And your dad thinks you need to focus on the future and not relive a nightmare. Frankly, I think it's a blessing you don't remember. Move forward in life and not dwell on the past."

As we stare, almost standoffishly, I believe Dad is genuinely concerned for me, and it's why he won't talk about the murder. Until six months ago, I didn't either. Now I do.

"Dad, I'm not sixteen. I can handle it."

"Carlen, *please*." He lowers his head, moans aggravatedly and runs his fingers through his hair. "Maybe *I'm* the one who can't handle talking about it. If I had been in the kitchen with Marion and helped her with the groceries, she'd still be alive."

Dad feels guilty? I've been so focused on how Mom's death affected me, it's never crossed my mind how it affected him.

I take his forearm and lean against him. "If you had been in there, the guy could've killed both of you."

"No. I could have stopped him."

"You don't know that. No matter how Mom treated us, I'm really sorry what happened to her. But I'm glad you were not in the kitchen. Dad, I couldn't have handled it if I had lost you that day. It would have broken me."

Dad wraps his arms around me and rests his head on top of mine. "Now do you see why I don't like to talk about that day?"

"You should have told me."

"I didn't want to burden you. Can we please not talk about this?"

"Consider the conversation over. I don't want to end our visit talking about her. Let's finish it on a happy note."

He leans me back and kisses my forehead. "I like the sound

of that."

I smile at him, still in awe at how much he's let his hair grow out. Stacy isn't going to believe me. But, she would if I had proof. "Dad, let's take a picture. I want to show Stacy how long your hair is." I reach for my phone on the coffee table and swipe it.

Dad laughs and protests, waving his hands. "No. My hair's a mess, and this shirt is old as dirt."

I tap the camera icon on my phone. "Oh stop it. I want a picture of us."

"One picture, and that's all," he grumbles but puts his arm around me.

While holding the phone, ready for our selfie, I smile. "Say…*cheese.*"

Snap

"Dad, speaking of pictures, where are the ones of me growing up?"

"Why?" He leaves the couch and pokes at the fire. The embers crackle and flutter up the chimney flue.

Gloria wants me to connect with that little girl. I thought it might help to look at my childhood pictures, but I'm not going to tell Dad that's why. At the same time, I hate to lie to him.

"Me and Stacy were talking about how we looked when we were young. She showed me some pictures of her when she was growing up. I didn't have any to show her and thought, while I'm here, maybe I could grab a few."

Dad's phone rings.

Since I'm closer, I fetch it from the table next to the recliner and offer it to him.

He frowns at the screen. "It's work. Let me see what they want." Dad swipes the screen and puts the phone to his ear. "Hello?" Dad listens. "Yeah. We ran out of them Monday. Ken, hold on a second." Dad looks at me. "I think Marion put them in a box in the hall closet upstairs."

That closet? I should've known. "Okay. I'm going to get a few to take back with me." I head up the stairs, and Dad continues his call.

My hand is on the doorknob, but it's not easy to turn it and enter the closet. Or what we referred to as Mom's private quarters. Dad and I were banned from stepping foot in here. The only time I've seen the inside of this closet, I was probably seven or eight. The door was cracked. I was curious and peeked inside.

"Get away from there. I'll teach you not to get into my things."

It took one flogging with a belt from Mom to douse any further curiosity what was inside. Although the closet is no longer off-limits, whatever is in there means nothing to me, because it's all her stuff. Sometimes I forget this closet is even here.

My heart races at the thought of going in there, but I turn the knob and enter. I flip the light and look around. Everything isn't neat and organized as I expected, but that's because Dad put Mom's things in here after she died and didn't care about it being perfect.

"God, it's creepy being in here," I murmur, then shiver, feeling her presence. "Let's get this over with."

Since Dad isn't like Mom and didn't label the boxes, I grab one off the shelf that is and set it on the floor. "Wow." It's Mom's school memorabilia, report cards, and research papers. I thumb through her schoolwork, impressed she made all A's. If Mom was so smart, why wouldn't she help me with my homework? Before the memory has a chance to sting, I put the box back and go through another one.

"Oh, my gosh." A very old porcelain doll is carefully wrapped in a blanket. It's hard to imagine Mom as a little girl playing with it. It's beyond spooky.

The next box I pull off the shelf is light. I set it on the floor and remove the lid. "No way." I stare at a wedding dress. Mom didn't seal it in a protective bag. My fingertips tenderly trail over the lace. Something possesses me to take it by the shoulders and lift it out of the box. To think Mom wore it, pregnant with me.

There are other things in the box, so I set the dress to the side, get on my knees, and rifle through it. There's a pair of white-laced shoes, a long white veil, a bouquet of dried flowers, and a wedding book.

"Why does he keep this stuff? Talk about not letting go of the past." I continue to rummage through the box but stop when something catches my eye. Something that should *not* be here. "No, it can't be." My heart races, hoping it's not what I think it is. I ease my hand toward the item, breathing harder the closer it gets.

"Did you find them?"

Still on my knees, I look up to see Dad standing in the doorway. Now I know the real reason he doesn't want to talk about Mom.

"What's wrong?"

"How can you *possibly* have this, Dad?"

He steps inside the closet and laughs lightly, confused. "How can I have what?"

"This." With my eyes on him, I lift the item from the box, not only exposing it, but his secret.

Dad glances at my hand. When he realizes what I'm holding, he tries to take it from me, but I jerk my hand back before he can. I hold it to my chest and lean away from him, cowering.

As we stare, he squats in front of me. "Carlen, give that to me," he tells me softly like it's not a big deal what I found.

"No," I tell him defiantly with my crossed arms securing it to my chest.

With his hand outstretched, he wiggles his fingers and even smiles. "Come on. Hand it over."

"Hand *what* over? Mom's wallet?" I squint and tighten my face at him. "How can you have it if the guy who killed her ran off with it?"

Dad raises an eyebrow at me. "Calm down." A grunt escapes as he stretches out his legs and sits on the floor in front of me without a look of shock, alarm, or distress. "It is your mom's wallet, but it's not the one she had that day."

His words repeat in my head like a soft echo until it registers. It's a different wallet. That means Dad isn't the one who stabbed Mom. Of course he didn't. How could I have made such a horrible assumption? With my arms locked against my chest, I look at him guilt-ridden and make a sad face. "I'm so sorry. I, I thought it was, you know, the wallet she had in her purse."

"It's okay. Don't worry about it." He laughs like it doesn't bother him, still motioning with his fingers. "Let me see it. I'll put it back, and then we can get out of here." He looks around the closet. "I've never liked being in here anyway."

I hold the wallet with both hands and stare at it. Curiosity tells me to open it. If it's Mom's old wallet, it would be empty. I thumb back the snap. Before I can open it, Dad takes it from my hands and gets to his feet. I have a what-the-heck-just-happened moment.

Dad reaches for a box on the top shelf and offers it to me, still sitting on the floor. "This is the one with your pictures."

"You really should mark what's in these boxes." I remove the lid but watch Dad to see what he does with the wallet, still curious if anything is in it. While going through some of my pictures, Dad puts the wallet back in the box. Then he stuffs the dress in it, clearly not as neat as Mom had it. She would have a hissy fit if she saw what he did.

"Ah, remember this one?" I hold up the picture for him to see. "We went to the zoo for my birthday."

Dad squints, leaning in for a closer look, then frowns. "Wow. I've gained a lot of weight over the years."

"You look better with meat on your bones."

I skim through the pictures. There are good memories growing up, but only because of Dad. We had some good times, him and I. Dad was like a candle guiding me through my darkness.

"This is enough." I put the lid back on the box. "Can you put this back for me?"

"Sure." Dad puts it on the top shelf.

I get to my feet. "Ready to get out of this closet?"

"After you." He motions for me to go first.

We head downstairs.

I can't believe it's dusk outside. Where did the time go?

"It's getting late. I should head home."

"Already?"

"Yeah, I know. Seems like I just got here." After tucking the pictures in my pocketbook, I take my coat from the hook on the wall and slip it on. "Thanks for making the chili."

He adds a few logs to the fire and pokes the embers, causing the flames to rise. "Sure you can't stay a few more minutes?"

"I'd give anything to stay longer." I walk toward him and button my coat, always dreading this part of my visits. "I have a long drive home, remember?"

"How can I forget?" He returns the fire poker and faces me, releasing a long sigh of sadness. "Guess I won't see you again until Thanksgiving."

"Speaking of…" I grab my purse and throw the strap over my shoulder. "We need to make plans. Call me in a few days." I hug him. It's never easy to leave and why I make my exits fast. If not, there'll be tears. "I already miss you."

"I miss you too. It's lonely after you leave."

"And it's lonely driving home." I release him, then tease him. "You need to come to Hendersonville."

"Maybe after the holidays."

"I'll hold you to that."

Dad walks me to the door. "Let me know you made it home."

I open the door and smile at him. "I will. Love you, Dad."

"Love you too."

After another quick hug, I rush outside, get in my car, and prepare for that lonely drive home.

~ ~ ~

It's almost nine when I walk into the apartment. Stacy and Dillon are snuggled on the couch in the dim light, watching a movie.

"How did it go?" Stacy mutes the television and sits up.

"It was nice." I plop down in the recliner and throw my arms over the sides and my head against the back. I'm tired. It's been a long day.

"So…" She raises one eyebrow. "It was a good visit?"

"I need a beer." Dillon stands and stretches with his hands together above his head. "Anybody else want one?"

"Yeah," Stacy tells him. "Bring me one."

Dillon turns to me. "Carlen, do you want one?"

"No thanks."

Once he's out of the living room, Stacy quickly scoots to the end of the couch closest to me and whispers, "So, tell me honestly. Everything okay?"

"Ask me that in the morning."

"Do you think you'll have nightmares?"

"I hope not," I mumble, my tired body taking in the comfort of the recliner. "Dad and I talked about Mom, so there's a chance."

"You should leave your television on to distract you."

"I've already thought about that."

"You know if you have one, you can come and sleep with me."

"No. I'll wake you up, and I know you have to get up early."

"Oh stop it." She pops my arm, dangling over the side of the recliner. "Don't be silly."

Dillon enters the room, so we'll have to finish our talk later. As much as I want to tell her about the wallet I found, I can't. Not that there's anything to tell. Like Dad said, it was an old wallet. Not the one that was stolen.

"Okay, guys. I'm calling it a night." I drag my tired body from the recliner and stretch while yawning.

"Remember what I told you."

I give Stacy a thumbs-up and tell Dillon, "See you later."

After gulping his beer, Dillon holds up his hand. "Have a good night."

Tired, I slip my shoes off and lie on my bed with my ankles crossed and my intertwined hands behind my head, replaying the visit with Dad. It was probably one of the best, minus that dark shadow. Even though I still have the memories of Mom, at least I seem more in control and not some terrified kid. Still, I long for the day I no longer hear her voice.

"Yeah, I know Gloria. It's up to me to delete the messages."

The longer I lie here, my eyelids become heavy, blinking slowly. It's tempting to close them and go to sleep. As tired as I am, maybe I'll sleep through the night and avoid *her*. I roll my eyes.

"Carlen, you look just like your aunt when you make that stupid face. God, I couldn't stand that woman. You're just as hateful as she was."

"Aunt Jean was *not* hateful. She was a sweet woman. Just like Dad. The reason you didn't like her is because she told you what she thought and called you out when you were ugly to us."

Wonder if Aunt Jean is in the handful of pictures I brought home from Dad's. With a second wind hitting me, I sit up and reach for my pocketbook at the foot of my bed. Once I have them, I quickly thumb through them.

I stop and stare at the picture of me when I was in the first grade, holding a finger painting. My arm is in a cast. Looking at it is a painful memory, so I continue to go through the pictures. With only a few left, hope dwindles that I have one of my aunt.

And then, there it is. I smile at one of the few good memories growing up. It was Aunt Jean's birthday. Dad stands next to her with one arm around her. I'm standing in front of them in a white dress that fluffs out at the knees and wearing white patent leather shoes. Mom always dressed me like a doll. She said how I looked was a reflection on her.

"What about the way you treated me, Mom? Wasn't *that* a reflection on you?"

If only I could ask her that question and make her answer it, along with all the others that are stored up, waiting to be asked.

"Carlen, you know that's never going to happen. Why continue to store them when you know it's toxic?"

Now I have Gloria's voice in my head.

"Because I want to know why."

"Since it's not possible to ask your mother these questions, perhaps you could write them out and let them go."

"It's not the same."

"Maybe not, but isn't it worth a try?"

Am I suddenly in a therapy session? First, Mom takes up space in my head, and now I'm having a conversation with my therapist. I close my eyes and rub my forehead. Maybe I should try journaling. Mom is still fresh in my head. Maybe the words would come. I lower my hands and look around my room. "Where did I put that thing?"

When I started seeing Gloria, I bought a notebook at her suggestion and tried to journal. After a few attempts, I gave up. Although I know I didn't throw the notebook away, I can't remember where I put it. I leave the bed, open my closet, and search through my box of miscellaneous things. Sure enough, there it is with the pen still poked through the spiral.

I lean against the headboard and bend my knees with the notebook on my thighs. After turning to the first blank page, I begin.

"Mom…"

Where are the questions that live in my head? Dang it. I chew on the inside of my mouth and try again.

"Mom, I don't know why you hated me so much…and…"

Why can't I write down what's in my head? This is frustrating and why I stopped journaling the first time. I sit back and take a moment. This is too much mental work. I tap my pen against the notebook and roll my eyes at the two lines. Even though I'm frustrated, there's some determination brewing, so I try again.

I don't know what I did that was so wrong to make you hate me. A mother is supposed to love her child. All you showed me was hate and fear. A fear that consumes me and disables me. It didn't go away when you died, but you won't win. I'll find a way to rid my head of your voice.

Finally, the words come, and my pen scribbles across the paper.

I was just looking at a picture of me when I was six and had a cast on my arm. Remember that day, Mom? Do you? It was summer. I was outside playing and fell out of the swing and hurt my arm. Do you remember that day, because I sure do?

I stop writing, suddenly that little girl.

"Mommy, my arm hurts really bad." With tears streaming down my face, I walk toward her, holding my arm with my other hand. "I, I fell down."

Mommy stops the sewing machine and looks at my

arm and then at me. "You're fine. Kids fall all the time. Stop crying." Mommy goes back to her sewing.

"But it hurts." I cry more tears. "It, it hurts really bad."

Mommy stops again and looks at me, but this time she has those mean eyes. "I said, you're fine. Go back outside and play. Can't you see I'm busy?"

"It hurts too much to play."

She points at the couch. "Then go sit down and quit crying, and it will stop hurting." She goes back to sewing. "You're such a baby. Now, go on like I said. I'm busy here."

If I keep talking, she will yell at me, so I go to the couch. It's hard to get on it with my hurt arm. I wiggle onto it and use my foot to push the coffee table. Once I'm on the couch, my legs stick to it, because it does that when it's hot weather. My legs stick to the seats in Daddy's car too.

"Ow, ow, ow."

Every time I move, it hurts more. I scoot to the end and put my arm on the arm of the couch so I won't move it. Then I sit and wait for it to stop hurting. That's what Mommy said. It would stop hurting if I sat here and stopped crying. But it doesn't stop hurting. My arm don't look hurt. It's just dirty from playing. Maybe that's why Mommy don't believe me. She can't see a boo-boo. It makes me want to cry, because my arm really does hurt.

It's been a long time. Mommy is still sewing. That's what she likes to do, and no one is supposed to bother her, or she gets really mad and screams. That's why I don't want to tell her my arm still hurts. I don't want her to scream at me.

The front door opens. "I'm home."

I can't run to Daddy. I like it when he picks me up and gives me a hug. He's always happy to see me.

Daddy looks at me. "Hey, pumpkin. Why are you crying?"

"Because I fell down and hurt my arm. Mommy told me to sit here and don't cry, and it'll stop hurting."

Daddy comes to me really fast. "Where did you fall?"

"Out of my swing."

"Let me see." He almost touches my arm.

"No, Daddy, don't." I push his hand away with the one that don't hurt.

Mommy marches to the couch, slinging her arms. "She's fine. She's just being a baby."

Daddy stands up and looks at her. "Our daughter is

hurt. Why didn't you call me or take her to the doctor?"

Mommy's eyes turn scary, and she points her finger at Daddy. "Don't raise your voice at me. I told you she's fine. Kids fall all the time and get hurt. That's what they do. She should be more careful."

"And good parents take their kids to the doctor when they're hurt. How long has she been sitting there?"

"I don't know. Maybe…two hours. I was busy."

"Busy? How dare you let her sit there hurting."

I don't think Daddy is happy. He never talks that way to Mommy, because he's scared of her too. But he never runs to his room and hides like I do because that's her room too.

Mommy makes that mean face and yells at him. "She's fine. She just wants attention. She does this every time I try to sew."

"Attention? She's hurt, Marion." He screams, and it scares me. Daddy never screams. Only Mommy. "How dare you not let me know she's hurt. What if she's broken her arm? Some parent you are."

Mommy slaps Daddy. "Don't you ever talk to me like that again."

Oh no. The scary Mommy is here. I don't want to see her. I wanna go to my room and hide, but I can't. She makes me cry, because I'm scared, and it made me move my arm. Now it hurts more.

"We'll talk about this later." Daddy looks at me. He must not be mad anymore because he's smiling. "Carlen, I need to take you to the doctor so he can look at your arm. Where does it hurt? Point to it."

I'm scared and crying, but I show him where it hurts. Where I bend my hand.

"Okay, I won't touch it." Daddy gets one of Mommy's books on the table.

"Don't mess with my catalog."

"Damn your catalog."

Mommy pulls on it, but Daddy pulls harder and takes it from her. "Back off. I mean it."

Now Daddy scares me. He's never been mad before.

"Just be careful with it. I need to order more patterns from it."

"Carlen, I'm going to have to pick your arm up, but I'll try to be gentle."

"Ow, Daddy, no, it hurts." It makes me cry really loud.

Daddy lays my hand on the book. "I'm done. Hold still a minute." Daddy takes off his tie and wraps it around my arm. "That should stabilize it." He picks me up and looks at Mommy. "One day you're going to push me too far, Marion."

"That's enough." I stop the memory and close my eyes. My heart is in pieces. Not for me, but for the little girl whose mother didn't care her child broke her arm. For the girl who still loved her mother, even though she neglected her. For the little girl who thought that's how all mommies were. That little girl was me.

"How could you do that to your own child?" Sobbing, I wipe the tears running down my face. "Why didn't you care about me?" The hurt quickly turns to anger. I stop the tears, then bear down hard on the pen and write in huge letters, I HATE YOU.

Chapter 5: Surprise

Gloria's office is crowded. There must have been a full moon last night. Of course, the seat I always sit in is taken. My second option is next to an older woman, flipping through a magazine. The lady doesn't glance my way when I sit next to her. My eyes are on the floor, hugging myself from an internal shiver of anxiety. Every time the door opens, I shudder, wishing it was Gloria coming to rescue me.

"Carlen?"

When I hear Gloria's soft voice, I look up and see her standing at the doorway, waiting for me. I leave my chair and head toward her, still hugging myself. "Thanks for seeing me today."

Gloria smiles, but she always does. "I'm glad I had an opening."

We walk the short hallway to her office. The only sound, her stilettos pecking the floor. Almost in rhythm with my pounding heart.

"Would you like something to drink? Some water or hot tea?"

I draw my shoulders in and shake my head, unable to look at her. "No thanks."

She opens the door to her office. I bolt inside like it's a safe haven and take my seat. As soon as I do, I curl up in the oversized thick-cushion chair and hug my legs. Although I'm still anxious and trembling, there is a sense of comfort here knowing Gloria will get me out of the flashback I'm stuck in.

"We're having messy weather today." She presses the back of her skirt and settles in the seat across from me and crosses her legs.

My stomach rumbles like a prewarning I might have a sudden case of diarrhea. "Yeah. It's supposed to rain all day." It's hard to look at her, so I stare at the flower pot on her desk and eye the long vine full of leaves that almost touches the floor. When I started coming here, it was only a few inches long.

"How did the visit with your father go?"

With a shaky hand, I tuck the hair behind my ear. "Um, it actually went really good."

"Oh." Her dark brows narrow as though she didn't expect my answer. "So, what's going on?"

"I'm not in a good place."

"But, you said your visit went well." Gloria reaches for the legal pad off of her desk and rests it on her lap.

"For the most part, it did."

"Did you hear your mom's voice?"

I nod. "A few times, but that's not what has me in a bad place. It's not the reason I had to see you."

"Did something happen?"

"Sort of," I mumble, resting my chin on my knees while she writes. "When I got home, I tried to do some journaling."

Gloria looks at me and presses her thin rosy lips together to hold back a smile, but her beaming brown eyes tell me she's pleased with my effort. "How did that go?"

"It was hard at first. The words wouldn't come out on paper." My body begins to relax. My stomach even settles. "Then it took off. I was on a roll and had a whole page in no time. Then things…changed."

"How so?"

"I brought some pictures home with me when I was young. One of them was when I was six and broke my arm. The more I wrote about that day, I became that six-year-old girl."

Gloria quickly scribbles like she's a reporter capturing a story for the six o'clock news. "What do you remember most about that day?"

"How Mom was too busy sewing to bother with me. She told me to sit on the couch and stop crying. I sat there with a broken arm until Dad came home and took me to the doctor."

Gloria continues to take notes.

"The more I wrote in my journal, the more I was six. When I woke up this morning, I was still six. I can't shake it. How do I make her go away?"

She stops writing and eyes me. "Carlen, you can't make her go away. That's you."

That's not what I wanted to hear. Frustration builds, causing my eyes to water. Gloria doesn't get how creepy and scary this is. I hug my legs tighter. "It feels like I'm going crazy."

"I assure you, Carlen, you're not going crazy."

"Why can't I shake it off? It's like she's haunting me. It's like…" What words could possibly describe what's inside of me? There are none. My anxiety rises at the thought of leaving here and still feeling like that six-year-old. "Gloria, I need her gone," I tell her with deep desperation, knowing she's my only hope. "If I can't shake this feeling, I'm not going to be able to go to work when I leave."

"Then let's find a way for you to cope," she tells me encouragingly, brushing her salt and pepper bangs to the side. "Do you think talking about that day will help?"

I give her a confused glare. "Um, no. Journaling about that day is why I'm here. I'm trying to forget, not remember."

"I understand that, but sometimes talking about it seems to satisfy that little girl in us. She's obviously still upset if she doesn't go away. Maybe we should listen to her." Gloria scribbles on her legal pad. "What does that little girl keep saying?"

I look down and think. The visual of me sitting on the couch is still there but grainy like an old home movie in black and white. "Her arm hurts."

"Does she feel ignored?"

"She doesn't know what that means. She believes her mom. That if she sits down and stops crying, then her arm won't hurt anymore."

Gloria stops writing and looks at me. "But you, the adult, knows that six-year-old was ignored and neglected?"

"I know now. A loving mother would have rushed her injured child to the hospital."

Gloria nods. "Yes, she would have, but sadly, your mother didn't."

Hearing her say that is validation, but my heart hurts for that little girl, still seeing her sitting on that couch. "Mom knew I was hurting." My eyes well up with tears. I look away before I cry. "Why wouldn't she take me to the doctor?"

"Carlen, it sounds like your mother had some mental issues that were never addressed."

I laugh and use the end of my sleeve to wipe a tear that seeps out. "You think?"

"Is it possible for you to accept you will never know why she neglected you?"

I wipe another tear. "No." Surely Gloria sees how my insides are a valley of broken shards, and the only way to be whole is to put them back together. "I need to know why she didn't love me."

"Is that so you can convince yourself your mother is the bad guy and not you?"

Sometimes I swear Gloria can read my mind.

"Maybe."

"Carlen, you have to believe it wasn't you. It was her. You do see that, right?"

"Rationally, yes, but in my screwed-up head, no. A part of me will never understand how she could turn her back on me and let me sit there hurting."

Gloria's eyes light up. "Listen to what you just said. You may never understand why."

That doesn't make me feel better, seeing that little girl sitting so compliantly on the couch, needing her mother, only to be ignored. And not just that day, but every day of my life. Overwhelmed from all the memories and the hurt, I lose it and burst into tears.

"Let it out, Carlen." Gloria offers me a box of tissues.

I snatch two, wipe my tears and babble, "It hurts she couldn't love me."

"I know it does," she whispers with compassion. "Don't hold it in."

I curl up in the chair and cry for that little girl.

Gloria pats my shoulder. "I'm here, Carlen."

I press the tissues against my mouth and nose, sniffling.

Gloria sits back. "I know you're hurting, but this is good, Carlen. This is how the healing begins."

"It doesn't feel like it."

"Sometimes what we feel isn't what's real. Kind of like wanting those answers. Even though you feel like you have to have them, logically you know you can move on without them, right?"

"You forget. I'm not a logical person."

"Yes you are. You really need to give yourself more credit than you do."

"Why should I?" I fold the tissues and wipe under my eye. "Look how screwed up my life is."

"Oh, I can think of many reasons why you should give yourself some credit."

"Name one."

She shrugs and twirls her hand. "Well, you didn't take the path of using drugs or alcohol, which is how many people cope with their past. You also work and pay your bills. I have so many clients who would give anything to be as functional in life as you are. Some of my clients struggle to work and be self-sufficient. Some end up homeless."

"I would be one of those clients if it wasn't for my dad."

"I'm glad you have him in your life. Carlen, you have a good head on your shoulders. We just need to work on cognitive thinking. Getting rid of old messages. Discovering what is real and what isn't."

"Gloria, it's more than stopping the old messages. I need to know why my mother didn't love me. If I don't know why, then it has to be because of me. I obviously did something wrong as a child to make her hate me."

She gasps horrified and places her hand on her chest. "Carlen, that's *not* true. What could a small child possibly do that's so wrong her mother would hate her?"

"I don't know. When you're a kid and your mother acts like she hates you, it's easy to convince yourself it's because you did something wrong."

Gloria shakes her head and passionately tells me, "No. You did nothing wrong. That might be the message you got from her, but again, I believe your mother suffered from an undiagnosed mental disorder."

"Would it sound weird if I said I believe you, but it's still hard to accept it was her, not me?"

"Not at all. Unfortunately, I see this a lot with my clients. They associate neglect or abuse with something being wrong with them when they were a child. As an adult, it's hard to reprogram your mind to stop believing something you've lived all of your life. That's why they say knowledge is power. When you know different, it empowers you to be different. You know, change that mindset."

"You make that sound easy." I wave my hand and sing sarcastically, "Now that I know it was Mom and not me, I can go live my life and function like normal people."

Thankfully, Gloria doesn't take my sarcasm personally. Instead, she gives me that sweet smile. "No, I'm not saying it's easy, but it is possible."

"How?"

Her smile is gone, and she gives me her serious gaze. "By stopping those old messages. Your mother may have put them there when you were a child, but as an adult, you have the power to stop them."

"Where's the 'stop' button so I can press it?"

She tries so hard not to smile at me being facetious. "You fight words with words."

I narrow my brows. "Huh?"

Gloria taps the pen against her cheek. "Can you imagine if you were to say…" She sits up straight and holds her chin in the air. "Mom, guess what? I don't need those answers anymore. It doesn't matter why you neglected me, because it's not going to stop me from living my life."

I laugh at her spunky personality. "Like that's going to ever happen."

She scowls. "There's that negativity again."

I raise my shoulders and squeal, "But it's true."

She points her ink pen at me. "I want you to say it."

"Say what?"

"What I just said."

I hate when she does this, but since I'm a compliant client, her wish is my command. After clearing my throat, I hold my head high and fake some spunk. "Mom. Guess what? I don't need answers anymore. So there."

She glows with pride and sings, "Nice. How did it feel when you said that?"

Now I'm the one smiling. "Like I was doing what I was told."

She frowns. "Carlen."

"Okay, so maybe there was a little something in saying it. But as sure as I'm sitting here, I'll be wanting those answers before the sun goes down."

Gloria taps her ink pen against her index finger and hums. "Your homework assignment is to write 'Mom, I don't need answers anymore' one hundred times a day over the next week."

My mouth opens wide. "Do what?"

"You don't have to do them all at once. In fact, write a third, three times a day. Bring it with you next time you come."

"Are you serious?"

She laughs wickedly. "Oh, I'm very serious."

Somehow, Gloria has brought me back to myself. That little girl is gone. I hope she's okay. Now, to the other thing that's bothering me. "Something else happened when I was at Dad's."

"What?"

It's hard to tell her. She might think I'm crazy for sure. But I need to talk to her about this.

"Carlen?"

"Um..." The words don't want to come out, but I force them. "When I was at Dad's, I saw something."

"What was it?"

My heart beats a little faster at the notion of talking about this. I take in a deep breath and prepare myself. "I was in the kitchen. When I turned from the fridge, I swear I saw a shadow walking toward the door. It happened so fast, I questioned if I really saw anything at all. Whether or not I did, it felt like someone was there. It scared the heck out of me."

"Oh, I'm sure it did. Have you seen it before?"

"No."

"Hmm." She frowns like she's in thought. "Do you think it was your mother?"

"No. I'm sure it was a guy, but it doesn't make sense. Mom never let anyone come in the house. We never had visitors. The only person I think it could be is the guy who stabbed her."

Gloria, clearly drawn in to what she's hearing, sits back in her chair and narrows her brows. "Did you talk to your father about this?"

"No. I wanted to talk to you first. See, the thing is, Dad said I was upstairs when it happened, so how could I have seen the killer?"

"Maybe it's not the killer and another memory you've suppressed."

"Gloria, no one else was *ever* in that kitchen."

"Do you think it was your father?"

My mouth opens to counter, but I can't. "Um, I haven't thought about that. Guess it could've been him. But why would a memory of my father scare me?"

Gloria, with her elbows on the arms of her chair, twirls her ink pen. "Memories often come in bits and pieces and can be scary."

"So, you think that's what it was? A memory trying to come back to me?"

"It's possible." She exhales. "Carlen, remember what I told you. If that memory does come back, it's because your mind thinks you can handle it."

"Dad said the only thing to remember is running into the kitchen and seeing Mom on the floor. Is that traumatizing enough to make me block out those few minutes?"

She nods. "Yes."

"So, I either have a memory trying to scare me or a ghost."

Gloria laughs. "Oh, I don't think it's a ghost. It could turn out to be something not even related to your mother's death."

"What should I do?"

She holds up her legal pad. "I know something that might help."

"Journaling isn't for everyone. I tried that last night, and it's the reason I'm sitting here right now. I can't go through that again."

Gloria lowers the legal pad on her lap and gives me her therapy gaze. "Keep in mind, Carlen, you have all the control. You just have to tap into that power. Remembering your past is like visiting someone. The door is always open for you to walk out. Maybe if you journal, you could have short visits. When you feel overwhelmed, then stop. Over time, you might find you're able to cope with what you're feeling and brave those moments."

I look away, not wanting to listen to her suggest journaling, because I'm not doing it anymore. I'm trying to run from my past, not have it follow me like a lost puppy.

"Carlen, somewhere along the way, you will have to face the past if you want to come out of that cage."

As much as I want to argue with her, I know she's right. I just don't like hearing it.

~ ~ ~

I plop down in my chair and notice a customer with his arms crossed, watching people walk by. "Can I help you with something?"

The middle-aged gentleman in a suit marches toward my desk and sighs. "I'm waiting for my wife to get here." He pushes the sleeve across his wrist and looks at his watch. "She's late, and I can't wait much longer."

"Is there anything I can help you with before she gets here?"

He laughs, suddenly less tense. "Me, make decisions? I'm only here because I have the credit card."

It's hard not to laugh at his humor. "Feel free to have a seat until she gets here."

"Mark, I'm coming," a panicked voice announces. A woman in a blazer and pencil skirt shuffles toward us and waves. "Sorry I'm late."

He thumbs through his wallet. "Babe, you know I only have a few minutes."

She opens her hand to him and sings, "That's all it takes to give me the card."

"You know the limit." He places the credit card in her hand, kisses her cheek, and then scurries away.

The lady looks at me, smiling like the bird that got two worms. "Show me your most expensive granite countertops."

"Sure. If you'll follow me." Per her instructions, I show her what we have.

She scowls. "Nope. Not me."

"Okay." I continue to the next counter. "This is one of our top sellers."

She shakes her head. "Nope. Looks cheap."

We're about to run out of 'the most expensive' countertops we have when she finally ponders over two. With her arms crossed, her eyes shift from one to the other. "Hmm, one of these might work."

I don't mind helping her decide which one. After all, that's what I love to do, but I need to use the bathroom. My poor bladder is growing impatient. "They are beautiful, so you can't go wrong." I trail my fingers across the one I like. "This one, the colors are softer, which would be awesome with a dark background. Maybe with trim or valances. Oh, and I can just see copper pots hanging over it."

"You know what?" She places her hand against her cheek, her eyes wide in awe. "I *love* that visual." She softly caresses it. "I think this one has my attention like a flea ready to jump on my poodle."

I laugh at her comment.

"Okay, I've made up my mind. I want this one." She looks at me with energy in her bubbly eyes like she's ready to remodel right now. "When can we have it installed?"

I motion to my work area. "If you'll have a seat, we'll arrange a time for someone to come out, take measurements, then give you an estimate."

She walks with me. "You know, I went to two other places, and they acted like they didn't want to help me. It's not like I knew what I wanted. Now, place diamonds in front of me, and I'll spot what I like immediately."

"Well, your search is over."

She exhales, exasperated. "Finally."

I settle in my chair and bring up the app on my computer.

"I sure hope you have something soon." She sits across from me and rests her big pocketbook on her lap. "Thanksgiving is right around the corner, and I have to have my kitchen ready."

"I understand."

She lucks out. There's an opening the next day. Once I have her taken care of, I practically run to the restroom. While sitting on the commode, I check my phone. Stacy sent a message.

How did things go with Gloria? Feeling better?

I send a reply. *Yes, much better. Sorry I couldn't talk about it this morning.*

She responds. *Just glad you're better. See you tonight.*

When I come out of the restroom and turn the corner, I almost run into Matthew.

"There you are." He jerks his head to shift the long black bangs out of his eyes. "I was beginning to think you were playing hooky today."

"No, I had an appointment this morning and came in late. Wanna hang out tonight?"

"Can't. Got plans."

What? Matthew has plans? He's more of a homebody than I am.

"Oh well. Have fun with your *plans*," I tease, curious what they are.

"Gotta run. Heading to lunch." He walks away and adds, "We'll talk later."

"I'll be here," I mumble, still in shock he has plans and didn't tell me what they are. I continue on my way. A customer stands at the end of the aisle with his back to me, glancing right and left. Once I'm close enough, I ask, "Can I help you with something?"

The customer spins around. As though I ran into a brick wall, I come to an instant stop with my mouth open and unable to breathe. It's *him* nestled in that big puffy coat and wearing a baseball cap.

"Ah, there you are." Grinning, Andy approaches.

"Um, I'll find someone else to help you."

He comes to a stop two feet in front of me. "No, I want *you* to help me."

Of all days, I can't deal with Andy. Not after an emotional

session this morning. I politely tell him, "Do me a favor and walk away."

He shakes his finger and sings, "Oh, no, no, no. You have to help me. That's your job."

With my jaw clenched, I hiss through my teeth, "I'd rather be fired than help you."

Andy raises his shoulders and covers his snicker. "Oh, someone woke up on the wrong side of the bed."

I'm not even going to respond and walk past him.

Andy grabs my arm. "Wait."

I turn and face him at the same time jerk my arm from his hold. "Don't *ever* touch me again. I'm going to find someone else to help you."

"No don't," he quickly pleads, suddenly submissive. "Look, I don't need help with anything. I came to talk to you. I tried calling, but it didn't go through."

"That's because I blocked you. And you wasted your time coming here, because I have *nothing* to say to you. Now or ever." Proud of myself for not crying, I step closer and stare him down. "You have *no* idea what you did to me that day. Yeah, I might have issues, and I'm not some blonde bombshell, but I'm not stupid enough to ever give you another chance."

"Carlen, I, I'm sorry." He reaches out to me but quickly withdraws his hand. Probably at my glare, daring him to touch me. "I'm the one who's stupid. I made a big mistake. I get it." There's sincere remorse in his eyes. His shoulders slouch, and he pleads, "Can we at least talk? Let me make it up to you."

For a split second, I almost fall for his sensitive side. Andy genuinely seems to mean what he says. My heart might have been broken, but we did have some good times. Then my last memory of him flashes before me like a billboard, and I question what I ever saw in him.

"You think I'm stupid enough to give you another chance after seeing you screwing someone on your couch?"

He holds his hands up in defense. "I'm not saying we have to get back together, but I really miss you."

I frown and almost laugh. "Well, I don't miss you."

He tilts his head and smiles. "I know how much you like Jump Off Rock and looking at the mountains. Let's go there and talk. We can take a blanket and some hot chocolate."

I cross my arms and smirk. "You mean, go there so you can

59

gawk at other women? That's what you did every time we went there."

"And I was wrong. I get it now."

"I'm not going anywhere with you. Get your whore to go with you."

A man behind me clears his throat. "Is everything alright?"

When I turn to see who spoke, my heart almost stops. There stands Mr. Handsome. The guy who looked at refrigerators. Right now, he's looking at Andy.

"She's helping me," Andy blurts out in a territorial tone.

I turn back to him. "No I'm not. We're done here. I have nothing else to say to you."

Mr. Handsome steps closer to me. "I think the lady wants you to leave."

Andy gives him a sinister glare. For a moment, I fear he might make a scene. Andy gets upset when things don't go his way. He looks at me. His lips part to say something, but he doesn't. After rolling his eyes, he simply turns and walks away. I watch until he disappears.

"Hope I didn't cross a line by butting in."

That sweet voice makes my heart flutter. I'm sure my face is embarrassingly red, but I turn and look at the most handsome man I've ever seen. Then I remind myself there's a girlfriend lurking somewhere. "No. I appreciate you running him off. Did you need help with something?"

There's that adorable smile. He even blinks so cute. "Well, I still need a fridge."

"Would you like to see it again?"

"If you wouldn't mind showing it to me."

"Not at all. Follow me."

And he does, walking so close his arm almost graces mine.

"This is the one you were looking at." I open the doors for him.

He massages his jaw and scans the inside. Then he nods. "Yeah. I want this one. How soon can it be delivered?"

"If we have one in stock, maybe a few days, depending on the schedule. Would you like for me to see?"

He closes the doors. "If you don't mind."

"Of course not. Let's go to my desk, and I'll check."

He motions with his hand. "After you."

We saunter to my work station.

He clears his throat. "Again, I'm sorry if I crossed the line back there."

"Oh, you're fine."

"Was that your boyfriend?"

"Ex-boyfriend. We broke up four months ago."

"Sorry for being nosy. I was concerned with the way he was pushy."

"He can be, but I think he got the message."

Mr. Handsome sits in the chair across from my desk.

I settle in my seat and pull up the page on my computer to search our inventory. "Looks like we have one in stock."

"Awesome."

"When would be a good day to have it delivered?"

"Let's see…" He gently finger-scratches his temple. "I can take off Friday. Will that work?"

I turn back to my monitor and check the availability. "We have a morning opening from nine to eleven. Or that afternoon between two and four."

"The afternoon works for me. That will give me time to haul off the old one to the scrapyard."

"Let's get you scheduled, then." I click here and there, input his information, then set up the time for him. "Would you like to purchase the extended warranty?"

He singsongs, "Do you get a commission if I do?"

I laugh. "No."

"Well, you would deserve it."

"Thanks, but it's something we have to ask."

"Sure, go ahead and add it."

"It's ready for you to swipe your credit card."

While he does, I steal a glance at him.

The transaction is approved, and a receipt pops out. I offer it to him. This is it. Goodbye Mr. Handsome. "You're all set."

He stands and tucks the receipt in his front pocket. "I'm definitely out of line when I say this, but I heard what you told that guy. Don't ever sell yourself short. You're a beautiful woman."

If I wasn't sitting in my chair, I might be on the floor. My eyes mist over at the most beautiful words I've ever heard, leaving me speechless.

"One of the reasons I came back wasn't only to buy a fridge. I wanted to ask you—"

"Carlen. This gentleman needs some help."

I look at Janet and want to strangle her for interrupting. Thankfully, I smile instead. "Sure. As soon as I finish with this customer."

The older gentleman waves his hand. "No rush. I can wait."

"I should be going," Brad, aka Mr. Handsome, announces. Then he winks at me. "Remember what I said."

He's gone. It's all I can do to face the next customer and keep a smile. "How can I help you?"

Chapter 6: Flowers

Dad's ringtone plays. I grab my phone off the dresser and swipe the screen. "Hey. What a nice surprise." After sitting on my bed, I struggle to get my shoe on with the phone sandwiched between my head and shoulder.

"Hope I'm not calling at a bad time."

"No, I, um…" I tug my other shoe on. It might help if I untied it first, but I'm in a rush. "Sorry, I'm getting ready for work. Someone called out, and they asked me to come in early. Is everything okay?"

"Everything's fine. I was just thinking about you."

"I'm off tomorrow. Why don't you come up for a visit?"

"Kind of short notice."

"It's not like you're across the country." Then a better idea hits me. "Why don't you come here for Thanksgiving? That gives you a week to plan for it. I've never cooked a turkey and would like to try it. And, you can meet Matthew."

"What about your roommate?"

"Between spending the day at Dillon's family and her family, Stacy will be gone all day."

Dad hesitates, but that tells me he's thinking about it.

"Please come. I'll take you to Jump Off Rock, and you can see the snowcaps."

Dad chuckles. "That's an…unusual name."

"It's a really nice lookout. Way back in time, an Indian woman lost her love and was so sad she jumped off to her death."

"I would love to, but it will be cold. I can't handle it like I used to."

"We don't have to go there. We can plan that this summer, but come next week." I beg like I did when I was little. "Pretty please."

A long, contemplating sigh rumbles. "The thing is, Patty is going to be alone. Her sister can't make it this year, and she's not about to fly to Texas. I told her she could join us. That's why I called, to let you know. I didn't think you would mind."

I leave my bed and pace, smiling with my lips parted. "Dad, are you and Patty—"

"No, sweetie. We're just good friends. That's all."

"Why don't you bring her here with you?"

"Are you sure that's alright?"

"Dad, I would *love* for you guys to come. And I know Matthew would be fine with it."

"I'll ask her tomorrow and let you know."

"Okay, because if you are coming here, I need to run to the store for groceries."

"Do you need me to send you some money?"

"No, but thanks." I glance at the time, which has flown by way too fast. "Dad, I really hate to go, but I'm going to be late for work if I don't."

"Don't mean to hold you up. I'll call you tomorrow about our plans for next week."

"Sounds good. Love you," I tell him in a rushed voice, running out of my bedroom.

"Love you too. Bye."

After grabbing my coat and slipping it on, I grab my lunch cooler and head for the front door.

~ ~ ~

Luck is on my side. With three minutes to spare, I clock in. On my way to my work station, I put on my orange apron and tie it. I predict that older man making eye contact is going to stop me.

"Um, Miss…" He holds up his hand. "Can you tell me where the things are you use for caulking?"

"Yes, they're on aisle four where the paint department's at."

He looks that way and gently scratches his jaw, then narrows his brows. "Oh, okay."

I continue to my work station.

Shannon pages me through the handheld radio. "Carlen, if you're not with a customer, come to the front desk for a minute."

"On my way."

A young lady with a small boy comes out of an aisle. When she sees me, she darts toward me with panic etched across her face.

The toddler holds his hand between his legs as they walk fast. "Where's the bathroom?"

"Turn right at plumbing." I point in that direction, sensing the urgency. "You'll see the sign."

"Johnathan, hold on one more minute." The woman picks up the small boy, holds him against her chest, and makes a mad dash toward the bathroom.

I step behind the service desk and approach Shannon. "What's up?"

"Oh, hey." She abandons the computer, takes my forearm, and escorts me to the counter and whispers, "I have to show you something." At the counter, she points at a vase with assorted flowers. "These just came for me. Aren't they beautiful?"

I stare in awe and a bit jealous. "Um, yeah. They are." I didn't know she was dating someone. "Who sent them?"

"You have to promise not to tell." She picks up the vase and brings the flowers to her nose and inhales.

"Like I'm going to know the guy."

"Oh, you know him." Shannon sets the vase down and faces me, blowing a bubble with her chewing gum. "He works here."

"Who?"

She smiles and chews her gum at the same time. "Matthew."

Matthew? But he said she wasn't his type. I'm having a 'what's going on' moment, a bit confused. "Wow. I didn't know you guys were dating."

"We're not exactly dating." She motions for me to follow her away from the other employees who have gathered around us. "I asked him to go out." She scrunches her nose and whispers, "Not like on a date-date, but to hang out. I couldn't believe he said yes."

Me neither.

"Last night, I mentioned today is my birthday. You can't imagine my surprise when I come in and find these flowers sitting here."

"Happy birthday," I mumble, still in shock.

"Thanks." She smacks her chewing gum. "Matthew is taking me out tonight, but he won't tell me where."

So that's what his plans tonight are and why he didn't tell me. Matthew does like Shannon, although he told me he didn't. I fake a smile. "Hope you guys have fun."

"Oh, we will."

"I need to get to my department. Let me know how tonight

goes."

She winks. "Might not can give you *all* the details, if you know what I mean."

Geez, like I want *those* details. "Gotta go. Catch you later."

I head through the store and dart down the aisles, looking for Matthew. I spot him stocking a shelf and run to him.

Matthew, putting a box of nails on the shelf, notices me coming. "Hey."

"Hey yourself." I tuck my hands in the pockets of my apron and sway, giving him an impish grin and sing, "I heard about the flowers."

He shakes his head and exhales. "She wasn't supposed to tell anyone."

"You can't blame her. It's a proud moment in a girl's life when her...*boyfriend* sends her flowers to work on her birthday."

He puts another box on the shelf and gives me a scolding glare. "I'm *not* her boyfriend. We hung out. That's it."

"But, you sent her flowers?"

Matthew stops stocking and looks at me with defensive eyes. "I only did it because I felt bad for her." He puts the box on the shelf. "She told me it was her birthday today, and all she's ever wanted was someone to send her flowers at work. I told her not to tell anyone they're from me. You know how everyone's going to talk if they find out."

I'm confused and not sure if he really likes Shannon or not. Either way, it's his business.

"Don't worry about what people say. I've gotta go. Talk to you later." I walk away and sing, "Have fun tonight."

Matthew rolls his eyes and continues to put up stock.

~ ~ ~

For supper, I have chicken nuggets, tater tots, and baked beans. While I eat, I think about Brad, aka Mr. Handsome, and wonder what he was going to tell me. What was the other reason he came to the store? Guess I'll never know.

The front door shuts. Stacy is home. And it sounds like Dillon is with her. Odd, because she mentioned this morning they had plans tonight. Not that I mind company.

"Carlen?"

"In the kitchen." I dip my nugget into the honey mustard sauce and devour it.

The cute couple enter the kitchen, holding hands.

"I thought you guys had plans tonight."

Stacy has this weird smile. "We stopped by for a minute."

Another guy enters the kitchen. He's tall and very skinny with messy dark hair. His thick eyebrows are just as dark.

"Carlen." Stacy places her hand on the stranger's shoulder. "This is James. He works with Dillon." She introduces him like one of those models on *The Price Is Right* would to a new car.

Still chewing, I wave my fingers. "Hi. Nice to meet you."

"You too," says the nervous guy rocking on his heels and stuffing his fingers in his front pockets.

Stacy can't stop smiling. "Since he didn't have plans tonight, we invited him to go out with us."

"We?" Dillon cackles, reaching into the fridge for a soda. "You practically dragged him out of his house when we left."

She huffs. "No I did not."

I dip another nugget and eye my best friend, nonverbally telling her I know what she's doing.

Miss Matchmaker shuffles toward me with innocent eyes. "We stopped by to see if you wanted to go out with us."

"Nah. I'm gonna hang out here." I spoon my beans and notice the guy is watching me.

Dillon pops the tab on his soda. "You should go with us. Get out and have some fun, Miss Hermit," he mutters, bringing the can to his lips.

"I'm not a hermit." I reach for a tater tot and pop it in my mouth. "I'm tired."

"Oh please." Stacy leans over the island bar, looks me in the eye and whispers, "Put on a nice outfit and go out with us."

I whisper back, "No. I know what you're doing."

She smirks, proud of herself. "So, do you think he's cute?"

"He's okay. Seems shy."

Dillon burps. "Hey, are we going or not?"

Still leaning over the island bar, Stacy turns and tells him, "Yeah. Give me one second."

"One." He grins like he's so funny.

"Ha, ha."

"We're leaving." Dillon and what's-his-name walk out of the kitchen.

Stacy pops my wrist. "Come with us."

While chewing, I stare at my best friend and try to come up with a good excuse. "I would, but I had a bad morning, remember? And a tense session with Gloria. It's not a good day for me to go out." To make my case, I give her a sad, pouty face. "Say you understand."

Stacy stands up straight, her palms leaving the island bar. "Does this mean you'll consider going out with him another time?"

Before I can tell her no, not going to happen, Dillon hollers, "Stacy, you coming or not?"

She yells over her shoulder, "Coming." Then she looks at me. "Text me if you need me."

"Will do. You guys have fun."

"You know we will."

Stacy leaves the kitchen.

The front door shuts.

I finish my supper, wash the dishes, then settle on the couch. My first instinct is to text Matthew to come over, but then I remember he's out with Shannon. I'm still in shock he bought her flowers, although it is in his good nature to do something so sweet. Then again, maybe he really does like her, but why keep that a secret? That's not like Matthew.

"Oh well." I grab the remote and surf the channels.

Murder Mystery? Hell no.

Romance? No, I'll think of Brad.

A romantic comedy? Maybe.

Girl gets dumped and meets a new guy who sweeps her off her feet. Love is in the air. After a few minutes of watching, I stretch out on the couch and get comfy.

"What the heck?"

The boyfriend's ex-girlfriend shows up and vows she's going to get her man back.

I scream at the television. "No. Don't you dare take her back."

The man goes back to his ex-girlfriend. New girl gets dumped…again.

"What an idiot."

The credits play. I yawn and punch the button to turn off the television. After dragging myself off the couch, I yawn again and head to my bedroom, ready to call it a day.

After I brush my teeth, I drop the toothbrush in the holder

and stare at myself in the mirror. I could look prettier if I wanted to. Some eyeliner would bring out my brown eyes. My fingers delicately trail across my pale cheek. A little foundation would give my face some color. With my palm, I push my bangs up and expose my eyebrows. They definitely need some attention. Mom never showed me how to use makeup. Not that I care.

I gather my hair into a ponytail and twirl it into a bun. I do a right profile check and then a left profile check. This isn't me. I'll never be a dress-up woman like Stacy and Mom. My hands part, letting my hair fall. It's dull and boring. Like me. Maybe I should get a new hairstyle and add some highlights. I think back to when I was twelve.

Mom said girls were supposed to have long hair and no bangs. I didn't think anything about it until I turned twelve. That puberty thing kicked in, I guess. All the girls at school wanted to have a grown-up look. My friends were getting stylish haircuts. It took me months to get up the nerve to ask Mom if I could get mine cut.

She always washed my hair in the kitchen sink. That particular day, things in the house had been calm. Mom even washed my hair with gentle hands. When she was having a bad day, she would claw at my scalp with her fingernails. I never told her how much it hurt, knowing she would dig her nails in harder. Even though it seemed the best time to ask, I was scared and chickened out. While she put conditioner on my hair to control the tangles, it was now or never, so I worked up the courage and asked her.

"Mom, I've been thinking about something."

"What?"

"My hair hasn't been cut in a long time. I was thinking, the next time you go to the beauty shop, can I get my hair cut?"

She didn't answer right away and rinsed my hair. It was clear I had upset her because of the vibe in the air. One I was all too familiar with. Then her cold tone confirmed it.

"You want your hair cut?"

It was a trick question. She wanted me to say no. Any other time, I would have quickly told her what she wanted to hear to tame the evil. There wasn't a brave bone in my body to tell her yes, I do. But that day was different for some reason. I defied Mom.

"Yeah. All of my friends at school are getting their hair cut and styled. I was thinking maybe I could have mine cut and see what I look like with bangs."

Mom didn't even finish rinsing my hair and jerked me upright so fast I didn't see it happen, although my body felt the instant snap. I had caused the monster to come out. All I could do was endure her wrath.

"You want your hair cut? Then by God you can get it cut."

Mom told me this as she gripped my hair like it was a rope. It hurt so much, I thought she had pulled half of it out of my head. Still wet and dripping, she dragged me down the kitchen counter with me sliding and having no control, knowing the worst was yet to come. Mom dragged me off the end of the bar. As soon as I was on my feet, she gripped my forearm and dug her fingernails into my skin.

"I'm going to show you how your hair is going to be cut."

Although the tears came, I knew better than to say anything. Mom escorted me down the hall like a tiger having a grip on his prey, determined not to let it get away. My arm hurt so much from her fingernails in my flesh, I shuffled on my tiptoes. I thought for sure she was going to take me to the bathroom and give me a buzz cut like she did Dad. I was already mourning the loss of my hair.

When we passed the bathroom, there was relief, but that was temporary. I had no idea what Mom was going to do, which made a scared little girl even more terrified of her mother. She took me to my room and stood me in front of a picture of me hanging on the wall. It was my graduation from kindergarten. I'm standing on the stage in my ocean-blue robe, holding my little diploma and smiling with pride. My short, baby-blonde hair barely comes out from underneath my cap.

"Take a good look at that picture, young lady. That's how short I'm going to have your hair cut. You'll look like a boy. When everyone at school laughs at you, maybe you'll learn not to ask for a haircut."

She left me standing there, sobbing for so many reasons. At twelve years old, how could I comprehend her words were anything other than to slice my soul into pieces, and that's exactly what she did. Even after what she had done, I considered it merciful, because she didn't cut my hair. Maybe the fear of her doing it was her intention. With Mom, who knows? Nothing she did ever made sense. Especially the day she took me to get my hair cut.

I couldn't believe she let me tell the lady how I wanted it cut. While she layered my hair and gave me bangs, Mom explained how I was almost a teenager and needed a more mature and age-appropriate style. I didn't care if she was being fake or lying, I was proud of my new look.

Back in the present, I stare at the sad person in the mirror. Not me. The twelve-year-old girl. "I'm sorry she was so mean to you." I flip the switch and head to bed.

Chapter 7: A Holiday

I flap the white sheet over the kitchen table and line it up. "Are the sides even over there?"

Matthew steps back from the table and eyes both corners. "Um, bring down the left side a little."

I move the sheet. "How's that?"

He gives me a thumbs up. "Perfect."

Next, I set the cornucopia on the table. Then I rotate it, trying to find the right spot. "How does this look?"

"If you ask me, those things are ugly."

I give him an oh-hush glare. "They're not ugly." I sprinkle artificial leaves in the center of the table. The fall colors are perfect. Then I place a brown candle near the center. I'm so proud of my table. It puts me in the holiday spirit.

"Got anything to snack on?"

"Matthew, you know where everything is. Help yourself." I'm dying to ask him about Shannon but don't want to make him uncomfortable. However, the words come out before I can stop them. "Are you going to see Shannon for Thanksgiving?"

He digs through my basket of snacks. "No, why?"

"Just wondering."

The doorbell rings.

"Dad's here." With the energy of ten horses, I run out of the kitchen and through the living room. When I open the door, there he stands. "Dad," I squeal all giddy, my heart exploding with excitement he's here.

"Happy Thanksgiving, sweetheart." He hugs me. "If you only knew how much I missed you," he groans, holding me tighter.

"Can't be as much as I've missed you."

After our hug, I don't forget he brought a guest. I almost don't recognize her. Patty is all dressed up in slacks and a pretty red sweater. Her short-layered hair is styled like she just walked out of the beauty salon. She even has on makeup. This is quite the contrary look of the garden lady I'm used to seeing.

"Hello, Patty. I'm *so* glad you came."

"Thank you for inviting me." She smiles and holds up an aluminum pan. "Hope it's okay, but I had to bring something. Just didn't feel right not cooking for the holiday. It's stuffing."

"Of course it's okay. And thanks for bringing it."

Dad slips his coat off and tosses it across the arm of the recliner and takes the dish from Patty so she can remove her coat.

"Thank you, Paul."

Dad sniffs the air. "Something sure smells good."

"Hopefully, that's the turkey." I take the dish from him but look at Patty. "I hope it's okay we have the meal for lunch. With you guys having a long drive home, I didn't want you to have to rush off after dinner."

"That's fine. Makes perfect sense."

"Eating turkey can make you sleepy."

Dad gives me a one-arm hug and laughs. "Carlen, don't worry. It's fine."

It's so good to have my dad here. I'm on top of the world. "Let's go to the kitchen. I want you to meet Matthew." I lead the way with a spring in my step. When I enter the kitchen, I proudly announce, "Matthew, this is my dad, Paul."

Matthew's eyes are wide, always the shy guy until he gets to know someone. "Um, hi, Dad." He shakes his head. "I mean, um, Paul. I mean, Mr. Dupre."

I laugh at my nervous friend. He's so cute.

"You can call me Paul." Dad offers his hand. "It's nice to finally meet you, Matthew. Carlen speaks highly of you."

My friend shoots me an oh-no-you-didn't eye, hiding behind his long bangs swept to one side.

Knowing he's embarrassed, I tell him, "Hey, you were there for me that day I needed someone, so let me brag what a good friend you are."

He playfully retorts, "It's not like you haven't been a friend too. You did get me that job."

"No, you got the job because you're a good worker." I continue with the introductions. "And this is Dad's neighbor, Patty."

"Hello, Matthew."

The bashful guy nods. "Hi. It's nice to meet you."

I set Patty's dish on the counter. "Would anyone like

something to drink?"

Dad holds up his finger. "I wouldn't mind some coffee."

Patty shakes her head. "I'm fine for now."

"Dad, you and Matthew can watch television while we take care of things in here. I'll bring your coffee when it's ready."

"Thank you." Dad turns to Matthew. "Do you watch football?"

Matthew shrugs. "Sometimes."

My heart warms, watching them leave. My two favorite men in the world.

"What can I do to help?"

"Let's see." I press my finger against my lip and ponder. "I was going to peel some potatoes. If you wouldn't mind doing that for me, I'll make Dad some coffee." If she's willing to peel the potatoes, I don't have to deal with using a knife.

Patty shoves her sleeves up her arms, ready to dive in. "Just tell me where everything is."

We prepare the meal and have small talk. Not only does Patty know how to garden, she also knows what she's doing in a kitchen, unlike me. It's a reminder how Mom and I never had mother and daughter moments. Even though it hurts, I'm okay.

"Patty, I didn't invite you so you could do *all* the work. You're a guest."

"Nonsense. I'm enjoying this." She turns the burner off, takes the pot and pours the green beans into a bowl. "I miss cooking for people. It's no fun cooking for myself." She carries the bowl to the table. "Matthew seems like a really nice guy."

"Oh, he is." I reach into the cabinets for plates. "He's shy, but once he gets to know you, he's a talker."

"Paul mentioned he would be here, but he didn't say if he was your boyfriend or just a friend."

"No, we're just friends." I set the plates on the table and open the drawer for the silverware. "I think he likes someone at work, but he's too shy to admit it."

Makes me wonder if maybe Dad is too shy to admit he likes Patty. Then again, maybe they are simply good friends like me and Matthew. If they are more than friends, I wouldn't object. I really like Patty. I set out the silverware and remember how Dad and I were not allowed to talk to her or John. We couldn't even go outside if they were. After Mom died, we got to know them. That's when we found out John had cancer.

The oven beeps.

Nervous, I put on the gloves. "Let's see how it turned out."

Patty opens the oven for me. "Carlen, it looks perfect."

"Let's hope it tastes good." I take the turkey out and carry it to the table. It's heavy. My luck, I'll drop it. Thankfully, I make it to the table.

Patty follows me. "I'm sure it's going to be delicious."

I laugh and warn her, "You do know this is my first time cooking one?"

"And you did a very good job."

"Thanks."

Besides Gloria, I'm not used to a woman complimenting me. Hope I'm not smiling too big.

Patty rests her hands on her hips and scans the table. "That's it. Looks like we're ready to eat."

"I'll let the guys know." Before I do, I light the candle.

We gather around the table and fill our plates. Everyone takes a nice helping. Hope that means the food looks good. I was nervous about cooking a big meal, but with Patty helping me, I think everything turned out fine. The candle burning cast a pleasing aroma of butterscotch.

I hold the spoonful of mashed potatoes in front of me and hesitate to eat it. Patty added mayonnaise in them. Who does that? I put the spoon in my mouth, expecting to pucker my face at the unusual concoction. To my surprise, it's creamy and satisfies my taste buds. "Patty, these potatoes are *delicious*." I quickly spoon another bite.

She smiles and forks her green beans. "Thank you. I'm glad you like them."

"And this turkey is the best I've ever had." Dad looks my way and winks. "You really did good, Carlen. I'm not just saying that."

His compliment makes me smile, and I can't stop. And I don't want to. I love my dad so much, sometimes it makes my eyes water.

Everyone is busy enjoying the food, so the conversation is light. Matthew is still in his shy phase, but he will come around. Patty is keeping an attentive eye on Dad. She makes sure he has everything he needs. Maybe that's her nature. It's just…different seeing a woman treat him with care and kindness.

"So, Matthew…" Dad reaches for a roll and glances his way. "Were you born in Hendersonville?"

Matthew nods and wipes his mouth. "Yeah. I mean, yes."

Patty spoons mac and cheese onto her plate. "This is a beautiful town. It has a historic look. I've always loved the mountains. Especially in the fall."

"You guys should come and visit more often." When Dad looks my way, I wink.

After the meal has been devoured, everyone is so full, we postpone dessert for later and continue to talk. We share personal tidbits with each other. I learn something new about Matthew. He was on a hockey team when he was young. Patty informs us how she loves to paint when it's winter and she can't enjoy the outside.

My mouth opens wide in shock. "*You* painted that picture of the Eiffel Tower in your living room?" I've only been in her house a few times but remember the painting very well.

"I sure did. It took me almost two years. John wanted to go to Paris." She drinks some tea and adds, "We were planning on going there for our twenty-fifth anniversary, but then he became ill. I decided if we couldn't go to Paris, I'd bring Paris to him."

"That's so sweet."

I'm in awe of Patty and what a good wife she was to John. I thought all wives were like Mom, but I was wrong.

It's hard to believe we have sat here talking for two hours. Matthew is finally over his shyness and joining in on the conversations. I'm glad Dad is giving him attention. Matthew's father isn't in his life. I don't know why, but I know it's a sensitive subject. I don't ask questions the same way he doesn't ask me about Mom. Come to think about it, all I know about my friend is he lives with his sister and brother-in-law.

Dad sits up straight and looks around the table. "I don't know about you guys but I'm ready for some of that pie."

Matthew shifts those pesky long bangs to the side. "I've *been* ready. Just waiting on someone to say something."

"Then, let's have dessert." I stand and gather the dishes. "Dad, would you like some coffee with it?"

"That would be nice."

Patty gathers dishes and follows me to the kitchen counter. "What can I do to help?"

"If you wouldn't mind, go ahead and slice the pie, and I'll start the coffee. Would you like some?"

"No thanks, but I would like some more tea."

"Sure."

"Do you have small plates?"

"Yes." I point to her left. "They're in that cabinet."

Since I'm standing in front of the utensil drawer, it seems natural to open it and fetch a knife for her to cut the pie. After reaching for one, instead of placing it on the counter for Patty, my eyes become fixed on the blade. I slip into a daze, like everything is slowing down. Blood appears on the blade. Instinctually, I try to throw the knife in the sink, but my hand grips it harder. It's happening in front of them, and Stacy isn't here to help me.

"Carlen, are you alright?"

I look at Patty, but the words won't come out. Only a gargle like I'm choking.

"Paul, come here." Patty steps back, looking me over with holy terror in her wide eyes. Not that I blame her, watching me gasp for air and holding a knife.

Dad and Matthew are already on their way to see what is wrong. Dad holds out his arm to stop Matthew. "Let me handle this."

Although Matthew stops, his eyes tell me he wants to help me.

Dad pinches the blade and tries to take the knife from my hand, but my fingers are locked around the handle. "Carlen, try to relax."

Like I'm not trying? I'd rather be holding a snake. Every muscle in my body has locked up. I'm stiff as a two-by-four.

Dad takes a kitchen towel, wraps it around the blade, and wiggles it out of my hand. He tosses it in the sink, takes my forearm in one swift move, and escorts me out of the kitchen. In passing, he tells Patty and Matthew, "Excuse us for a moment."

Patty, still wide-eyed, keeps her distance.

Dad rushes me into my bedroom and closes the door. As we stare, he pants like he just ran a race. "What happened in there?"

I press my lips together. Guess I can't hide it from him anymore. I hug myself, trying to find a way to say it without him freaking out. "Um, sometimes when I see a knife, I flash back to seeing the one in Mom's chest."

Dad throws his hands up and huffs. "Carlen, why haven't you told me?"

I shrug, feeling scolded. "Because I didn't want you to worry."

He inhales hard, then lets it out, trying to calm down. "How long has this been happening?"

"About six months. It's why I started seeing Gloria."

He gets upset again. "What else are you not telling me?"

I harp back to calm him down. "Nothing. That's it. Honest."

"Carlen, you should have told me about this."

"We're not supposed to talk about it, remember?"

His brows narrow, and he waggles his finger at me. "You *know* that's different."

I cross my arms and pace. "Now you know."

"That's no way for me to find out."

I was hoping he wouldn't find out.

"Come home with me. I don't feel comfortable leaving you here alone."

I stop pacing and shake my head. "Dad, I can't stay in that house. You know that."

"Then I'll stay here a few days. Patty can drive my truck home. Once I know you're okay, I'll rent a car to get back to Charlotte."

"No. Matthew will stay with me until Stacy comes home."

"What if it happens again?"

"Stacy knows what to do. She's helped me through this before."

He takes my hand and sandwiches it between his. "But I'm going to worry about you."

"Trust me, if I wasn't okay, I would let you know. You would see it."

"Will you tell Stacy to call me if something happens?"

"Yes. And I'll give you Matthew's number if that'll make you feel better. I have two good friends who will look out for me, so you don't have to worry."

Dad smiles. "That guy likes you."

"Yes, he does. As a friend."

"Don't be so sure of that. Did you see how fast he came to your rescue?"

"Like I said. We're good friends. He's actually seeing someone at work. But, speaking of liking someone." I eye him and grin. "There's something between you and Patty."

He holds his hands up in defense. "Sweetie, we're only friends. That's it."

I'm disappointed. It would be nice to hear him confess there is more. "If that ever changes, I'd be happy for you. I really like

Patty."

"She likes you too. She told me on the way up here how I had raised a girl into a beautiful woman."

I smile with my lips parted. "She really said that?"

He frowns. "Would I lie about something like that?"

"No. I'm not used to hearing that from a woman."

"I'm sorry you never heard that from your mom."

I can't believe he mentioned her. It must have slipped out. "Thanks for saying that, Dad."

"Are you sure you're okay?"

"I'm fine. In fact, I'm ready for that dessert. How about you?"

"Give me a hug first."

I throw my arms around him.

"Promise me you're alright."

"Dad, really. I'm fine."

After our hug, we leave my bedroom and saunter down the hall.

"You mind if I explain to them what happened?"

"Not at all." He gives me a one-arm hug. "I'm so proud of you."

I never get tired of hearing that.

We enter the kitchen. It's an awkward moment. Matthew and Patty sit at the table with coffee, tea, and pie.

While enjoying dessert, I tell Matthew what happened to Mom. Patty already knows since she is our neighbor.

"Sometimes when I look at a knife, it triggers me, and I see Mom."

"It would me too." Matthew jerks his head to shift those long bangs out of his eyes and brings another forkful of pie to his mouth. "From now on, I'm in charge of knife duty," he announces like he's my protective brother.

Dad's fatherly eyes dart to Matthew. "Thank you. I appreciate that."

Patty finishes drinking her tea and gently sets the glass down. "Carlen, I, I didn't mean to…"

"Hey. It's okay. I'm sorry I spooked you."

"Don't be sorry. I can't imagine what you've been through. It's just, I didn't know what was wrong or what to do."

Patty's kind words melt my heart in a way it's never experienced before. Why couldn't I have had a mother like her?

With eyes that tell me she cares. Eyes that comfort me and not scare me. I'm so touched I can hardly get my words out. "If I'm lucky, it won't happen again."

"If it does, I'll know what to do. And if you happen to be alone, call me. I'm always here if you need to talk."

"Thank you, Patty. That means a lot."

When I was given a woman therapist, I almost canceled the appointment. To me, all women are like Mom, or so I thought. Thankfully, I gave Gloria a chance. And now that I'm getting to know Patty, it's clear all women are not like Mom.

The time comes, and we say our goodbyes, which are never easy. At least I don't have a lonesome drive home. Or Dad, since Patty is with him.

After they leave, Matthew hangs out with me. For supper, we have a turkey sandwich and finish off the pie. With our bellies stuffed a second time, we relax on the couch, put our feet on the coffee table and watch a movie.

Halfway through, Matthew tells me, "I'm really sorry about your mom and how you had to see her like that."

"It was horrible."

"No wonder you freak out when you see knives."

"It only started six months ago, which is weird, because she was murdered five years ago.

"If you ever need to talk about *it*, you know where to find me."

With my head against the back of the couch, I look at him. "Talking about my mother's murder isn't exactly my favorite conversation."

"That's not what I meant."

"What did you mean?"

"Inner demons."

I tense up at his words. We have never had this kind of conversation, and I'm suddenly uncomfortable. "What makes you think I have inner demons?"

"Because I know what it's like. I have them too."

Chapter 8: Brad

Only an hour into my day, I regret not calling in sick. Wonder if mental nausea even counts as being 'sick'? Whoever came up with Black Friday never worked in retail. It's not the crowd that has my anxiety at a ten. It's not the reason I can't focus or have yet to smile. All I can think about is Matthew and his confession last night and my response.

"I don't have inner demons."

And I didn't dare ask him what his were. I was already pushing having nightmares after the knife incident, so I had to shut down that conversation.

"Can we finish watching the movie and enjoy what's left of this day instead of talking about the past?"

"Sure, forget I said anything."

How could I cut my friend off after he opened up to me and confessed something so deep and personal? Matthew has inner demons? The shock still lingers, because whatever haunts him, unlike me, he hides it. Something tells me it has to do with his dad not being in his life. He's never mentioned his mother. If they were close, I would think he would talk about her the way I love talking about my dad. When I see Matthew, I have to tell him how sorry I am for being an ass last night. I should have turned the television off and let him talk.

"Can you *please* help me?"

I quickly turn to see who called out in desperation as though there is an emergency. I face a young lady in sweats and her hair still in a messy ponytail. "Yes, of course. How can I help you?"

"My sink won't stop leaking." She winces and flings her hand. "You know, at the handle. I've got water going everywhere on my vanity. I called my dad, and he said I need a new washer. I told him no I don't, it was my *sink*," she squeals so dramatically I almost laugh. "Dad said to come here, and you would know what he's talking about."

"Yes, it's those little black rubber rings."

She frowns and puckers her face as her agitated body comes to a sudden halt. "Oh. One of those." She whacks her forehead with the heel of her hand and rolls her eyes. "Duh. Now I feel stupid. But after the Thanksgiving-from-hell last night at my parents, and then I wake up and get a shower when I turn on the faucet, I'm deserving of a brain fart." She rolls her eyes and rocks her head, then cuts a smile. "Okay, so I'm exaggerating, but you get what I mean?"

"I do. At least it's a simple and cheap fix."

She snort-laughs. "At the rate my day is going, nothing is going to be simple."

I laugh at her sudden comical behavior.

"So, can you point me in the direction I need to go? If not, I'll starve to death before I find those darn things."

Again, I laugh. She's got a sense of humor once she's out of panic mode. "They're in the plumbing department." I point in that direction. "Sam should be there. He's an older guy and will be glad to help you if you don't find them."

"Oh, Sam is going to be my new best friend," she sings in a spirited voice and walks away in her pink fuzzy slippers.

When I turn to continue on my way, I collide with someone. It's *him*. And my hands are on his chest. And he's smiling at me with his luscious lips together. "Oh gosh. I'm so sorry." I quickly step back and stare into his beautiful brown eyes.

"I was hoping I would run into you." He chuckles. "Or, you running into me works too."

"My bad." I tuck my trembling hands into the front pockets of my apron. He's here. Right in front of me. "Is there something I can help you with? Need another refrigerator?" I can't help but laugh at myself because I'm nervous.

"No, but if I did, I'd only buy one from you."

"Hope you are enjoying it."

"I sure am."

"So, what can I help you with?"

He looks around like he's searching for someone or something. Then he looks at me and lowers his voice. "Mind if we step out of the main aisle?"

"Not at all."

Mr. Handsome walks me down the carpet aisle and stops halfway. When he looks at me, that adorable smile is gone. "I didn't come here needing anything. I was hoping to see you. I'm not sure if you remember, but the last time I was here I was trying to ask you something."

"I remember we were interrupted. What was it you wanted to ask?"

"I know you don't know me, but I was wondering if you would like to go out sometime?"

He's asking me out? What a jerk. I cross my arms. "What about your girlfriend?"

"Girlfriend?" His brows narrow with sincere confusion. Then he shakes his head and tells me slowly, "I don't have a girlfriend. At least not for the past three months."

"When you were here the first time, there was a blonde-headed girl with you." I won't point out she was pretty and dressed hot-to-trot.

Once he remembers, he laughs. "Oh, that was Cindy. She lives across the street. Her car was in the shop, so she asked me to bring her here to return a light fixture."

Did I hear him right? Miss Feisty isn't his girlfriend? "It's just, when she said that…" Dang Carlen, pull that foot out of your mouth so you can talk. See what you get for assuming? "So, she's not your girlfriend?"

"Cindy?" He cackles and scratches his sexy five o'clock shadow. "No, she's a little wilder than I can handle."

"Yeah, she did seem hyper."

"So, would you like to go out tomorrow?"

I clear my throat. "Where were you thinking of going?"

"Anywhere you want. I'll leave it up to you." Brad reaches into the pocket of his shirt and offers me his card. "I really hate to run off, but I need to get back to work. Think about it, and call me if you want to go out. Here's my number."

I take his card. "But I have to work until six tomorrow."

"That's not a problem." He waves, walking away in a hurry. "Call me tonight, and we can talk."

I watch until he turns at the end of the aisle and disappears. Did this really happen? Brad wants to go out with me? I look at his card and cover my giddy smile. Guess it did happen.

Bradly Austin. Co-owner of Austin Electrical Company.

I tuck the card in my back pocket and look for my best friend. We need to talk.

"Hey, Robert? Have you seen Matthew?"

He heads toward me. "I think he's in the garden area today."

"Okay, thanks."

My heart beats a little faster, heading to the garden center, not sure what I'm going to say to Matthew. He's not on the first row, or the second, or the third. I finally spot him in the corner of the store. "Hey, got a minute?"

Matthew picks up a bag of salt slag from one pallet and drops it onto another one. "What's up?" He continues to move bags from one pallet to another to combine them into one.

"Do you have plans after work?"

He jerks his head to shift his bangs and looks at me, catching his breath. "No. Why?"

"Come over and hang out."

"I don't know." He continues to move bags.

Matthew has never talked to me with distance in his tone. I don't blame him. What I did was wrong. He would have never shut me down the way I did him.

"Please come over so we can talk. I feel bad about last night."

He continues to stack bags onto one pallet. "It's fine. No big deal."

I have to get back to my department before Scott catches me socializing. "Please come over, and let's talk." Before he can tell me he's not going to, I walk away.

~ ~ ~

While leaning against the headboard with my laptop on my thighs, I scroll through Facebook but my thoughts are on Brad. How can someone so perfect want to go out with someone like me? Watch, he's going to break my heart. I just know it. He'll sweep me off my feet and either cheat on me or turn out to be an asshole.

The front door opens and then shuts.

I'm bursting to tell Stacy what happened and yell, "Hey, come here for a sec."

"Hold on. Let me get out of these high heels. My feet are *killing* me."

While I wait for Stacy, I continue to scroll through my timeline and read posts. "Geez, Stephany, the world doesn't need to know you're sitting on the toilet because you ate something you shouldn't have."

My former coworker doesn't have a TMI filter. Before she goes into detail, which she will, I scroll some more.

"What's up?"

I move the laptop to my side and sit up, anxious to tell Stacy the news. "Remember that guy I told you about at work? The one who's gorgeous and was flirting with me but had a girl with him?"

Stacy, in her robe, sits on the foot of my bed and pulls the clamp from her hair to free it. "Yeah. What about him?"

I bat my eyelashes. "He came into the store today and asked me out."

She laughs like she doesn't believe me. "No way."

I nod slowly and flash his card. "Yes way."

She frowns and holds up a finger. "Wait, you said he has a girlfriend."

"Turns out she's a girl who lives across the street and needed a ride to the store to return something."

She pops my leg and sings, "Good for you. When are you going out with him, and where?"

"Tomorrow, but we haven't decided where. I'm going to call him later, and we'll figure out a place."

"I'm so happy for you. And you look excited about going out. It's about time you get out of this apartment and have fun. And, I wanna meet this guy."

"You will, but give it some time to see where this goes." I look at his card. "He might see the real me and decide to run as fast as he can."

Her jaw drops in repulsion. "Girl, you need to stop talking like that."

"Come on, Stacy." I tilt my head and raise my eyebrows. "You know I have issues. Guys don't want a girl who has baggage."

"If that's the kind of guy he is, then hit the pedal and run the red light." She places her hand on my knee and shakes it. "You're an amazing person, Carlen. If someone doesn't see how hard you've struggled to get through your past, then the hell with them. This guy included. If he can't accept the real you, then he doesn't deserve you."

"That's so sweet," I coo, a little embarrassed.

"Speaking of going out..." Stacy leaves the bed and tightens her robe. "I need to take a quick shower before Dillon gets here. We're going out to eat at Renzo's. Want to come with us?"

"Can't." I sit back and pull the laptop onto my thighs.

"Matthew is coming over when he gets off work."

Stacy squints one eye, crosses her arms and hums.

I laugh at her. "What? Why are you looking at me that way?"

"Someone might end up with two guys liking her."

My glare warns her, don't-go-there. "Stop it. You're like the sister I never had, and Matthew is like the brother I never had."

"That brother of yours needs to do something with his hair. Those bangs are always in his eyes, and he has to jerk his head to get them out of his way so he can see."

I grimace, coming to Matthew's defense. "He's fine just the way he is."

Stacy gasps and leans away from me. "Oh, touchy, aren't we? I still say he likes you."

"No, he doesn't." I look at my laptop and mumble, "He's seeing this girl from work."

"Whatever. I've got to jump in the shower. Dillon will be here any minute." Stacy leaves.

My attention is on Brad and where to meet him tomorrow.

Donuts and coffee? No. Too simple.

Definitely not a steakhouse. Way too fancy for a first meet.

Sandwiches? Maybe.

Stacy walks into my room, dressed in slacks and a red fuzzy sweater with her hair braided to the side.

"Aw, don't you look cute."

"Thank you." She grins and curtseys. "Dillon and I are leaving."

"Don't get into any trouble."

"Who, me?"

I laugh at my friend but envy how easy it is for her to go places and not give it a second thought. Especially a social place where it's loud and crowded. I would have to be medicated to go there, or I would have a massive panic attack.

"See you tomorrow."

I wave my fingers. "Bye."

When Stacy leaves, my attention turns to Matthew, wondering when he is coming over. He should be here by now. I check my phone, but he hasn't left any messages, so I send one to him.

Are you coming over?

The dots dance, so I wait for him to reply.

Give me ten minutes. Got food?

I laugh. That's a sign things are alright between us if he's asking for something to eat. *Want some leftover potato soup?*

With lots of cheese.

See you in ten. With my phone still in my hand, I tap Brad's number. When it rings, I'm so nervous I almost hope it goes to voicemail. But then I hear the sweetest voice.

"Hello?"

"Hey, it's Carlen. Is this a good time?"

"Yes. I'm on my way home in this lovely traffic," he sings in an alluring voice. "How was your day on this Black Friday?"

"Busy, but I would rather open than close. You wouldn't believe how people can mess up a store."

He chuckles. "I can *only* imagine. So, have you thought about tomorrow and where you'd like to go?"

"I was thinking we could meet somewhere simple. Where it's not too crowded."

"Any ideas?"

"How about the Mountain Deli?"

"The place on Main Street?"

"Yes."

"Sounds good to me. I love their sandwiches. I can pick you up, or I'd understand if you're not comfortable with that and would rather meet me there. It's up to you."

Before I lose track of time, I leave my bed and head to the kitchen to heat up the soup for Matthew. "Um, I think maybe I'll just meet you there."

"That's fine. What time?"

I take the leftover container out of the refrigerator. "I could meet you there after work, unless, maybe I should come home and change first." I put the container in the microwave and press the start button.

"No need to go home and change. Come as you are."

I like the way he said that and smile. "Okay. I'll be there about twenty minutes after six."

"I'm looking forward to it."

I grab a bowl from the cabinet. "Just so you know, I'm shy until I get to know someone."

"There's nothing wrong with being shy, and...I did kind of notice."

"Sorry."

"There's nothing to be sorry about. Be who you are."

"In a nutshell, I'm a simple girl." The microwave beeps. I take the container out, dodging the steam. "And my life is pretty simple too. Nothing fancy about me," I add, warning him.

"I'm not looking for fancy in a girl. I wasn't looking at all, but your beautiful smile caught my eye. Oh, and I like your sense of humor."

"Who? Me?"

"Yes, and you have this perky spirit."

"That's the shyness."

"Maybe, but you do have a sweet spirit."

The doorbell rings.

I head to the living room. "Okay, that's enough compliments for today." I open the front door and nod for Matthew to come inside. After he does, I mouth, "Give me a second," and shut the door. Then I motion for him to follow me.

"Hope I'm not embarrassing you."

"A little."

"Trust me, I don't give compliments lightly."

"I believe you." And I really hate to end this amazing phone call, but Matthew is giving me an I'm-starving-over-here face and rubbing his stomach. "Since you're driving, I should probably let you go."

"Yeah. I'm almost home. I'm looking forward to tomorrow."

"Me too. Bye."

"Um, Miss Daydreamer over there," Matthew sings to get my attention. "Didn't you mention food?"

Back to reality. After reaching for a spoon in the drawer, I carry the bowl to the table. "Here you go, Mr. I'm-starving-to-death." I rest the bowl in front of him.

Matthew looks at the soup. "Hey, I thought I ordered cheese." Those pitiful hazel eyes meet mine.

"Oops, forgot." I fetch the bag of shredded cheese out of the fridge.

"Who was that on the phone?"

Once I have the bag open, I sprinkle cheese into the bowl. "Brad." I seal the bag and return it to the fridge.

"And who is this…Brad?"

I take my seat at the table and rest an elbow on it, then place my chin in the palm of my hand and watch him eat. "A customer. He asked me out."

When Matthew's eyes dart to mine, one eyebrow rises.

"You've got a date?"

"No, it's not a date. We're just going out."

He eyes me, spooning soup. "Do you like this guy?"

"It's not like I know him. We've only talked a few times in the store, but he's *so* gorgeous," I moan, visualizing his eyes, his smile, and his five o'clock shadow.

"What is it with girls? Looks aren't everything."

"Um, excuse me. I know a girl who thinks you're handsome and practically drools when she talks about you."

"Stop it."

An idea hits me. I pop his elbow, almost making him spill his spoonful of soup. "Maybe we could double-date one day. Me and Brad. You and Shannon."

"Don't think so."

I sit back and cross my arms. "And why not?"

"Don't ask."

"Why?"

His spoon scrapes the inside of the bowl. "Let's just say, it's not a good idea."

"Tell me why."

"No."

"Matthew." I call out his name, agitated. "I thought we were friends. Why won't you tell me?"

He stirs what little soup is left. "If you must know, Shannon is jealous of you. That's why."

I laugh hysterically. "You're kidding, right?"

"No." His eyes cut to mine, and he points the spoon at me. "And if you tell her I said that, I'll never forgive you."

"You know I won't say anything."

"If you do, it's going to cause drama at work. We don't need that."

"Why is she jealous of me?"

"She said guys don't have just *girl* friends and asked if our friendship included benefits."

"Are you serious?" If Shannon were here, I'd take her pretty blonde hair and stuff it in her mouth. This makes my blood boil. "And what did you tell her?"

"Carlen, she just turned eighteen. I told you she's…" He shakes his head and spoons more soup. "Don't let it bother you."

"But it does. I haven't given her a reason to be jealous."

"Can I ask you a question?"

"What?"

Matthew jerks his head to shift his bangs out of his eyes. "If a guy really likes a girl, but he's afraid to tell her, what can he do to, you know, let her know?"

I try hard not to smile, thinking he's finally going to confess. "How much does this guy like the girl?"

"Don't assume I'm going to propose to Shannon. Gee whiz." He lowers the spoon in the bowl and pushes it to the side, then rests his crossed arms on the table. "The reason why I'm asking is because some guys were talking about it the other day. I didn't have an answer, so they teased me. I thought I'd ask you the way you asked me why men cheat."

"Fair."

"So?"

"But every girl is different."

He throws his head back and moans. "Oh my gosh. It's a general question. There's no right or wrong answer."

"Well…" I ponder an answer as we have this playful staring contest. "Flowers work." He's already done that. "A card once in a while with something sweet written in it."

"You mean, something cheesy?"

"Anything to let her know you're thinking about her. A text in the morning is sure to put a smile on her face."

Matthew nods like he's paying attention.

"Also, leaving notes here and there. Maybe cooking for her. That's sexy as heck."

"What if I don't know how to cook?"

"Then learn. The thing is, get to know what she likes. Listen to her."

He raises his hand for me to stop. "Got it. Ready to watch a movie?"

Not yet. We have one more detail to take care of first.

"Before we do, let's talk about last night."

He shrugs. "There's nothing to talk about."

"Yeah, there is. You told me you had demons too."

He rolls his eyes and sits back in the chair. "I exaggerated. Don't take what I said so seriously."

"Sure you don't want to talk?"

"I told you, there's nothing to talk about."

We stare. I'm not trying to push him, but it's hard to tell if there is something and he regrets telling me or there truly is nothing to talk about.

"I'm sorry I cut you off last night, but I'm here now if you want—"

Matthew raises his hand and tightens his face. "You know what, forget I ever said anything and forget about the movie. I'm out of here." He abruptly leaves the table.

"You're going home?" I turn in my chair, but he's already out of the kitchen. "Matthew. I'm sorry. Please come back."

The front door shuts.

I sit here in shock. What the heck just happened?

Chapter 9: He's Too Perfect

One more light. I place my palm on my chest and exhale through my puckered lips, trying to simmer my pounding heart. My stomach is beyond soothing. It's agitating like a washer. If it hits the spin cycle and causes me to throw up my food in front of Brad, I'll die of embarrassment.

The light turns green.

I cruise Main Street until I come to the Mountain Deli. When I arrive, I pull into a parking spot across the street. Before going inside, I need a moment to settle my anxiety, if that's even possible. Why am I so nervous? What is it about Brad? It was never like this with Andy or Terry.

The longer I sit here, the more the anxiety attacks me. Then the negative thoughts flood my head. What does Brad see in me? I look at the diner and know it's either bite the bullet and go inside or leave. Thanks to the negativity, it's tempting to start my car and go home. It's the tiny voice that says, *Come on, Carlen. Don't run*, that empowers me to open the door and exit my car. Dusk consumes what's left of the descending sun. It's also bitterly cold. I huddle in my coat and cross the street. When I reach the entrance, I'm so cold I open the door and enter, anxiety or not.

And there he is, next to the wall. Brad stands and holds up his hand to let me know he's there.

I make my way to the table. He's so handsome in his blue dress shirt.

"Hey. You made good time." Brad pulls a chair out for me.

"The traffic wasn't too bad." I settle in my seat and scoot closer to the table.

Brad returns to his chair across from me. "Hope you're hungry."

"I am. My lunch was six hours ago."

"Hello." The waitress in a burgundy chef's shirt with a black collar offers us a menu. "My name is Katie. How are you guys doing this evening?"

Brad takes his menu. "Fine, thanks."

"Are you ready to order, or do you need some time?"

I open my menu and tell her, "I need a few minutes, please."

"Sure thing. What would you like to drink?"

"Sweet tea."

Brad tells her, "Um, I'll have water."

"Okay, I'll be back with your drinks."

We ponder over the menu with light chatter in the background from other patrons. My anxiety hasn't lessened, but my hunger kicks in looking at the delicious sandwiches. If I eat something heavy, it might not agree with my stomach.

"Here you go." Katie places our drinks on the table. "Do you still need some time?"

Brad closes his menu. "I'll have the roasted turkey breast and some chips."

"Okay." She scribbles his order on a notepad, then looks at me. "And for you?"

I offer her my menu. "Um, I'll have a grilled chicken salad with ranch dressing."

She reaches for my menu. "Would you like soup to go with that?"

I smile and shake my head. "No thanks."

She reaches for Brad's menu. "Alright. It'll be ready in a few minutes," she sings before walking away.

Brad's eyes are on me, hard. "You seem nervous."

I shrug and smile, embarrassed. "Just a little."

"Thought so." He exhales. "So, do you like working at Home Depot?"

My hands are sweaty, so I rub them across my jeans. "I actually love it. When I got the job, I was supposed to be a cashier, but I ended up in home improvements and appliances."

He sits back in his chair without a lick of anxiety. "Strange how things work out sometimes."

"It is. My first week, I hated it because it was boring. But now I love it. I'm so glad they put me there." Slow down Carlen. You're going to end up babbling and bore him. Talk about something more interesting. Like him. I sit back and act casual like Brad. "I saw on your business card you're an electrician."

He nods and taps his fingertips on the table. "I am. Dad started the business when I was ten. The summer I turned sixteen, he let me go with him on small jobs. Some of the best memories I have growing up are from that summer."

My memories of being sixteen are someone murdering my mother.

"After I graduated high school, Dad brought me on board. My older brother opted for the suit and tie lifestyle. He takes after Mom."

"Are your parents still married?"

Brad laughs like I asked a weird question. "Yes, they are. Thirty-five years last March." He reaches for his glass of water and brings it to his lips. "Are your parents still married?"

I would rather walk barefoot on a hot street than have to talk about this. But it's not like I can hide it if we're going to get to know each other. "No. My mom died five years ago."

As expected, the shock appears on his face with the bulging eyes and his mouth open. Brad lowers his glass and clears his throat. "Oh, I, I'm sorry to hear that."

"It's okay. You didn't know."

"So, it's just you and your dad?"

The mention of him makes me smile. "Yes. And we're *really* close. He was just here for Thanksgiving."

Brad drinks some water. "That's nice. I guess you're going to Charlotte for Christmas."

Ah, he remembers where I grew up. How impressive. "Yes."

"My parents make a big deal over holidays. Especially Christmas. They hire someone to put up the decorations. Inside and out. Mom loves to entertain."

I cringe. Entertain? Like, dress up fancy, act proper, and sip wine with a house full of people? Is it me, or is it suddenly hot in here? Either way, my coat has to go, so I wiggle out of it. "That sounds amazing."

"It is. People drive by just to look at it. You should come over once they have it decorated. You'll see what I mean."

Meet his parents? I'm doing good to sit here with him. I laugh to counter my nervousness. "Your mom might not like a stranger coming over to look at her decorations."

"Of course she would," he singsongs. "That's why she does it. Mom loves having people over."

And my mom never let anyone come into the house. It's obvious we come from different worlds. He's not going to understand mine. Heck, I don't understand his.

I sip my tea and try to think of something to say. "Do you still live at home?"

"No. I bought my house when I was twenty. I'm in the process of remodeling it."

"Wow, that's impressive. You're first home at twenty." Then it dawns on me. I don't know how old Brad is. He must be older than I thought. "Can I ask a question?"

"You can ask me anything you want."

"How old are you?"

For the first time, Brad seems a bit uneasy. His sweet smile is gone, and he clears his throat. "I turned thirty back in September."

Thirty? He's nine years older than me? I'm not sure how I feel about that.

"Mind if I ask how old you are?"

Still in shock, it takes a second for me to answer. "I'm twenty-one."

With his hand around the glass, he taps his finger against it. "I figured you were younger. Hope the age difference doesn't bother you."

It does, and it doesn't. I'll have to process this later. And I'm not telling Dad. He'll flip out if I tell him I met a guy who is, let's see… Dang, Dad is only eleven years older than Brad. "You are a lot older than I thought, but…" There's no need to let it bother me. We might end up only friends, so it wouldn't matter. "I'm not worried about it."

"Okay, guys. Here you go." Our waitress places Brad's sub in front of him. It looks delicious. The melted cheese covers the meat, resting on open buns. She places the salad in front of me. It's a big bowl, but there's not a lot of chicken unless it's hiding under the lettuce. "Is there anything else I can get you?"

I pick my fork up and shake my head. "I'm good."

"Me too." Brad picks up his sub halves and puts them together.

"Enjoy your lunch, and I'll check on you later."

Brad takes a big bite of his sub, obviously not embarrassed to eat in front of me. I'm scared to take my first bite. What if I chew my food funny? Or smear dressing on my face.

"What's the big city like?"

"Um…" I fork a small bite and shrug. "There is a lot of traffic. Everything is fast-paced. Everyone is always in a hurry."

"Bet the clubs are nice."

95

"I don't go to those." I take my first bite and wipe my face just in case.

"What about concerts?"

"Never been to one." And I don't ever plan on going to one either. I would leave with a case of PTSD.

He laughs, surprised. "Wow, you've never been to a concert?"

"Nope."

"What do you like to do for fun?" He continues to devour his sub.

"Well, I have to admit, I don't go out a lot." I use my fork to toss the salad.

"Do you like to hike? Triple Falls Trail is really nice."

I cover my mouth while chewing. "I've never been hiking."

Brad's so shocked he almost chokes, then coughs. "You've been here three years and never been hiking? You're missing out. There's about ten of us who go once a month during the season. If you want to go, I can show you the ropes. No pun intended."

A giggle slips out, but not at his joke as much as the thought of him putting a harness on me.

"That's a cute smile."

Embarrassed, I look down and poke a piece of chicken. My cheeks are surely red as fire, because my face is warm.

"You're not like most girls."

My smile is gone. Not unless 'most girls' have issues and are damaged. "No, I'm not."

"Carlen, that's a compliment."

A compliment? I look at Brad but can't say anything, feeling a bit vulnerable.

His brown eyes soften, as does his voice. "You really don't take compliments easily, do you?"

I shake my head.

"We'll have to change that." His phone rings. Brad takes it from his pocket and looks at it. He swipes the screen and slides the phone back inside his pocket. "You come across as being a sweet Southern girl. I like that."

"Brad, I'm a simple girl who lives a simple life," I confess honestly and without thought, my words spilling out on their own. And I don't care. I'm tired of hiding who I am because someone might not accept me. "I don't go out a lot, because I don't like crowds. I don't drink or party." There, I said it. That's who I am. If he walks out, so be it.

"There's nothing wrong with that." Brad takes the last bite of his sandwich and wipes his hands.

"But guys like girls who go out and do things."

He finishes chewing and winks. "I'm the kind of guy who likes being with a nice girl more than what we do or where we go."

It's the sweetest words ever and warm my heart. It also makes me more comfortable with Brad. He really is Mr. Perfect. So far. I smile and eat my salad and don't care if I have dressing on my face.

Brad tells me about an upcoming job he's going to be doing at the school. How he hopes to one day expand the company and have employees. Brad is very motivated. Surely Dad would find that impressive and approve of Brad. He's nothing like Andy who job-hopped the whole time we dated. The more I listen to Brad, he seems so sincere. I'm ready to test those waters again.

"What's your dream, Carlen?"

I finish my last bite and lower my fork to the bowl. "Since working in the appliance department, I'd love to someday have my own decorating business."

"Hey, if my dad can start his own business, so can you."

Our waitress places the tab on the table. "Can I get you guys anything?"

I raise my hand and shake my head. "I'm good."

"No, thanks." Brad hands her some cash. "Keep the change."

"Thank you. You guys come back and see us."

I was so nervous coming here, but now I don't want this evening to end.

Brad tucks the receipt into his front pocket. "I'll walk you to your car."

He doesn't want to talk a little longer? Maybe I've bored him or said the wrong thing.

We exit the restaurant and wait to cross the street.

"You picked a good place. That sub was really good."

"Thanks for the salad."

"You're welcome."

A tall, skinny guy strolling across the street catches my attention. My undivided attention. It's not the first guy I've seen wearing a hoodie, but that guy reminds me of Terry, my first boyfriend. My first love. And my first broken heart. But it couldn't be him here in Hendersonville.

"Carlen, is something wrong?"

The young man turns the corner and disappears. Why does it bother me? What was it about that guy?

"Um, no. I thought I saw someone I went to school with back home." I turn to Brad. "Were you saying something?"

"I asked if you have plans for the rest of the evening."

We cross the street.

I guide him to my car and smile at the thought of our evening not ending just yet. "No. No plans. This is my car." I stop at the drivers door and unlock it with the fob.

Brad opens the door for me. "Would you like to come to my house?"

Maybe I didn't bore him after all. But go to his house? Even though I trust Brad, I'm not sure that's a good idea.

As we stare, and I still ponder what to do, the handsome man grins and tempts me. "You could see what I've remodeled and give me pointers on decorating since that's your thing."

I'm not turning down this invitation and perk up with excitement. "I would love to. Mind if I follow you there? I don't want to leave my car here."

"Not at all. I'm in the blue truck. You have my number if we get separated."

"Okay." I slide into my seat, pull the strap over my shoulder and buckle up, ready to race over there.

Brad closes my door, then waves before walking to his truck.

After starting my car, I back out of the parking spot and wait for him. Brad leads the way. I try to send Stacy a message and let her know what's going on, but of all days, we hit every green light. I'll have to send her one later. I'm not going to do it while trying to follow Brad. I manage to keep up with him on Sixth Avenue and follow him into Laurel Park. "Wow. He lives here? Nice."

Brad's taillights lead the way through the community. He signals and turns into a driveway. I pull in next to his truck. When I exit my car, the anxiety returns.

Brad meets me at the front of my car, opens his arms and sings, "Welcome to my home."

I laugh at his sweet personality and love how he makes me feel safe and comfortable. "It's a beautiful home."

He walks me to the front door. "It's an older neighborhood, but I love it here."

Who wouldn't love Laurel Park? If I could live anywhere, it would be here.

Brad unlocks the door and motions for me to enter. "Ladies first."

Smiling from the butterflies dancing in my stomach, I step inside. The living room is spacious with a vaulted ceiling. A leather couch lines one wall and part of another one with a footrest the size of a table. The hardwood floor is beautiful. Not too dark or too light. And it blends well with the tan walls and white crown molding. Of course, there's a massive television on the wall.

"What do you think?"

With my arms crossed, I continue to look around the room. "It feels like a new home."

Brad stands next to me, exhales and rests his hands on his hips, also looking around the room. "It pretty much is. I took out the carpet and put in a new floor and new windows. It had a popcorn ceiling, so I got rid of that. I just finished this room about a month ago. Now I'm working on the kitchen."

"Speaking of windows, I love those curtains. The blue adds a soft touch."

"Mom picked those out for me."

"So, what did you need my advice on?"

"The kitchen. Mom and I don't agree on what to do with it. Come on, and I'll show you."

It's hard not to stare at his backside, but it's right in front of me, following him.

We enter the kitchen, and my attention is diverted to a big mess. Sheetrock is stacked against a wall, the one ripped down and the frame exposed. New light fixtures rest on the island bar, waiting to be installed. The windows are new and still have the label stuck on the glass. There are no cabinets on the bare wall, only the outline of where they once were. Then I spot something that makes me smile. "Aw, now *that's* what I call a really nice refrigerator." I can't resist letting a giggle escape, but quickly cover it.

Brad nudges my forearm and winks. "So do I. And it's got cold beer in it." He heads to the fridge and looks over his shoulder at me. "Would you like one?"

He must not remember me saying I don't drink. No big deal. "No thanks."

"Sure?"

I nod. "Yes."

He opens the door and takes out a can. On his way back to me, he pops the tab. "Any suggestions on how to make this kitchen look nice?" He gulps the beer.

With my arms crossed, I scan it and let a visual come to me. "The first thing I would do is come up with a color scheme."

"What color?" He leans against the island bar and gulps more beer.

"A bold color to get your attention. Then a soft color to calm it."

"Mom wanted teal and brown."

I shake my head and cringe. "Tell me you said no."

He laughs. "I said no."

"What colors were you thinking?"

Brad looks around the kitchen and exhales. "That hasn't hit me yet." His eyes meet mine, and it makes my heart flutter. "You should come with me when I buy the paint and help me pick out the colors."

This night continues to be full of sweet surprises. I have a buzz and didn't have to drink any beer. "I would love to. Let me know when."

"Maybe we can schedule a time next week." He guzzles the rest of the beer and tosses the can in the trash, then gracefully walks toward me. "Blinds, or no blinds?"

Brad is like static electricity. Every hair on my body stands at attention. I swallow hard so I can speak. "Um, blinds?"

"Yeah. For the kitchen window. Should I buy them or just have curtains?"

My fluttering heart is now pounding with fury when he comes to a stop in my personal space. Those alluring brown eyes pierce into mine. It's hard to take in air, wondering if this means he's going to kiss me. He can if he wants to. I clear my throat. "Um, that's…probably more of a…personal preference." I can hardly get my words out, staring at this handsome man in front of me. "Some things you should probably decide, because it needs your touch."

"Spoken like a woman who knows her stuff."

I've got goosebumps multiplying from my toes to the top of my head. The way Brad is staring at me, I'm almost positive he doesn't have paint or blinds on his mind. Me neither.

Kiss me, Brad.

He must have heard my thoughts, because he leans in slowly, in sessions, as though to ask for permission. I ease closer, letting him know he has it. Just before he kisses me, I close my eyes, anticipating our lips touching. When they do, I've never felt so breathless and weak. His kiss is gentle and cautious like I'm fragile. But I'm not and want him to know, so I deepen the kiss.

Brad parts my lips. Without missing a beat, his tongue encircles mine. A warmness builds inside of me, which causes certain parts of my body to come alive. It's been so long since I've been touched that it would be easy to let him do whatever he wants to me. I've never felt this deep desire to drop all of my defenses, ignore what consequences may come from my actions, and let a man have me.

His hand goes to the small of my back. Then he eases my lower body against his. I place my hands on his sides. I was hoping for a kiss, and now I'm hoping he'll rip my clothes off and do whatever he wants to me. I'm sure it would be heaven.

When he runs his hand under my shirt and up my back, I'm ready to beg him to please me. I want this, and from the feel of his lower extremity, so does Brad. I don't know why reality has to interfere and remind me this handsome, sexy man with his hands all over me is not my boyfriend. We're not a couple. As much as I want to get naked with him right here in his kitchen, I can't give him that part of me. At least not today.

"Um, Brad." With my hands still on his sides, I ease him back but can't look at him. He's going to be frustrated I've put the brakes on this passionate moment.

He takes my face in his hands. Those warm brown eyes hold me captive and take me away from life. From the things that haunt me. "I'm sorry if I crossed the line."

I smile at his understanding and that he's not upset. "No. You didn't." And for a second, or two, I have regrets I stopped him.

"Listen, if I ever do cross the line, you have to let me know."

"I will."

"Promise?"

A girlish smile escapes. "Yes."

"Good." His eyes shift, perusing my face. "You're different, Carlen. There's just something about you. And I like it."

"But, Brad, you don't know me. Not really."

"Then let me get to know you."

"Just don't have any high expectations of me, okay?"

Still holding my face, he looks so deep into my eyes it's like he's holding my heart instead. And he probably is. What's happening to me? I've never felt so weak in my life.

"All I ask is to be who you are. I can't stand fake. And be

honest with me."

With words like that, how could I not smile? Maybe I've finally met the one. The right one.

"That, I can do."

The doorbell rings, interrupting our moment.

Brad narrows his brows. "I have no clue who that could be, but let me get rid of them." After a quick kiss, his hands leave my face, and he scurries out of the kitchen yelling, "Coming."

With my hand on my cheek, I smile like I haven't in so long. Perhaps never before.

A nice-looking man in a wool coat sprints into the kitchen like he's on a mission. The second he sees me, he comes to an instant stop, and his eyes bulge. "Oh, hey," he tells me, obviously surprised at my presence. Then he reaches for a glass in the cabinet. "I didn't know anyone was in here. Sorry if I startled you."

"I think I startled *you*."

He laughs and fills the glass with water.

Brad and a petite girl stroll into the kitchen. She's beautiful with a model face, pretty eyes, and long dark hair.

"And that's when I told him…" She also stops in her tracks when she sees me. "Oh. Why didn't you tell us you have company?"

Brad stands next to me, places his hand on my back and introduces us. "Carlen, this is Ron and his wife, Josie. I did some work on their house a few years ago, and now we're like family."

"Family?" Ron, holding the glass, walks closer and unbuttons his wool coat with his free hand. "Why are we the last to know you've got a girlfriend?"

I thought, *That was presumptuous.*

"Yeah, Bradly." Josie crosses her arms and playfully scolds him, squinting one eye. "How dare you not tell us."

Brad chuckles. "Guys, we just met. There's nothing to tell you."

"I have an idea," Josie sings, spiritedly. "Why don't you guys come over one night for dinner? I'll make my killer chicken alfredo casserole."

Ron gulps the rest of his water and sets the glass in the sink. "I have a better idea. Let's go to the Season's at Highland Lake in Flat Rock. We haven't been there in a while."

Oh, no, no, no. That place is way too fancy for me. I would have to dress up and eat proper. Surely Brad will save me from this invite after telling him I'm a simple girl.

Josie's pretty eyes light up at the suggestion. "That sounds like a *great* idea." She flips her hand. "I just love their maple duck breast. How about we plan something for next week?"

Brad glances at me. That smile tells me he loves the idea too. "It's a really nice place. Have you ever been there?"

No. And I don't want to. I can't handle going somewhere that fancy. The Mountain Deli is my kind of fancy. I'll remind him after they leave, but for now, I force a smile and act just as excited. "No, but I've heard it's nice."

Josie gasps in shock. "You've never been there?"

"No."

"Oh," she mumbles like she doesn't understand why. Then she smiles, once again, energetic. "We'll just have to change that, won't we? It's truly an experience."

All I know to say is, "I'm sure it is." What I want to say is, that's not going to happen. A formal restaurant is out of the question. My anxiety would blow the roof off the building.

"How about we have coffee this weekend?" In my hesitation to answer, she adds, "My treat."

It's sweet she's offering, but I also feel backed in a corner. And I'm not lying when I tell her, "With the holidays, I won't have a weekend off until after New Years."

She tsks, disappointed. "Oh."

Ron raises his hand. "Hey, Brad, speaking of the holidays, Josie and I are having our traditional Christmas party on the twenty-second. You guys are officially invited. No need to RSVP. Just show up with empty stomachs and ready to have fun."

"Wouldn't expect anything less at one of your parties."

Josie turns to me. "You will come?"

I say the only thing I know without committing. "I'm not sure. I spend the holidays with my dad in Charlotte, so I'll have to let you know."

"I sure hope you can make it."

Ron leans over the island bar and tells Brad, "Before I forget, we're planning a ski trip the third weekend in January. We rented the same cabin we had last year. You want to join us?"

Brad looks at me and then he turns back to Ron. "Let me get back with you on that."

"Sure, but don't wait too long."

"Ron, let's head out. We've got places to go and things to do."

Still leaning over the island bar, he taps it and straightens his back. "Right behind you, dear."

"No, you're in front of me."

"Not for long." He raises his hand. "Good to see you, Brad." His eyes meet mine. "And it was nice to meet you, Carlen."

I nod. "You too."

Josie waves her tiny fingers. "Bye, Carlen. You and Brad come over any time."

"Thank you."

Brad follows them but looks over his shoulder at me. "Be right back. I'm going to walk them out."

"Okay."

The kitchen turns silent, but the living room once again fills with their laughter. Why do I feel like the odd person in an even game? Ron and Josie couldn't have been nicer and seemed to accept me. So, what's wrong?

I know what it is. I'm deluding myself into thinking I could ever fit into a life I try so hard to avoid—Brad's life. Can I really leave the comfort of my world and step into Brad's?

The front door shuts, then the living room is silent. Seconds later, Brad enters the kitchen and heads to the fridge like he found a second wind. "Sorry about that. Sometimes they just show up."

"It's fine. Don't worry about it." Why are my eyes misting over, and my heart is sad?

He opens the fridge. "Sure you wouldn't like something to drink?"

"No thanks."

And it hits me. A surge of anxiety shoots through me like an injection. The kind I have to fight to run out of the house like it's on fire and run home so I can hide from the world and everything that scares me.

Fight it Carlen. Come on. Don't run out that door. You'll regret it.

But Brad and I are so different. The likelihood we could ever be a couple seems implausible. Even a friendship seems doubtful. Brad isn't going to put up with me dodging places and doing things he enjoys. I know I'm letting my negative thoughts assault me, but this is my reality.

"Carlen, is something wrong?"

I blink and come out of my thoughts. "No. Why?"

He pops the tab on a beer can. "You seem, I don't know, like you were somewhere else just now. Are you upset they stopped by?"

"No, not at all." I tell him sincerely, hoping he believes me. It's not that they showed up, it's that 'odd person syndrome' bugging me, pecking at my insecurity. It takes everything in me to pretend I'm alright inside. "Ron and Josie are nice. And lively."

After taking a gulp, Brad sets the beer can on the bar and walks toward me. With the back of his hand, he wipes the wetness from his lips. His eyes bore into mine like he's reading every thought I have. "Carlen, are you sure you're alright? Something seems different."

"Like what?"

He eyes me and shakes his head. "You seem timid. Like you're afraid or uncomfortable. Or like something's bothering you." He places his hand on his chest. "Did I do or say something to upset you?"

I lick my dry lips and ponder what to say without lying, at the same time hiding my secrets. "No. I promise." I tell him honestly, because in reality, it's me, not him.

Brad studies me. Then he smiles. "Just making sure. Now, where were we before we were interrupted?"

He leans in to kiss me. This time, it's not what I want and turn my head.

"Okay, something *is* wrong. Are you going to tell me or make me guess? You were fine before they came over, and now you're like cold as ice."

How can I blame Brad for his irritated tone? I lied to him. Something is wrong. The least I can do is say something before I run out the door. Perhaps for good. It's not easy to force the words, but I do. "Sorry if I seem cold. Nothing is wrong, it's just that…" What the hell do I say now? Confess who Carlen really is? Sugar-coat things?

"Just what?" He steps back, cups his beer can, and guzzles it.

"I really like you. Maybe too much. And it scares me. This talk about going to a fancy place to eat, the Christmas party, and hiking, I don't do those things."

Brad sets the can on the counter and straddles a bar stool with his not-so-warm eyes piercing mine. "What are you saying, Carlen?"

What the fuck? At this point, I don't care what happens. I'm tired. "Want the truth?" I raise my eyebrows, cross my arms and wait for him to answer.

"Nothing but."

Still having a brave moment, I spill my guts. "The truth is, I suffer from panic attacks, so I don't go out in public unless it's a necessity. I also suffer from depression, so some days I can't even get out of bed. I see a therapist because I come from a screwed-up home, so *I'm* screwed-up." I fling my hand and continue, even though I'm out of breath. "I have insecurity issues. Any self-esteem I have wouldn't register on a meter if I turned the dial myself. My only motivation in life is to eat, sleep, and work. Again, because it's a necessity. I don't go to parties. I don't drink. I don't go to strange places and have fun. I don't live life other than working and sitting on the couch, because I'm afraid of life." Winded and out of breath, I stop. "Now that you know what Carlen is really like, I'll do the honors of showing myself out." I turn and head out of the kitchen, hoping I don't cry before I'm out of his house.

Within a couple of steps, Brad has my forearm and turns me around. Still out of breath, I look at him. "Carlen, I didn't ask you to leave."

"Doesn't mean you don't want me to."

He scowls and lets go of my arm. "Says who?"

"My insecurity."

"What if it's wrong?"

"It hasn't been yet."

"How do you know if you always run away before giving someone a chance?"

My lips part to answer, but I can't.

Brad rests his hands on his hips. "What you just said took a lot of guts. I appreciate your honesty. And I'm being honest when I tell you that I want you to stay."

This is where he's supposed to tell me to get lost, but he wants me to stay? With everything in me, I want to believe Brad. A part of me does, but the insecurity has power over me, unable to forget Mom's prophecy.

"Oh, Carlen, don't fool yourself. He says this today, but somewhere down the road when he sees the real Carlen come out, he's going to throw you out the door."

Unfortunately, this is one time I believe her. "Brad, I just told you what I'm like. I'm damaged. I'm not like other girls, trust me."

"Carlen, I know what you told me. Maybe I *like* the fact you're not like the other girls."

"That's easy to say now, but when you get to know me, *truly* get to know me, you'll want me to leave." I tell him in a monotone voice, defeated, already resolved to the reality we never had a chance.

"You're assuming again. That's a little costly, don't you think?" He squints one eye. "Are you going to tell the next guy this too? And then the next guy?"

His words hurt, even though he's right. I look away and mumble, "I told you I'm insecure."

"Aren't we all to some degree?"

"My degree has a chain around my ankle. Your degree doesn't stop you from living life."

He laughs, then quickly covers it and massages it away. With a straight face, he tells me, "Sorry, but you have a sense of humor."

"No I don't," I counter in a feisty but playful voice.

He laughs again. "Oh yes you do."

"If you're trying to compliment me, you know I don't do those either."

"I know. But I'm still here and trying to convince you not to walk out the door."

I look away. He's supposed to want me to leave after telling him I have a lot of baggage, so I'm a bit confused why he's wanting me to stay.

"Carlen, don't take this the wrong way, but nothing you said has caught me off guard or surprised me. Some, I already suspected. But that day I saw you in the store, your smile said so much more. Maybe it wouldn't work out between us, but I'm willing to see where this goes. Are you?"

If Brad only knew how much, but then I hear Mom's voice.

"Go ahead, Carlen, stay. Don't listen to me. Find out the hard way. No guy in his right mind would ever tell a girl he wants to be with her after she just told him she has issues."

Again, I believe Mom. With teary eyes and my heart breaking, I tell him, "Brad, it means a lot what you said." I cover my mouth, fearing I might throw up. "I'm really scared right now and have to go." I leave the kitchen and rush through the living room.

"You're leaving after I just told you I want you to stay?"

I stop at the front door and look at him. "I'm truly sorry, but yes, I need to go."

"Does this mean you'll come back?"

Even though I'm on the verge of a complete panic attack, what he said makes me smile. "Yes. I'll come back."

"I'll hold you to that."

"Why? I just told you I have issues. Most men would tell the girl to hit the road."

"You said you're not like most girls. Well, I'm not like most men."

"Before I come back, make sure that's what you want."

"Carlen." He throws his hands up and squeals, "Who says *you* won't be the one who walks away?"

I laugh and then quickly cover it. "I'm damaged, not stupid."

He laughs harder. "I love your sense of humor."

I think he really believes I have one.

"Sure you won't stay?"

What do I do, Gloria? Stacy, help me here. I can't fight the fear. With the deepest regrets, I tell him, "Sorry, but I have to go."

He rolls his eyes and exhales with exasperation. "I can't stop you. If you want to leave, then go." When he opens the door for me to leave, it stings.

I can't look at him when I say, "Bye."

"See ya."

With my head lowered in shame, I walk out. When he shuts the door, I'm convinced it's the last time I'll see Brad.

On the way home, I have the biggest pity party. Of course, once I leave the situation the anxiety is gone, but then the guilt sets in. Now I feel stupid for leaving.

My phone rings. It's Dad. I can't let him know I'm upset. I tap the touchscreen and sing, "Hey, Dad."

"Hope I'm not bothering you."

"Never. It's always good to hear your voice. What are you doing?"

"Oh, just sat down and fixing to watch a western and thought I'd check on you."

"I'm good. You don't have to worry."

"Carlen, after what happened on Thanksgiving, it's hard not to worry. I had no idea you were having those moments, or whatever they are."

"That's why I didn't want you to know, so you wouldn't worry. Gloria is helping me work through them."

"Are you remembering anything?"

I come to a stop at a red light. "No. I just get triggered when I see a knife, but it's not all the time."

"So, you're really okay?"

"Dad, really, I'm okay. How are things at work?"

"Oh, the same old stuff."

"How's Patty?" The light turns green, so I continue on.

"She's having a hard time. Next week is John's birthday."

"That's right. I'll have to call her."

"That would be nice. I'm sure she would enjoy hearing from you. After we left your apartment, she told me how much she enjoyed getting to know you more."

"And I really enjoyed getting to know her. I'm so glad she came. It was the best Thanksgiving."

He doesn't say anything.

"Dad?"

"Yeah?"

"Is something wrong?"

"Dang it. I think those raccoons are in the trash can again. Or either the Taylor's dogs. I need to go check. They made a mess the last time they got into it, and I don't feel like cleaning up the yard again. Can I call you back after I see what it is?"

"Sure."

"I need to lock up the shed while I'm out there."

"Go take care of things."

The call ends.

When I pull into my parking spot next to Stacy's car, I kill the engine and notice Dillon's truck is also here. Great. That means they're hanging out at the apartment tonight. Stacy is going to ask me how things went with Brad. Before telling her how I screwed up a nice evening with the perfect man, I need a moment alone.

I close my eyes and replay the evening with Brad. Then I think about the guy in the hoodie who was on the other side of the street when we came out of the sandwich shop. I've seen a lot of guys like Terry over the years, but something about that one bugs me. I replay and rewind those few seconds I watched him stroll along the sidewalk. Play. Rewind. Play. Each time, his image fades. He's dissolving. It's hard to tell it's even a guy in a hoodie. He's simply a grainy shadow floating by.

"Holy shit." I sit upright with my eyes wide and gasp for air like I just surfaced from the depths of the ocean. "That shadow I saw in Dad's kitchen was Terry. It was him."

But Terry was never in the house. So that shadow couldn't have been him.

"Geez, Carlen. You really are going crazy." I close my eyes

and fall back in my seat and let out the biggest sigh ever.

Sometimes my poor brain malfunctions, and this is one of them. Terry was never in the house, but he came close. Dad was okay with me dating Terry, but not my dear controlling mother. I couldn't believe Dad talked her into letting him come over for supper so she could meet him and decide if I could date him. But that never happened, because Terry broke up with me.

"Guess I'll have to face Stacy sooner or later. Might as well get this over with."

I open the door and exit my car. It still bothers me that I don't know why Terry broke up with me. Gloria was right when she said some things in life we'll never know why.

When I walk into the apartment, Stacy and Dillon aren't here. They're probably off with Dillon's friends or at the hot tub. Either way, I don't have to tell her about Brad. I head to my room and call it a day.

Chapter 10: A Gut Instinct

What I wouldn't give to fall asleep before my alarm goes off, even if it's only twenty minutes. I've been awake for hours. My brain won't shut down. Not with nagging regrets I walked out on Brad. Why was it so hard to stay? Why can't I be normal?

"Oh for Pete's sake, get over it and stop pouting like a baby. What are you going to do, lay in bed all day and play the victim?"

"I'm not pouting, Mother. It's called, thinking about my mistakes. And what do you care if I lay in bed all day?"

The alarm blares.

So much for any sleep now. I reach over and tap the snooze button. Maybe Mom is right, and I should lay in bed all day and play the victim. It would be so easy to call Scott and tell him I'm not coming in to work.

The alarm blares again.

After tapping the snooze again, I blink slowly.

The sunlight is consuming the darkness. A new day is coming to life, unlike me. This is one of those days I might not be able to get out of bed.

The alarm blares again.

This time, I don't hit the snooze and tune it out. I'm numb. Lifeless. Don't care. Depression is kicking my butt.

"Carlen, what the hell?" Stacy snatches my clock off the nightstand and silences it. Then she looks at me, slamming it back on the nightstand. Her hair is wrapped in a twisted towel on top of her head. One eye has makeup, and the other waiting its turn. "Are you trying to wake up the whole damn complex?"

I haven't moved. Not sure I've even blinked. Still numb, I mumble, "No."

"What's wrong?"

"Nothing."

"Liar." Stacy pops my leg and sits on the bed. "Tell me what's wrong, but it has to be the short version. I've got to get to the

111

office."

She wants the short version? "I went to Brad's yesterday. Told him about my issues. Then I walked out on him."

"Okay, maybe not *that* short. What did you tell him?"

"Everything. I mean everything."

"Can you be a little more specific?"

I exhale and try to make my brain function. "I told him about my depression. My insecurities. That I'm screwed-up because of a shitty childhood and how I'm a homebody and never go anywhere."

Stacy gives me an 'Oh wow' frozen face. "Why?" She quickly raises her hand and adds, "Don't get me wrong. I'm not saying you shouldn't tell him, but that's not like you. You're very private with that."

"It just came out." I yawn and stretch. "Maybe I had a 'don't fucking care anymore' moment."

"Carlen, what's going on? This isn't like you."

"Short version? While I was there, I realized how different we are. It'll never work."

"Is that what *he* said, or you?"

"Me." I yawn again. "He said he still wanted to see where things go."

"So, what's the problem?"

I sit up and lean against the headboard. "Stacy, what guy still wants to see a girl after she just told him she has issues?"

She huffs. "Uh, one that likes you, that's who."

I roll my eyes.

She stands and gives me her don't-be-so-negative glare. "We'll have to finish this talk tonight. I have to get to work."

"See ya later."

"Don't you have to be at work in an hour?"

"Yeah."

Stacy walks backwards and points at me. "When I get home, me and you. We're gonna talk."

I give Stacy a thumbs up and then she walks out.

Alone, I'm tempted to throw the covers over my head and go into my isolated world. But, I can't do that if I'm going to pay bills. I leave the bed and shuffle to the bathroom.

For a Sunday, it's been busy, but I'm not focused on work. Dad didn't call me back last night. Surely he forgot. Still, it gnaws at me. Enough that I send him a quick message.

Morning. You forgot to call me back. Still wrestling with the raccoons?

"Is it time to go home yet?"

I glance up and smirk playfully at Shannon. "Late night with Matthew?"

"What can I say?" She smirks back and tucks her hands in the pockets of her apron. "The guy can't get enough of me," she sings like a lovebird sitting on a branch.

"Are you two a couple now?"

Shannon looks right and then left. Then she leans over my desk and whispers, "You have to promise not to say anything. Matthew doesn't want anyone to know."

My mouth opens in shock. "Wait, you guys *are* a couple?" I was joking with her, but it looks like the joke is on me.

"Like I said." She stands tall and points her finger at me. "You can't tell anyone. I mean it. You can't even let Matthew know I told you. We made a promise, but I trust you."

"Can you tell me where the door hinges are for kitchen cabinets?"

Shannon, still grinning from ear to ear, turns to the customer. "Sure, I'll show you where they are. Follow me." She leads the way.

I'm sitting there in shock. Matthew and Shannon are a couple?

My phone vibrates. I quickly grab it, thinking it's from Dad, but it's from Brad.

Any chance I can talk a simple girl who has a sweet smile into meeting me after work?

It's a very touching message, but I'm not making any plans until I know my dad is alright. My gut tells me something is wrong.

Can I let you know later? After I send the text to Brad, I send another one to Dad. *Hey, I'm really getting worried. Text me.*

~ ~ ~

Dad still hasn't replied when I take my lunch break. I bite into my sandwich, even though I'm not hungry, and call him. With each ring, needing to hear is voice, I can't even chew. When it goes to voicemail, I leave a message. "Dad, why are you not answering me?

I'm scared you're having some diabetic attack and in a coma. Call me."

It could be something as simple as Dad lost his phone. Or maybe the battery is dead and he doesn't know it. Or, work could have called him in. He could be taking a shower. Regardless of the possibilities it is nothing, my heart races, telling me it's something. I'm seconds from leaving and driving to Charlotte, but that's two hours away. I can't wait that long to find out what's going on.

Patty? She's next door and could check on him.

I quickly thumb through my contacts and tap her number. Then I pray she's not in the yard and answers. If she doesn't, I'm calling the police to do a welfare check.

"Hi, Carlen. What a nice surprise."

"Hey, Patty. Sorry to bother you. And I hate to ask, but would you mind doing me a favor?"

"Sure, what is it?"

"Can you please look out your window and tell me if you see Dad's truck?"

"Yeah, hold on, I'm walking to the window now."

I hope it's not there, because if it is, that means he's home, and there's no reason he shouldn't answer the phone or message me if he is.

"Carlen, his truck is home. Is everything alright?"

"I don't know. Have you talked to him?"

"No. Not since yesterday morning."

"We were talking last night. Dad heard something in the trash can, so he went outside to see if it was the raccoons. He said he'd call me back, but he didn't. I figured he forgot. I've been trying to reach him all day, but he won't answer my messages or my calls. Now you tell me his truck is there, so why isn't he answering? I'm scared something's happened to him."

"I'm sure it's nothing, but if you want, I can run over there and check on him."

"Would you please?"

"Sure. Let me get my shoes on."

I fan my face, on the verge of crying like a baby. "I can't lose my dad."

"Carlen, I'm sure he's fine. Let me go over there and have him call you."

I wipe a tear running down my cheek and plead, "Please hurry. I need to know he's okay."

114

"I'm fixing to walk out the door. Let me call you back in a minute."

"Okay. Bye."

After the call ends, horrible scenarios run through my head. What if someone attacked him last night when he went outside? What if he's dead?. With trembling hands, I send a text to Matthew. *I need you. Now. Breakroom.*

My hands shake so hard, I can barely collect what's left of my lunch and put it in the cooler. Once I have it zipped, I hold my phone, stare at it and will Dad to call me while trying to ignore the laughter and chatter of my coworkers.

The breakroom door opens. Matthew walks in, looking for me. When he finds me, he heads my way. I motion for him to hurry, which he does.

At my table, he places his hands on it and leans in. "What's wrong?"

"I think something happened to my dad. I just called Patty. She's the neighbor who was here on Thanksgiving. She's going over there to check on him." My eyes water, and I hold my breath to keep from crying. I fan my face and whisper, "Matthew, if I lose my dad, I'm not going to be able to handle it."

"Let's get out of here."

Once out of the breakroom, Matthew escorts me to the back of the store where it's private.

I clench my hands against my chest, still breathing too hard. "Why hasn't Dad called me? Patty's had plenty of time to go there and tell him. She knows I'm freaking out. And he wouldn't leave me hanging this long."

"Maybe she's explaining you called. Maybe he was in the bathroom. Give him a few more minutes."

"No, something's wrong. I feel it in my gut." Trembling, I hug my cooler and rest my chin on it. "It's bad, I know it."

Matthew rubs my upper arm. "Carlen, he's fine. You'll see."

"Maybe I should call him again."

"Give it a few more minutes."

"Matthew, it shouldn't take this long."

"When was the last time you talked to him?"

"Last night."

Matthew gives me a one-arm hug. "Don't worry. I'm sure there's a simple explanation. After he calls, you'll laugh at what it is."

"I sure hope so." I lean against Matthew, needing him to hold me.

"It's going to be okay."

"*Hey*. What's going on?"

Matthew and I quickly break away from each other and face the store manager strutting toward us with fury in his eyes. I can't speak, and Matthew doesn't answer.

Scott stands in front of us and throws his hands to his hips, looking at one and then the other. "I *asked* what's going on? What are you two doing back here hugging?"

"Carlen's upset. She's waiting on a phone call to see if her dad is okay."

Scott looks at me with a little less fury in his eyes. "What happened to him?"

With my fingertips over my lips, I sniffle and mumble, "He, he went outside last night, and now I, I can't get him to return my calls. His neighbor went to his house to check—" My phone rings, scaring me to death. "That's him." Relieved, I swipe as fast as I can and put the phone to my ear. "Dad, what's going on? Why haven't you answered my calls?"

"Carlen, it's me."

"Patty?"

"Yes."

I totally confused. "Where's Dad? Put him on so I can talk to him."

"He's um…outside."

"Outside? What was he doing? Why wasn't he answering my calls?"

"Carlen, I don't know how to tell you this, but I found him unconscious at the back steps. He must have fallen down them last night."

"*What?*" I squeal in horror and cover my mouth. "Oh my God. How bad is he hurt?"

Matthew put his hand on my shoulder to let me know he's here for me.

"I don't know. I came inside and called nine-one-one. An ambulance just got here."

"Is he going to be okay?"

"Carlen, I, I don't want to scare you, but you might want to come home."

"I am. As soon as we hang up. Will you call me and let me

know what's going on?"

"Of course I will. I can offer to ride with him to the hospital if you want me to."

"Yes, please. And make sure they know he's a diabetic. They need to check his sugar."

"I've already told them. They're getting ready to put him into the ambulance, so let me run lock up both houses."

"O-okay, bye." With trembling hands, I close out my phone and look at Scott. "Dad's hurt. He's on the way to the hospital. I have to go to Charlotte to be with him."

"What happened?"

"His neighbor found him unconscious at the bottom of the back steps." I turn to my friend and burst into tears. "Matthew, he was outside all night long in the cold." Even though I need to stay calm because I'm facing a two-hour drive, I can't hold it in and cry harder. "I knew something was wrong."

"Carlen, are you sure you're able to drive?"

Before I can answer Scott, Matthew takes my hand and tells him, "No, she's not, so I'm going to drive her there. Hope you understand this is an emergency, and we need to leave."

By the time Scott answers, "Keep me posted," we're out of the back of the store.

Still holding my hand, Matthew rushes me down the aisles. I keep my head lowered and let him guide the way. It seems like forever and then it seems like seconds before we are out of the store and in the glaring sunlight. Matthew hasn't slowed our pace. "We'll take my car."

"Matthew, are you sure? You don't have to drive me there."

"Carlen, maybe I want to."

Our pace turns into a mad dash through the parking lot. I grip my phone with my free hand against my chest. My hair blows across my face, making it hard to see, but Matthew's leading the way, still holding my hand.

We come to a stop at his car. I'm out of breath at the same time, fueled from the need to get to my dad.

Without breaking his stride, he opens the passengers door for me. "Get in."

I slide into the seat and throw my cooler in the back. Matthew gets in and starts the car, and then he slams it in reverse, then he peels out of the parking lot.

When we merge with the traffic on I-26, Matthew glances my

way. "Buckle up. I'm going to get you there as fast as I can, and I'd feel better if you were strapped in." He accelerates, weaving in and out of traffic like a race car driver.

I pull the strap over my shoulder and buckle up, then I burst into tears and wipe them with the end of my sleeve. "Thank you for driving me."

"You don't have to thank me. I want to be there for you."

"I don't even have my coat or my pocketbook."

"Your things are safe in the locker. I have money if you need anything. At least you have your phone. Maybe you can borrow a coat from Patty."

What would I do without Matthew? I rest my head back and look out the window at the mountains. Gloria told me when I have bad thoughts to find something to distract me. And I need distracting. I read every sign in passing. Every mile marker. Every tag on a car that passes. Every logo on commercial trucks. Nothing works. I cry, worried about my dad.

Matthew places his hand on my wrist. "He's going to be alright."

I turn to him, wiping my wet face. "You really think so?"

Matthew keeps his eyes on the road and tells me with confidence, "Yes, I do."

Why don't I believe it? I turn back to the mountains and pray the next time I talk to Patty she tells me Dad is alright.

Chapter 11: How Is Dad?

Carlen, I'm so sorry, but Paul didn't make it. Your father is dead, just like your mother.

A single tear runs down my face, fearing Patty's words.

"Talk to me." Matthew nudges my leg. "You haven't said anything in a long time."

Still staring out the window, I mumble, "Why hasn't she called? She has to know something."

"Think of it as good news. Like, they're running tests and stuff like that."

"But they're not running tests on her."

"Guess you got me on that one."

My phone rings, sending me into a panic and frantically trying to remember where I left it. I grab it from the console. "It's her." I swipe the screen and can't get my words out fast enough. "How is he?"

"I don't know. They won't tell me anything, because I'm not family."

"Where did they take him?"

"Presbyterian."

"Did he say anything in the ambulance?"

"He did come to a little, but he didn't say much, because the medics were asking him questions. That's all I know, Carlen. I'm sorry."

"It's okay. Thanks for riding with him."

"I wish I could tell you more. I worry about you driving and upset."

"Matthew is driving me. He was with me when you called."

"Oh, that's good, then. Where are you?"

"About an hour away. Can you ask if they'll let you see him? I mean, that's not like asking questions about his condition."

"I'll ask as soon as we hang up, but, Carlen, Paul is in good hands. He'll be okay."

Here come the tears again. I close my eyes and cover my mouth. "But what if he isn't?"

"Ah, sweetie. I know you're scared, but he's going to be alright. He was much better by the time we got here."

"You're not just saying that?"

"No. I'm not just saying that. He was still in and out of it but somewhat responsive. That's a good sign. You have to think good thoughts."

"I'll try."

"Maybe by the time you get here, they'll have good news."

"Thanks for everything, Patty. I need to go so I can save my battery since I don't have my charger, but call me if you find out anything."

"I will."

"Bye." After closing out my phone, I put it in the console and lean back, exhausted.

Matthew switches lanes to pass a slow truck. "What did she say?"

"They won't tell her anything, because she's not family, but she said Dad was more alert in the ambulance."

"That's good." Matthew glances my way with a smile and ruffles my hair. "See, I told you he's going to be fine."

For the first time, I'm ready to believe it. "Yeah, I think so too. I just need to get there." This is the only thing I hate about moving to Hendersonville—being so far away from Dad.

~ ~ ~

After running nonstop since we parked, I'm out of breath when we rush into the emergency room. I scan it, not sure where to go. When a nurse comes my way, I hold up my hand. "Excuse me." I swallow and catch my breath. "Can you tell me where my father is? An ambulance brought him in a couple of hours ago."

Although she's in a rush herself, thankfully, she motions for me to follow her. We come to secured double doors. She swipes her passkey, and then we enter. She points to the nurses' station. "You can ask someone which room he's in."

"Thank you."

We scurry to the semi-circular desk. Before I get there, I'm already asking, "Can you tell me where my father is? His name is

Paul Dupre."

Surely my plea alerts her I'm freaking out over my dad, but she looks up at me with little concern. "He's having a CT scan done, so he's not in his room."

"Can I talk to the doctor? I don't even know what his condition is."

"The doctor is with other patients and will speak to you when he has the results."

I huff, frustrated. "Can we at least wait in his room?"

"If you want to." She motions down the hall and points with her pen. "Room seven."

We head that way, and I mumble, "What's her problem?"

Matthew keeps up with my fast pace. "Ignore her."

"Trust me, I am."

We enter Dad's room. The first thing I see is an empty bed with the sheet and blanket in disarray. My eyes tear up. It hits me how real this is.

"Carlen." Patty, holding her phone, quickly stands from the chair. "They just took him for a CT scan. I was sending you a text."

"That's what the nurse told me." I place my hand on his bed, needing to feel his presence. "Has he said anything?"

With her lips pressed together, she shakes her head. "Not really. Other than mumbling."

"If the CT scan comes back that everything's okay, do you think they'll let him go home?"

She shrugs. "I'm sure if he's okay, they'll release him."

It's not that I don't trust her, but there's an unsettling feeling in my stomach. Slowly, I make my way to the end of the bed where she's standing. "Patty, you wouldn't hide something from me, would you? You'd tell me if it's bad?"

She places her hand on my forearm. "I don't know anything. Honest. They barely talked to me."

And I believe her.

There's nothing to do but wait. I sit, then pace, and sit again. Every time someone walks by, there's disappointment it's not my dad. Time seems to have stopped, but not my racing heart.

"What's taking so long?" I exhale and look out the window for something to distract me.

Patty stands next to me. "I know the waiting is hard, but it means his condition isn't serious, or they'd be rushing here and there. It's a good thing, Carlen."

I look at her. A kind woman trying to soothe my fears instead of causing them. Something foreign to me, but something I desperately need. If only Mom could have... Before the past invites itself into the moment, I look out the window and focus on Dad. "I suppose. It's just, this not knowing is hard. Why can't they tell me something?"

"I'm sure they will as soon as they know."

More waiting. It seems longer than it is, because I keep looking at the clock.

"Anything I can get you?"

Without looking at Matthew, I shake my head.

"Mr. Dupre, we're back in your room." A nurse helps a man in scrubs push a gurney into the room.

"Dad?" I leave the window and rush to him.

Matthew takes my forearm and holds me back. "Give them a minute."

The nurse is on one side of his bed, and the male attendant is on the other. They use a sheet to transfer Dad. He grunts during the process but doesn't open his eyes.

"Mr. Dupre, I'm going to hook you back up," she tells him in an attentive voice, taking the wires that rests on his chest and inserts them into a monitor. Without missing a beat, she places an oxygen tube across his mustache and guides it behind his ears. "Try to wake up, Mr. Dupre. You have visitors." She slips the blood pressure cuff around his arm and then covers him. "I know you're cold. This warming blanket will help."

I gnaw at a fingernail. "When will they know the results of the CT scan?"

She looks at me, still tending to him. "As soon as the doctor knows, he'll come talk to you."

After the attendant pushes the gurney out, I rush to his bedside and take his hand. "Dad, it's me, Carlen. Can you hear me?"

He blinks like he's half asleep.

"Dad?" I put his hand against my cheek, hoping he will sense my presence.

He squirms a bit but doesn't seem focused.

Patty stands on the other side of the bed. "Paul, can you hear us?"

"Car-len?"

His first word, and it's so precious.

"Yes, I'm here. What happened?"

While moaning, his face contorts, and I'm guessing it's because he has one major headache. There's a huge knot on his forehead. "Don't say a word."

I shake my head, confused. "About what?"

He mumbles something incoherently.

I look at Patty. "What's he talking about?"

She shrugs. "I don't have a clue."

Twenty-five minutes pass, and still no word. Patty tries to convince me that's good news. Waiting for the results is better than the doctor rushing in to announce Dad has a serious injury.

"Be right back. I need to use the restroom," Matthew announces and leaves.

"Dad, *please* wake up."

A man in a white doctor's coat walks into the room. "Hello, I'm Dr. Stanton."

"Hi, I'm Carlen. How's my dad?"

The doctor looks Dad over and feels his cheek, then his forehead. "The CT scan shows that he has a concussion."

I have no clue what that means other than Dad has a head injury. "How bad is it? I mean, is there damage? Does he need surgery?"

The doctor turns to me and shakes his head. "No. Fortunately, it's a mild concussion."

"How do you treat that?"

"We don't. It's something that heals on its own. He'll probably have a headache when he comes to. We can give him some Tylenol for the pain."

It sounds so simple. So far, the news is better than I could ask for. I nod, almost in happy tears. "Does that mean he can go home?"

"I'm afraid not. Miss Dupre, your father came in with life-threatening conditions. His sugar was at a dangerous level, along with being severely hypothermic and having a head injury. This could've been much worse. He'll need to be monitored until his levels are safe. If he's better in a few days, he can go home."

It feels like he's scolding me. What do I know about medicine and injuries? It's not like anyone has told me anything about his condition. I'm just a scared daughter worried about her father.

"But he's going to be alright?"

"Yes. He just needs to rest and let his body recover." The doctor glances over the monitors. "His heart rate is still low, but his body temperature is rising."

"You don't think there's damage from the concussion?"

"No, but when he wakes up, we'll see how his motor skills and memory are. I may do a neurocognitive test, but at this point, I'm confident that won't be necessary."

"When will he wake up?"

With his hands in the pockets of his white coat, he exhales. "That's up to him. Some people bounce back sooner than others. If your father is one of them, perhaps he can go home sooner. Only time will tell. Does he have someone at home to take care of him when he's released?"

"Um, I live out of town, but I'm going to stay with him as long as he needs me."

"Good. At this point, try to talk to him and keep him awake."

I nod hard and even smile. "Don't worry. I will."

"Is there anything else?"

"No. Not that I can think of."

"If something comes up," he heads for the doorway, looking over his shoulder, "you can let a nurse know."

"I will. Thank you." When I look at Patty, I grin and sing, "He's going to be okay."

She laughs at my giddiness. "You know, Paul might milk this just to keep you around."

I look at Dad. "Yeah, I can see him doing that."

Matthew walks in with three soda cans and offers one to me. "Did I miss something? I swear that's a smile on your face."

"It is." I take a soda from him and pop the tab. "The doctor came in and told us Dad's going to be okay." I gulp the cold carbonated drink and don't stop until I have to catch my breath, unaware I was so thirsty.

"That's good news." He offers a can to Patty. "When can he go home?"

I ease out a burp without trying to be rude. "In a few days."

"Carlen, unless you need me to stay, I'm going to head out."

"How will you get home?"

Matthew raises his hand. "I can drive you."

"Thanks, but that's not necessary. I'll call a neighbor. She won't mind."

I don't want Patty to leave. Admittedly, I need her. "You know you're more than welcome to stay."

She makes her way around the bed and stands in front of me

with the warmest smile. "I know, but I can come back later. Do you need me to bring anything for you?"

"Not that I can think of."

Patty gives me a gentle hug. "I'll bring you guys some dinner when I come back."

I can't believe I'm hugging her. "Thank you."

She releases me and waves to Matthew. "I'll see you later."

"Sure you don't want me to drive you home? I don't mind."

"No, really. You stay here with Carlen."

After Patty leaves, it's time to take care of business. "Where's the restrooms?"

Matthew jerks his head to move his bangs. "Go down the hall, and it's on the right."

I gulp my soda, then set it on the table next to Dad's bed. "Be back in a few." On the way to the restroom, walking as fast as I can, I call Stacy, but it goes to voicemail. "Hey, I'm in Charlotte. Dad fell and is in the hospital. Matthew drove me here. Dad's going to be okay, but I'm not sure when I'll be home. Call me when you get this." As soon as I hang up, a text comes through from Brad.

Haven't heard from you. The invite is still good.

"Oh shoot. I forgot to answer his text." *Had to come to Charlotte. Dad's in the hospital. Will keep you posted.*

After my trip to the restroom, a reply comes from Brad.

Hope your dad is okay. Let me know if there's anything I can do to help.

~ ~ ~

Dad is moved upstairs to a room, but he's still groggy. It's been a long, exhausting day, mentally and physically. It would be easy to fall asleep in this chair. My eyes are heavy. It would only take a few more blinks.

Dad mumbles.

I spring out of the chair and rush to his bedside. "Hey, wake up."

"Where am I?" He blinks and looks around the room.

"The hospital. Do you remember what happened?"

He closes his eyes tight and moans. "My head is killing me. Did I get hit by a semi?" He reaches up and moves his hand toward the knot.

125

"No, Dad. Don't touch it." I ease his hand back to his chest. "You have a big goose egg there."

"What happened?"

"We think you fell down the steps and hit your head, but you're going to be alright. Do you remember going outside to see if the raccoons were getting into the trash?"

"No, but I'm sure they did."

Now he's acting like my dad, just tired and groggy. And I'm one happy daughter.

"How long have I been here?"

Over the next few minutes, I explain what happened, what the doctor told me, and how I'm going to stay with him until he recovers. The part where I'm going to talk him into moving to Hendersonville will come later.

"You're going to stay at the house?"

I frown, offended. "Someone has to be there to take care of you."

"But I know how you feel about sleeping there."

"Guess I'll have to deal with it," I singsong like it doesn't bother me. And for now, it doesn't.

Dad's face has never looked so peaceful or happy. "Thank you, sweetie."

"You don't have to thank me."

The day turns into evening. Tired, I gaze out the window at the Charlotte skyline while Dad and Matthew watch a western. Matthew must be tired as well, although he looks comfortable in the chair, sitting sideways with his legs dangling over one arm and his head resting over the other.

I leave the window, kneel in front of him, and whisper, "You have to work tomorrow and have a long drive home. You should probably head out before it gets too late."

"I can't leave you stranded," he whispers back. "How are you going to get around? You don't even have your pocketbook."

"I'm going to stay here with Dad until they release him. It's only a few days at the most. If I need anything, I can let Patty know. So, go home. I know you're tired."

"I'm fine. I don't mind staying."

"Matthew, if you really want to help me out, go home so you can get my pocketbook at work. I know it's safe in the locker, but I'd feel better if you got it. And see if Stacy and Dillon will drive my car home. The keys are in my pocketbook."

"Are you sure?"

"Yes, now that I know Dad's okay." I glance his way. He's still glued to the television. I look at Matthew. "If you leave now, you can be home by nine."

He turns in the chair, puts his feet on the floor, and leans closer. "Will you call me if you need anything?"

"There is something. Would you mind coming back to get me when this is over?"

"You know I don't mind. Just let me know when."

We stand at the same time.

"Be careful going home. And call me to let me know you made it."

"You worry too much."

"Oh hush." I turn to Dad. "Matthew's heading home."

He mutes the volume. "Thanks for driving Carlen here. I really appreciate it."

Matthew moves the bangs from his eyes. "Not a problem. Glad you're going to be alright."

"Me too. Drive safe."

"Don't worry, I will."

I give my best friend a big hug. "Thank you for everything."

Matthew wraps his arms around me. "You're welcome. I'll call you when I get home."

"Please don't forget."

"I won't." Matthew releases me and walks out of the room.

I already miss my best friend.

Chapter 12: Terry

Dad can recite every character's line in the movie. And he gets into it like it's the first time he's watched it. What is it about horses and cowboys? I'm bored. If I lie on this couch any longer, I'm going to fall asleep. I need to check in with Matthew and Stacy. I leave the couch and stretch. "Dad, my phone is almost dead. Where's your charger?"

"It's on my dresser. My phone is charging, but it should be finished by now."

"Do you need anything while I'm up?"

"No. I'm good."

"I won't be long."

Once upstairs, I stroll down the hallway. At the forbidden closet, I stop, but I'm not sure why. I've passed it several times today. Unconsciously, I know what it is. I'm curious to see if Mom's wallet is empty. Nothing is stopping me from going in there and looking. It would only take a minute. My hand goes to the doorknob, but I don't open it. There's no reason to go in there. Like Dad said, it was one of her old wallets and not the one that was stolen.

I enter the master bedroom and unplug Dad's phone from the charger and sit on the edge of his bed. After plugging the cord into mine, I swipe Stacy's number. The call goes to voicemail. "Hey, it's me. Just checking in. I know you're at work and can't answer. Dad came home this morning. Call me when you're not busy, and I'll update you." My next call is to Brad. Or rather a text.

Wanted to let you know I should be home in a few days. Dad is doing well. Hope you are.

Why am I avoiding talking to him? Fear? Insecurity?

Next on my list is Matthew. After swiping his number, I bring my legs onto the bed and sit Indian Style.

"Hello stranger," he sings in a chipper voice. "Did your dad come home today?"

"Yes. He's doing really good. The doctor said if he was up to it, he could go back to work Monday."

"Speaking of work, I can't talk long. We're busy."

"I figured. When are you off? I need to get home and back to work myself. Scott's been understanding, but I know it's the holiday season."

"I'm off Friday. Then I've got to work the weekend. I'm not off again until Wednesday."

I twirl a lock of hair and grin. "Wanna come get me Friday?"

"I'll mark my calendar," he tells me in a deep, professional voice.

"You're funny." The silly guy makes me laugh. "When I get off the phone, I'll text you the address."

"Brilliant, mate. Reckon I'll leave with that. This bloke has work to do."

I laugh, a bit confused at his new persona. "What's with the English accent?"

"I watched a movie last night. This cool dude was from England, and we were trying to talk like him."

Thankfully, I restrain myself from asking if 'we' means him and Shannon. Wonder why he doesn't confide in me? He knows I won't tell anyone.

"Sounds like you had a good time with your friend."

"We did. Look, I hate to go, but I don't want Scott to catch me on the phone."

"No need to explain. See you Friday. Oh, I keep meaning to ask. Did you get my pocketbook?"

"That's affirmative."

"Thanks. Bring it with you."

"Mak-ing a no-te as we speak."

Something has gotten into Matthew, and I like it. Goofy guy. "Just don't forget the note."

"Ha, ha. I'll call before I head there."

"Sounds good. Thanks, Matthew."

"No problem."

After swiping to end the call, I send him a text with the address and mosey out of the bedroom with a yawn. In the hallway, the closet door gets my attention again, but I don't stop. There's something else on my mind. Something I need to talk to Dad about. Once downstairs, I offer him his phone. "It's charged."

"Thanks." He rests it on his thigh and continues to watch the movie.

I sit on the couch, lean back, and put my feet on the coffee table. It's now or never. Time to tell him what's on my mind. "Dad, I've been thinking about something."

His wide eyes dart to mine. "Huh-oh."

"It's not bad."

His phone rings. Then he looks at it. "That's Patty."

"You should invite her over for supper."

Dad gives me that I-know-what-you're-up-to squint and answers. "Hello."

So much for our talk. And speaking of supper, it's time to start something. I leave the couch and mouth, "Invite her."

Dad waves me off as I leave the room. "Yes. I'm doing good. Thanks for asking."

In the kitchen, it's quiet. In a way that tells me she's here. Let her say something. I'm ready. Acting brave, I open the refrigerator and hum, searching for ideas. There's nothing in here I want, so I open the freezer. It's not the cold making me shiver, it's her. She's here, and I don't feel so brave. I'm scared to death if I turn around, she's going to be standing there with her dark eyes.

"You better get out of that fridge right now. And get out of my kitchen before I get the broom after you."

Logically, I know she's not here. It's that little girl who is afraid, not me. I would love to turn and see Mom so I could confront her. To say what that little girl couldn't. My brave moment returns, and I spin around and bark, "You can't scare me anymore, so leave me alone."

It's silent. In a way that tells me she's gone.

I'm proud of myself and smile. With the freezer door still open, I continue my search. "Hmm, let's see, what am I hungry for?"

Hamburgers? Tempting, but I don't feel like thawing the meat.

Pizza? Nah. Frozen pizza is for when you seriously have nothing else to eat.

Wow, Mom hasn't said anything. And her presence isn't here. I could get used to this. Now, where was I? Supper ideas.

Fish? My face puckers, deciding. My stomach says a winner. Fish it is.

I grab the box and shut the freezer door. When I turn around, a white flash blinds me like a light bulb exploded in my face. My heart races as I step back, expecting another flash. As the glare subsides, I blink and scan the kitchen. Everything appears normal. There's no shattered glass anywhere that I can tell. And Dad hasn't run in here to see what happened. I hesitantly make my way to the oven, still scanning the kitchen, then place the frozen box on the counter. As if things couldn't get any creepier, my head feels funny. Like the first and only time I got drunk, which is why I don't drink. Having something overpower my mind freaks me out.

The sudden chill in the air causes goosebumps to run up my arms, warning me she's here, but even more so, she is *not* happy. It scares me so much I try to run out of the kitchen, but when I look down, I don't have a body. Just like in my dreams. Maybe that's what this is. I will myself to wake up, but I can't.

I'm no longer in the kitchen but swirling in a foggy hurricane. Voices echo, but they're faint. I can't tell who it is, but at least it's pleasant, not hostile. The more I concentrate on the voices, everything settles, and I'm back in the kitchen, although it's black and white and grainy. Although I don't see anyone, I know I'm not alone.

"This is my mom. And Mom, this is Terry."

I blink at the grainy image forming next to me. Then I blink harder. It's Terry. I open my mouth to say something, but nothing comes out.

"Hello, Terry."

When I glance at the kitchen counter, I blink harder. Mom is there, getting a pot from the cabinet.

"So, you're the boyfriend?"

"Yes, ma'am."

"Guess you don't know the real Carlen yet, or you wouldn't come near her."

"Mom, please."

"Carlen, he needs to know what kind of person you really are. If you won't tell him, I will."

I'm confused, trying to make sense of what is going on. Why am I hearing a conversation that didn't happen if Terry never came to the house? He broke up with me before I could invite him to meet my parents. At least that's what I thought.

The more the fog in my head lifts, I remember something. "Oh my gosh. Terry *was* here."

I must have blocked that out. Why would I want to remember Mom bashing me in front of my boyfriend? My eyes water, recalling the things she said to Terry. The sweetest guy in school who told me he loved me slowly lowered his arm from around me after Mom made her speech. Then he broke my heart, because he believed everything she said.

"Um, Carlen, I should probably go. Maybe we shouldn't hang out anymore."

Gloria was right when she suggested the shadow was unrelated to Mom's murder and might be another memory I've suppressed. The shadow was Terry walking through the kitchen to leave after Mom warned him I was some crazy girl. Now I know why he dumped me. Because of her.

I bring my clenched hands to my temples and growl in anger. The only reason Mom let me invite Terry over was so she could say those things to him. She wasn't open to me dating him, she was on a mission to break us up, and that's what she did.

Between the anger boiling and the hurt slicing me, I release it and scream, "I hate you. I'm glad you're dead!"

"Carlen, what happened?"

I turn to see Dad running to me and scowl. "I remember what happened."

With wide eyes, Dad comes to a stop in front of me. "You remember?"

"Yes."

One simple word, and it seems to throw Dad into a panic, breathing harder than I am. "Um, sweetie, let's talk about this."

I'm angry as hell, but he's white as a ghost and looks like he's going to pass out.

"Mom's the reason Terry broke up with me."

He shakes his head like he didn't understand what I said. "Huh? Terry?"

"Yes. Remember that day he came over for supper to meet you and Mom? She only let him come over so she could break us up."

For some reason, Dad has a dumbfounded look on his face. Then he mutters, *"That's* what you remember?"

Offended this seems like something inconsequential to him, I lose it and yell, "Dad, she had *no right* to do that." A piercing tingle shoots through my head, distracting me. I blink, still having flashes of Terry walking away, but it's fragmented. I blink harder and try to focus, but all I see is a hoodie and someone walking out the back door. Oddly, it's the same story Dad told the police. Is that why

Dad doesn't want me to remember? Because Terry is the one who murdered Mom?

"Carlen?"

"Dad?" I can't swallow or breathe, preparing to ask him and preparing for what he says. "Was it him?"

"Who?"

"Terry. Did he murder Mom?"

His eyebrows rise, then he shakes his head. "No, sweetie. Terry didn't do it."

"But, you said the guy who killed Mom was young, tall and skinny, and wore a hoodie. You just described Terry."

"Carlen." He laughs with relief. "It wasn't him. I assure you. Terry didn't have a reason to hurt your mom. He left, remember?"

I did see him walk toward the door, but no, I didn't see him walk out, which makes me wonder if it was Terry, and Dad isn't going to admit it. Then again, maybe it's nothing. Maybe Terry walked out, and that was it. I just know my head is in overload.

"Carlen, are you okay?"

I rub my temple. "Yeah. I've had enough of the memories and flashbacks for now. I'm hungry. Hope fish is okay." I grab the box from the counter and open it.

"Fish sounds good."

"Did you invite Patty?"

He grins so proud. "As a matter of fact, I did. She said she's already eaten but thanked us."

"Oh well." After reading the directions, I preheat the oven. Then I reach for a baking pan in the cabinet. "Maybe she can come over tomorrow."

"We'll see."

I place fish portions on the pan. "You know, Dad, if you met a nice lady and got remarried, I wouldn't worry about you as much."

He heads to the fridge. "I'm fine being single."

"If you were married, you wouldn't have spent the night outside after falling."

Dad pops the tab on a soda can and sits at the table. "How are you and Matthew doing?"

I laugh, knowing he's throwing it back at me. "I told you we're only friends." I'm so close to telling him about Brad but don't. He'll flip out when I tell him how old he is. The oven beeps. I put the pan in and set the timer. Then I pull a chair from the table and sit in front of Dad, knee to knee like with Gloria. "I've got something on my mind." I raise my hand in defense and add, "I need you to be open and hear me out before you say anything."

"You have my undivided attention," he sings and brings his soda to his lips.

"Since your accident, I've been thinking about something." I stop, already fearing his answer. Then it just comes out. "Please consider selling the house and moving to Hendersonville."

He chuckles like 'my talk' has turned out to be something simple. "Sweetie." Dad leans over the table and places his hand on my wrist. "My home is here."

"You can have a new home in the mountains." Maybe my little girl pouty face will work. "I worry about you. Get out of the big city."

"But I like the big city."

I moan, disappointed. "You won't even consider the possibility? What if something else happens?"

"Would you feel better if I got one of those medical alert necklaces?"

I huff, not finding that funny. "No. I want you to move closer to me."

His tone deepens. "Carlen, this is my home. I've lived in this house for twenty years. You grew up here."

"But wouldn't you rather be closer so we can see each other instead of living with memories?"

Dad exhales, giving me the eye like he doesn't want to have this conversation. "It's not just that. I have my job that I enjoy. My friends. Some of the neighbors here, I've known half my life."

It finally occurred to me why he was resistant. "Is it because of Patty?"

He tried so hard not to smile, but I saw it. "That's part of it. She's a good friend. I enjoy her company."

That's when I realize he has a life here and not miserable the way I thought. Even though he's alone, he's not lonely, and when I look past my concerns, it's not hard to see he's happy.

"Then I guess we'll have to make more trips to see each other. And get one of those medical alert necklaces."

Dad chuckles, thinking I'm joking, but I'm not.

The credits play. It's been a long time since I've seen Dad laugh so much. That's why I picked a comedy to watch. We need to end the day with good thoughts. Me especially after remembering Terry was in the house and why he broke up with me.

Dad mutes the sound, still laughing. "That guy was hilarious. I still see him running out of the bathroom when the spider dangled from a web in front of his newspaper."

"I liked the part where he saw the snake in the kitchen and ran." The visual comes to me, which makes me laugh hysterically. "He fell three times, because he had on socks. It was like he was ice skating."

Dad laughs so hard, he has tears. "And it was a fake snake." His phone rings. Dad takes it from the side table and eyes the number, still laughing. "It's work." He swipes the number and leans back in the recliner. "Hellooo?" he sings.

I leave the couch and stretch, one arm bent, the other reaching to the ceiling.

"Yeah. That's what I told Gary."

I kiss Dad's cheek and wave as I walk backwards.

"Hold on a minute," he tells the person on the phone. "Are you going to bed?"

"Yeah. I'm tired." I cover my yawn, still walking backwards. "See ya in the morning."

"Night, Carlen. Love you."

"I love you too."

Dad continues his call. I march up the stairs. On the top floor, my hand trails along the wall while sauntering down the hall. I stop at the closet. Funny how so many years I've blocked out the small room, with good reason, and now it seems to scream at me every time I come upstairs. And I know why. That curiosity won't be satisfied until I go through that wallet. There's no need to. Dad wouldn't lie to me. Not about something like that. Or would he? I know he would do anything to protect me, but what would he be protecting me from?

The truth?

The truth being—that wallet isn't the one that was stolen.

But I believe Dad. I had to. If he lied to me, then that meant he was the one who murdered Mom. To end the doubts and suspicions, it was time to prove my dad wasn't lying to me.

My hand goes to the doorknob. I grip it and turn it slowly. The little girl in me knows any second Mom will catch me and beat the daylights out of me. But I'm not that little girl and open the door but only a few inches. I don't like the creepy feeling of going in there. My fear overrides the need to prove my dad's innocence. I pull the door closed and mosey to my room.

Chapter 13: Sad Eyes

"Carlen wake up." Dad gently rocks my shoulder. "Carlen?"

I moan, not wanting to get up. "What time is it?"

"Almost nine."

Nine? I spring upright and wipe my eyes. "I didn't mean to sleep so late."

"That's why I woke you up. And I've got breakfast waiting downstairs."

I yawn. "You fixed breakfast?"

"Yes, so hurry up."

"Be there in a minute."

He leaves my room.

I yawn again and throw back the covers. My feet hit the floor, and I slip on my shoes. I walk past the mirror. Nice morning hair.

In the kitchen, I yawn for the millionth time and take my chair. "I don't know why I slept so late."

"It's been a long week." He sets a cup of coffee in front of me and takes his seat.

"Just what I need." I sip the hot liquid, hoping it will bring me to life.

Dad sprinkles pepper over his eggs. "After we eat, I need to run over to Patty's. She called this morning and asked if I'd change the filter on her furnace."

"That's easy. She can't do it?" I reach for my fork and poke the scrambled eggs.

"Not where it's at. It's in the hall ceiling." He brings the coffee to his lips. "She almost fell off the ladder the last time she tried to change it, so I told her I would do it for her."

"Tell her to come over and visit. I'll make some lunch."

He bites into his toast. "Why don't you come over with me and invite her?"

"I need to take a shower." I spread jelly on my toast. "It's a shame we couldn't get to know her and John before Mom died.

There was no reason we couldn't be neighbors." The more I think about it, the more it angers me. "Because of her stupid rules, we couldn't even go out in the yard."

Dad's eyes scold me as he pokes his eggs a little too hard. "Carlen, don't let what your mother did make you bitter. It would be easy to become her. And I say that in a respectful way."

He's right. I wipe the jelly from my finger. "I'm sorry. I shouldn't have said that."

"No need to be sorry." He chews and points his fork at me. "Always try to find the good in something."

"Name something good about Mom," I counter in a dry tone.

He lowers his fork. A tired sigh carries. "I'm sorry she treated you the way she did, but—"

That's where I stop him. "It's not *your* fault."

"When you get older, sometimes you look back and wish you had done things different."

"Dad, you're the best father a girl could ask for. No regrets, you hear me?"

We stare.

"I mean it, Dad."

He nods and then forks his eggs.

"When you go over to Patty's, please invite her to lunch. Tell her I'm leaving this afternoon."

"Speaking of, I need to get over there." He wipes his face, leaves his chair, and kisses my temple.

"Don't forget."

"I'll invite her." His voice trails off before walking out the back door.

I finish my breakfast and head upstairs to change and to do something with my morning hair. When I come to Mom's closet, I stop and look at the door. One minute is all it will take to look inside that wallet to see if it's empty, which I know in my heart it is. To satisfy the nagging curiosity and end this once and for all, I open the door. With a flick of the switch, the darkness is gone. And so is that box.

My hands go to my hips, and a sigh rumbles. "That's weird." I bite the inside of my mouth and do another glance over, more careful this time. It's not here. Alarms don't go off, knowing there's a simple explanation. Maybe I overlooked it. One by one, I go through boxes, lifting the lid and glancing inside. After the last one, I step back and try to make sense of this.

Why did Dad take that box out of the closet? And where is it? My curiosity is now upgraded to unnerved. He would never throw something so sentimental away, so where could it be?

The shed.

While he's at Patty's, there's time to check. I run downstairs, grab the key to the shed at the back door, and head outside.

At the shed, I cup the cold lock in my palm and turn the key. The lock pops open, and I step inside, already scanning the shelves, feeling like a criminal breaking into someone's building.

If it's here, it's not in plain sight. I rub my bare arms to wipe away the cold air, still searching. I lean over the riding mower and check behind it. Nope. I lift back the corner of a tarp and expose a storm door leaning against the wall. Just as I'm ready to let go of the tarp, I look at the floor. My eyes bulge. Lo and behold, there it is.

There's only one reason Dad would've moved the box out here. The sick feeling in my gut tells me that's not Mom's old wallet, but the one she had the day she died. And if it is, that means Dad was the one who...

What now?

Do I walk away and pretend I don't know anything, or look inside to confirm my fears?

Can I go home without knowing the truth?

Can I handle the truth?

My heart races because time is limited, and a decision must be made.

Without giving it a second thought, I jerk the tarp back and reach down into the tight space for the box. With a couple of grunts and tugs, I manage to pull it from behind the storm door and set it on the floor in the center of the shed. Out of breath, more from the anxiety than the effort, I sit and lift the lid and expose Mom's wedding dress. My hands dig inside like a dog to dirt until I see Mom's leather three-fold wallet. I take it out of the box and sit back on my heels, staring at it as tears collect in my eyes. It's not too late to put it back.

But it is too late. I have to know.

"Please be empty," I whisper, preparing myself. My heart pounds so hard, I can hear it in my head. Once I open it, I can't take back what I know. I inhale a deep breath like I'm about to jump off a cliff, which wouldn't be as scary as this. I release the air through my parted lips and thumb back the snap and open the wallet. The first thing I see is Mom's driver's license and then her credit cards.

I've seen enough and close the wallet, then lean against the mower and whimper. Through the tears, a blinding flash explodes, startling me. I look to see if the door flew back and the bright morning sun pierced in, but the door is closed. Still blinking from the glare, I cower and somehow know I'm that sixteen-year-old girl. From the smell of spices and something cooking, I'm in the kitchen. The hairs on my arms rise, sensing someone is near me. Mom? I blink harder as the fog dissipates. No, it's Terry. It's that day he came to the house.

He walks away from me.

I reach out my hand for him to come back. *"Please don't believe her. She hates me."*

The door closes. He's gone.

I turn to Mom, heartbroken.

She's laughing, still preparing supper.

Any other time, I would run to my room and cry, but something is different this time. I'm not going to run or cry. I'm going to confront her and march toward the kitchen counter to do so.

"Carlen!" Dad barks my name.

I'm pulled back to the present and look up at him, standing in the doorway of the shed.

We stare.

I shiver from the cold as well as the truth finally exposed. "It was you, wasn't it?"

He snatches the wallet from me and flings it back in the box. "You have to forget you ever saw that." Within seconds, the box that holds his secret is behind the storm door, and he covers it with the tarp.

I get to my feet and hug myself from the cold. "You have her wallet. The one that was stolen."

Dad appears calm and unfazed at what's happened. "We're going inside, and we're never going to mention this moment ever again, you hear me?"

"You want me to pretend I don't know who killed Mom?"

His eyes bulge. "Carlen," he yells in anger and points to the door. "Go inside the house right now."

Dad has never spoken to me this way, scaring me more than Mom ever did. I step back.

His eyes soften with remorse. "Sweetie, I'm so sorry I yelled at you." He steps closer, but I back up, still scared of him. "Everything I've ever done is to protect you. That day, I did what I had to do. For you."

With my arms together at my chest and shivering, I ask the question I already know the answer to. "You killed Mom?"

As we stare, Dad's eyes water. He shrugs and tries to blink away the tears. "It happened so fast." He winces and bursts into tears, crying out, "I had to protect you."

My mouth opens to say something, but what? I don't know what to say and run out of the shed as fast as I can.

"Carlen."

I run to the house. When I enter the kitchen, there's another flash. The brightest one yet. Blinded and disoriented, it feels like I'm freefalling into an abyss. It's so fast. And it's quiet. So quiet. Then I'm still, not moving, as though I hit the bottom. Then I hear her. Mom's haunting laughter. With the glare gone, I see her standing at the kitchen counter, chopping carrots. Although I stand in place, I watch the sixteen-year-old girl march toward her. A very angry sixteen-year-old.

"How could you do that to me?"

Mom's cold eyes cut to me as her laughter simmers into a growl. *"Don't you ever speak to me like that again."*

I point at her and yell, *"What you did was evil."*

Mom slams the knife on the counter and gets in my face. *"What I did was save that poor boy from you. You didn't deserve him. You don't deserve anybody."*

I spew the words that have been stuffed for so long. *"What I don't deserve is a mother like you. A cold, heartless mother. I can't wait until I'm eighteen so I can slam the door in your face before I walk out of this miserable prison you call a house."*

She shakes her finger at me. *"You're gonna burn in hell for talking to me like that."*

"No, you're the one who's gonna burn in hell."

She raises her hand to slap me at the same time I grab the knife on the counter she was using to cut the carrots and point it at her. *"You're never going to hit me again."*

"You rebellious brat." Mom snatches potholders from the counter and reaches for the two-handle pot on the stove, then she comes at me. *"I'll teach you not to talk to me like that."*

I back up, still pointing the knife at her. *"Mom, don't. That's*

141

boiling water."

Mom blocks my path when I try to run by her. We stare. Those eyes are dark and evil, and they tell me she's going to burn me with that pot of water.

"Dad! Help me." I back up until I'm cornered in the U-shaped kitchen and have nowhere to go. *"Mom, don't. Please. I'm sorry for what I said."* Even though I plead with her and point the knife to keep her at bay, she continues to draw closer.

Dad rushes into the kitchen and screams, *"Marion, no! Don't you dare."*

Mom ignores him and lifts the pot in the air to pour the boiling water on me. Out of instinct, I extend my hands to keep her back and defend myself, forgetting the knife is in my hand. It penetrates her chest. I release the knife and scream in horror at what I've done. Mom gasps for air and lowers her arms, dropping the pot. Hot water splashes against the counters before puddling on the floor. Mom brings her sprawled hands to her chest but doesn't touch the knife.

"Carlen, go to the living room and call for help."

Paralyzed, I watch in horror as blood pools around the wound on Mom's chest. Dad takes her forearm. With her mouth open, she wheezes hard for air. Each breath is more labored than the last. She looks at me. It's the first time I've seen someone behind those cold eyes. She's scared. Dad eases her to the floor and yells at me again to leave and call for help, but I can't move. Mom collapses out of Dad's hold and hits the floor. Her head falls to the side. Her hands are flexed inward. She struggles so hard for air. I fear each one will be her last.

"Mom, please don't die."

With her eyes on me, she wheezes one last time, then it's silent. She's gone.

I scream, *"Mom, no,"* so loud that my head feels like it's going to explode. Once my scream echoes away, it's silent. Silent in a way I've never felt before. I feel like I've fallen into a deep sleep.

"Carlen, I need you to look at me."

Dad's voice is muffled like he's far away, but when I focus, he's standing next to me, gripping my arm to steady me, being the wobbly mess I am. My head hurts. "What, what happened?" Disoriented and confused, I look down but don't see Mom lying on the floor this time. My eyes water. My stomach jolts. I look at Dad and swallow. "Now I know why you didn't want me to remember."

"Carlen, don't say it," he pleads with his eyes welling up with tears as well.

"It wasn't you. It was me."

"Let's get out of this kitchen." And just like that day, he rushes me into the living room. After setting me on the couch, he takes the blanket from the recliner and covers me, although I'm no longer cold. Dad sits beside me, and we look at each other. "I had hoped this day would never come, although I feared it would."

Numb, probably from the shock, I sit motionless. "That's why you didn't want to talk about it."

"Still don't, but…" With his elbows on his knees, he lowers his head and massages his face. "Tell me what to do, Carlen, because I don't know."

"Like I do?" I can still see Mom's eyes. It's like I'm staring at a picture of her. For sixteen years, all I saw were cold, empty, evil eyes. The last seconds of her life, I saw a person. Perhaps the person Dad fell in love with. And I killed her. The numbness is gone, and the guilt of what I've done strikes me hard. I cover my mouth and cry. "Dad."

He quickly wraps his arms around me and holds me next to his chest. "It's okay, Carlen."

"No it's not," I babble. "She was scared. I think she knew she was dying and wanted me to help her, and I couldn't." I cry harder into his chest and grip his shirt. "I hurt her, Dad. I didn't mean to."

"I know, sweetie."

"How am I supposed to live with myself?"

"Because you didn't have a choice."

"Yes I did," I babble, wiping my face with the blanket. "I, I didn't have to stab her." The visual flashes over and over with my hand thrusting the knife into her chest. Then her sad eyes staring at me. I cower against him. "I'm scared, Daddy."

He holds me as tight as he can. "I'm here, baby girl. I'm here. It's going to be okay."

I cry out from the depths of my soul. "How could I do that to my mother?"

"Carlen, you reacted. You defended yourself."

"Then how come you made up that story?" I lean away and look at him, crying and trying to breathe at the same time. "Why did-didn't you tell them wh-what really happened?"

He slowly wipes his forehead with his fingertips and exhales. "After I called the police, you asked me what happened. It took a second to realize you had blocked it out." Dad moves the curtain of hair away from my wet face, then places his palm on my cheek. His eyes pool with tears, fighting each one. "In that moment, I had to make a decision. The hardest one I've ever had to make. I couldn't bear to see them question you when you didn't remember. I just couldn't, Carlen. You had been through enough."

"I have to tell the police what happened." I lean against him, needing my daddy, because I'm scared. "They'll arrest me and put me in jail."

"There's no need to tell them. It's better not to say anything."

"How can I do that? What I did was—"

He quickly leans me back and grips my forearms. "What you did was defend yourself."

"But, Dad—"

He places his finger over my lips. "It was self-defense. You won't go to jail, so why go through all of that?"

I shrug, pulling the blanket tighter around me. "Seems like the right thing to do. I mean, if they won't put me in jail, then maybe I should tell what happened. I'm scared if I don't, I'm going to have nightmares for the rest of my life."

He exhales as though he understands, then he nods. "If this is what you have to do, then I'll support you."

"I'm going to talk to Gloria about it before I decide. Dad, there's somewhere I need to go before Matthew gets here. Will you go with me?"

"Of course I will. Where do you need to go?"

"The cemetery."

~ ~ ~

Dad drives while I stare out the window with my head against the glass. Gloria said if I ever remembered what happened, it means I'm ready to deal with it. She was wrong. How does someone deal with remembering they killed their mother? At least for now, I do feel numb. Maybe my head is protecting me from short-circuiting like it did that day.

My phone pings. It's Matthew's reply to a text I sent earlier.
Should be there in an hour. Had to stop and get some gas.
No rush. Running an errand. Take your time.
There's also a message from Brad.

Are you still coming home today? Would love to get together.

I text a reply. *I'll let you know. Not sure when I'll be home.*

"Is everything alright?"

"Yeah," I mumble and rest my head against the window. "That was Matthew. He'll be here in an hour."

"Are you sure about this?"

It takes a second to realize what he's asking until I see we're at the cemetery. "Yeah, I'm sure."

So many times, I have driven this road and passed the cemetery. Not once have I stopped to see Mom's grave.

Dad turns into the narrow-gated entrance. The sky is gray. The grass is brown. The trees are mere skeletons. The only color is the poinsettias sprinkled amongst headstones. It's been so long I can't remember where Mom's buried. Dad clearly remembers, because he goes right to her grave. Someone put flowers in front of the headstone. I don't have to guess who put them there.

Dad pulls onto the side of the one-lane road and parks. "Do you want me to go with you?"

"Thanks, but I need to do this alone." I get out of the truck and saunter to her grave, buttoning my coat. The memory of her funeral is vague, but with each step, it grows stronger. There were only a handful of people here. Mom didn't have a family except for us, and she didn't have friends. A few neighbors showed up. Patty and John attended.

I stand in front of her headstone and look at her name.

MARION FAY DUPRE

On the way here, I prepared what to say to Mom. Now that I'm here, the words are gone. Whatever I say will have to do, because I'm not staying here long. I huddle in my coat, enduring a cold winter's breeze.

"Never thought you'd see me here, did you?"

I take in a deep breath and try not to let the anger come out. A confrontation isn't what I came here for.

"Mom, I haven't been here because I didn't have a reason to. You never loved me, so why should I…

Stop. Remember why you're here, Carlen.

Seems the words that need to come out are a bit rebellious. Regardless, I came here to say them, and that's what's going to happen no matter how long it takes.

Let's try this again.

"Mom, I came here to tell you how sorry I am for what I did

to you. I, I didn't mean to hurt you. I was only trying to stop you. Everything happened so fast. If I could go back, I would…"

Would what? Let her pour the boiling water over me?

"Mom, you cornered me. There was nowhere for me to go. And you would have poured that water on me. Your eyes told me so, but I'm really sorry for what happened."

For the first time in my life, I almost shed a tear for Mom. Not the one I knew, but for the one I didn't know.

"Maybe I'll be back one day. If not…" I'm not feeling so numb anymore and need to leave. I said what was on my heart. "Goodbye, Mom." I head back to the truck.

Dad watches out the passengers window. I've never been this emotional over Mom. It's overwhelming. I might end up crying over her after all. That's not to say it's a bad thing, but it's scary. My pace quickens, needing Dad. As though he knows I'm about to break, the drivers door opens, and he leaves the truck. He runs to me. I just need to make it to his arms. When we collide, I weep.

"I'm here, sweetie. Don't hold it in. Let it out."

And I do, letting out a gut-wrenching cry.

"It's going to be okay. I promise," he tells me, holding me tight under a light sprinkle.

I take in a deep breath and cry out in guilt and agony. "I didn't mean to hurt her."

"I know you didn't. This is why I didn't want you to ever remember. To have this burden of knowing."

"I wish I didn't remember," I babble, all choked up.

The sprinkle turns to rain.

"We need to take cover." Dad ushers me to his truck and helps me inside. He shuts my door and runs to the drivers side and jumps in. He takes my hand. "We can sit here if you still need more time."

I catch my breath and shake my head. "Please get me out of here."

"Okay."

Once we're buckled up, Dad eases down the path toward the exit. The clouds darken. Raindrops pound the truck. It lures me into a daze, and my thoughts wander. How can I live with knowing I killed my mother? Should I turn myself in to the police?

"I worry about you going home."

"Maybe getting out of Charlotte will help. You know, being away from the house."

He comes to a stop at the exit of the cemetery, and we look at each other. "Promise to call me if things don't get better?" The worry in his eyes grows heavy.

"Dad." I reach over and place my hand on his arm. "I'll be okay. It's just the shock of remembering." That's a lie. I'm anything but okay. "Look, Matthew will be here soon. I don't want him to see something's wrong, so for now, it will help if we don't talk about this. I have to block it out until I can talk to Gloria. If you want to help me, keep me distracted by talking about something else."

He nods and forces a smile. "I can do that."

"Did Patty say she was coming over for lunch?"

"Yes, but I can go over and explain it might be better to do it another time."

"No, don't. She will be a good distraction."

"Are you sure?"

"I'm sure."

His lips part to counter, but he exhales.

"Dad, trust me. If I couldn't handle it, I'd tell you."

He smiles like he's proud of me. "I believe you."

We leave the cemetery.

Chapter 14: Home

With Patty helping prepare lunch, it keeps me distracted. And I've noticed how she knows her way around the kitchen so well. She has yet to ask me where anything is.

"Patty, thanks for bringing the potato salad." I set the plates on the table.

"You're welcome." She stirs the chili. "When Paul invited me over, I thought I'd make some to go with our hot dogs. Since it's just me, I don't often make it. I miss cooking for someone. At least I still have my gardening to keep me busy."

"Your yard is always so pretty."

"I've always loved planting flowers. Since John died, it's become therapeutic." She turns the stove off and brings the pot to the front burner. "The chili is ready."

"I'll let the guys know." I saunter to the living room and announce, "Lunch is ready."

"Coming." Dad sits up from the recliner and mutes the television.

Matthew leaves the couch and pokes my side in passing.

I poke him back. "Come eat, hungry boy."

The four of us gather at the table. While everyone chats and fills their plates, I glance at the spot where Mom took her last breath. It haunts me differently now that I know what happened.

"Carlen?"

I quickly turn to Dad and smile like all is fine. "Yeah?"

"Could you pass me the slaw?" What Dad is really asking is, am I alright? He must have noticed I zoned out.

"Sure." When I hand Dad the bowl, I wink to let him know not to worry.

He winks back.

Without him knowing, I watch him spoon slaw on his hot dog. My time with Dad is coming to an end. After spending five days with him, it's sure to be an emotional goodbye.

"Oh, Patty's delicious potato salad," Dad sings, giving her an adorable smile and reaching for the bowl.

"I thought you might like some."

So that's why she made potato salad. It wasn't a coincidence. Patty obviously knows how much Dad loves it. Unfortunately, it's something I've yet to master, and he doesn't like store-bought, so he's sure to enjoy Patty's. The act of someone fixing a dish out of love or kindness is a foreign concept to me. Mom would have tainted the meal if she knew it was something I liked. And she did. A memory of her doing that still haunts me to this day.

Matthew nudges me. "Can you pass the chili?"

"On its way." I take the bowl and set it next to his plate.

Dad, forking potato salad, turns to Matthew. "Did you get caught in that downpour on your way here?"

"Not until I got to Charlotte."

"You guys be safe going home."

"We will."

Patty squirts ketchup along her hot dog. "I think the heavy rain has moved on. At least that's what the weatherman said before I came over here. Oh, Paul, before I forget, I heard the Petersons are expecting another grandchild."

Dad's eyes widen, and he stops chewing. "Another one already?"

She laughs. "That's what I said when Mildred told me."

"I'm sure she's already knitting a blanket." Dad glances my way. His eyes ask if I'm really okay.

Hopefully, my smile tells him everything is fine. For now, it is. I'm distracted by the pleasant meal at this table. Something I'm not used to. This is so unlike how things were growing up.

Patty dabs the corner of her mouth with a napkin. "I haven't had hot dogs in ages. I forgot how good they are."

Matthew is already putting condiments on his second one. "They're even better if you grill them."

Dad reaches for the bowl of chili. "Maybe the four of us could grill out this summer."

Dad doesn't know Matthew has a girlfriend and that I've met Brad.

Patty sure perks up at the idea. "We should do that."

"Carlen, what time do you want to head out?"

I lower what's left of my hot dog. "Soon," is all I can tell Matthew but glance at Dad. We have this unspoken dialogue. Me telling him how hard it's going to be for me to leave him. My eyes mist over, already missing my dad.

"Carlen, is something wrong?" Patty places her hand on my wrist.

I flinch at her touch. Perhaps because she is sitting in Mom's chair, and for a split second, I thought it was her. And I don't like a woman's hand near me. It's a trigger. "Um, yeah. I always get emotional when it's time to leave."

She smiles and retracts her hand. "I'm sure it's hard, but I bet as soon as you see those beautiful mountains, you'll be excited about being home again."

Matthew mutters, "There's something else back home she'll be excited to see."

I cut my best friend a sharp glare to warn him not to spill the beans about Brad.

"You'll be back for Christmas," Dad reminds me.

I tease him. "Unless you want to come back to Hendersonville. I can try my luck at baking a ham."

Dad looks at Patty, and I swear he has eyes for her. "We'll have to see how things go."

After we finish eating, we talk about our jobs, how fast the year has come to an end, and who we want to win the Super Bowl. I listen more than talk, because this moment overshadows bad memories. Today, we're making new ones, and I hope there's more to follow. When I glance at the clock and see how much time has passed, I gather my dishes. "Matthew, we should head out if we want to avoid the afternoon traffic."

"No, Carlen." Patty quickly piles dishes as well. "I can do these later. Don't worry about it."

"I don't mind."

"Let me help." Dad stands and gathers bowls.

"Me too." Matthew joins in and rounds up the glasses.

It turns into a four-man cleanup. We bump into each other and laugh. I run to the fridge with the condiments. Matthew and Dad tackle the trash. Patty runs into him on the way to the table to wipe it. I've never seen him have fun. He deserves this. *We* deserve this.

And then it's time to leave. I'm strong until Dad hugs me. "Don't cry. We'll see each other on Christmas."

"Dad, you know leaving you is never easy."

"I know. It's not easy for me either. Maybe when you come

to visit, you can stay more than a day."

Until now, spending the night in this house was not an option. It was hard enough coming for a day visit. Perhaps something good came out of Dad's accident. After all, I survived spending more than one night here. It's time to stop letting the past come between me and Dad.

"If I can get the time off work, I would love to spend a few days with you."

"Oh, sweetie, you don't know how much that means to me." Still holding me, he whispers, "Are you going to be okay with, you know?"

"If not, I'll call you."

"That's what I wanted to hear. I love you."

"I love you too."

Dad releases me.

I turn to Patty standing next to him. "I'm glad you came over. I really enjoyed lunch." I almost laugh, remembering cleaning up the kitchen.

"I enjoyed it too. We'll do it again on Christmas."

I cup my mouth and whisper, "Keep an eye on my dad for me."

She winks and whispers back, "Don't worry. I will."

If I have to leave, at least I know someone is there for him. Someone I've come to trust and care about.

"Matthew." Dad offers his hand. "Thank you for everything. Come back any time."

"Glad you're doing alright."

"Me too."

Patty offers her hand. "Matthew, take care and drive safe."

"I will."

The moment arrives.

I sniffle and fan my face and quickly force my words. "See you in a couple of weeks."

Matthew opens the door for me. I walk out and into the cold and a gloomy sky.

"Your dad's pretty cool."

I look at Matthew, walking beside me. "The coolest ever."

We get into his car.

Matthew buckles up and starts the car. "Is Patty your dad's girlfriend?" he asks, backing out of the driveway.

I buckle up. "No. He said they're only good friends."

Matthew puts the car in first gear and laughs jokingly. "I saw more than just friends."

We drive away.

My eyes are on the house until it's no longer in view. "If they are, I'm happy for them. Dad deserves someone who finally treats him right."

Matthew comes to a stop at the intersection and looks at me, frowning. "What's that supposed to mean?"

"You want to hear the story?"

He squints one eye. "About?"

"Why I have demons?"

"That's totally up to you." Matthew checks the traffic. It's clear. He continues up the road.

When we turn onto the highway, I challenge him. "I'll tell you my demons if you tell me yours."

Matthew picks up speed and changes gears. "You have to go first."

This is going to be an intense ride home. I wait until we are out of Charlotte and away from heavy traffic.

"You know how Mom died, thanks to me freaking out over a knife after Thanksgiving dinner. What you don't know is what kind of mom she was."

"That bad, huh?"

"Worse."

"Like how?"

Weird how a memory came to me while we had lunch.

"Like the time Mom destroyed a good meal just to hurt me."

"How did she do that?"

With my elbow propped on the door, I rest my head against my hand. "I walked into the kitchen. Mom was peeling potatoes. I asked her if she was going to mash them or fry them. She asked me why I wanted to know in a hateful tone. I told her I was hoping she was going to fry them. I *loved* her fried potatoes. The one nice thing I can say about Mom is she knew how to cook. Hands down, she had the gift. She could cook a full meal like she had ten hands."

You would think I'm telling Matthew a pleasant childhood memory the way I'm calm and my tone is light.

"She said she was going to fry them. I probably smiled because I could already taste them. Then she told me she was going to fry them in onions. She knew I wouldn't eat them if she did, because I hate onions." The memory stings, even years later. I can still hear her hateful tone and see those evil eyes.

Matthew frowns with disgust. "She put onions in the potatoes just so you wouldn't eat them? Out of spite?"

"Yep. I can still see those potatoes on the plate in front of mine and remember how it felt not to be able to eat any. How the smell of onions permeated from them. Every time I smell an onion, I think about that day."

He turns his eyes back to the road and mumbles, "That's just *wrong*. Why would she do that?"

"That's how she was. I swear her mission in life was to hurt me. Like anyone will ever believe that. Moms are supposed to love and protect us, right?"

"What did your dad say about it?"

"I didn't tell him." I watch cars pass, sensing that teenage girl trying to surface. "If he had confronted her, she would have lashed out at him, and I didn't want her doing that."

"Did she ever hit you?"

"Yeah. With a broom. Or she'd slap me. Or poke my forearm with something really hard while yelling at me. There was this one time she used Dad's belt on me. Patty and John had just moved in. I happened to be in the yard and watched Patty water her flowers. She came over to introduce herself. Mom yelled at me to come inside." I pause, remembering that day. Some memories are not grainy but as real as looking at my hand.

"Carlen, if you don't want to talk about this, you know you don't have to."

We look at each other at the same time.

"Seriously. You don't have to talk about it." He turns his eyes back to the road.

No, I absolutely don't want to talk about that day. Yet, there's this gentle tug inside of me, encouraging me to, telling me it's okay. And with Matthew, I feel safe sharing things with him. Except how I found out it was me who murdered Mom.

"It's okay. Really." I continue. "When I went inside, Mom asked me what I told Patty. I told her nothing, other than my name and how old I was. Oh, I did ask her if she had any kids. Mom slapped me for lying and told me to tell the truth." My shoulders rise, and I squeal, "I *had* told the truth, but she didn't believe me. Mom grabbed my forearm and shook me as hard as she could, demanding I tell her what I said to Patty."

"What did she think you told her?"

"Now that I look back, I think she was jealous of our new neighbor. Dad couldn't go outside if she was out there." The sun pierces through the clouds, and the brightness blinds me. I adjust the visor. "I kept telling her I didn't say anything to Patty. She still accused me of lying and told me she would beat the truth out of me. She dragged me to her bedroom. I cried and begged her to believe me. Mom still had my forearm when she took one of Dad's belts from the closet and whacked me across my back." I stare, remembering that moment all too clearly. "I screamed bloody murder, because I was wearing a white, ruffled, half-top, and she was hitting my bare skin."

"Oh, shit. That had to hurt like heck."

"Yeah, it did," I mumble, still able to hear myself cry and scream for her to stop. Each whack hit the previous one and caused more pain. "I tried to get away from her but ended up going in circles with her having a grip on my arm and still hitting me. When she finally stopped, I told her she was hitting my back and not my butt. She pointed the folded belt at me and told me it was my own fault for not being still. My back burned for the longest time."

"Tell me you told your dad what she did."

"No. She said if I did, she would make him move out, and I'd never see him again. I was too young to understand Dad would've never left, but I believed her and didn't tell him."

Matthew reaches over and puts his hand on my arm, just below my elbow. "I'm sorry you had to go through that."

"I guess some of us..." The car in the lane next to me suddenly drifts into ours. "*Look out.*" I instantly jerk away from the door, draw in and brace for impact.

BEEP.

Thankfully, with Matthew blowing the horn and able to swerve into the other lane, we dodge an accident but by inches. The young girl doesn't even look our way, still texting.

"You *idiot*," I scream, throwing my hand to my chest and wheezing. I shake my head and tell my body it's okay to relax now. "Dang. I think my heart just came out of my chest." I move my feet and look around the floorboard, still trying to calm from the near-collision. "Did you see where it went?"

Matthew laughs, almost snorting.

I look at him. "It wasn't *that* funny."

"I thought so."

"That scared the crap out of me." My hands still shake. It's going to take my heart a long time to settle. Going almost eighty and getting sideswiped isn't on today's list of things to do. "So, that's my story." I tell him like it wasn't a big deal. At least I'm not in that dark place. "That's my demons. What's yours?"

As quick as I made Matthew laugh, I'm just as quick to make it disappear. He rakes his bangs out of his eyes and stares straight ahead. "It's not easy for me to talk about it. I have some pretty horrible memories growing up too. Me *and* Michelle."

"Matthew, like you told me, if it's too personal, you don't have to share what happened."

"No, you told me your demons, so it's only fair I tell you mine." He looks at me without his funny, goofy expression I'm so used to. "Just warning you. It's not a pretty picture." He turns his eyes back to the road.

Guess I'm not the only one with a horrible childhood. Not the only prisoner of the memories. And from Matthew's dreadful tone, his might even be worse than mine.

"My dad is an alcoholic. And he's got one nasty temper."

"Is that why you don't see him?"

"That and, because he's in prison."

Prison? Wow. That's a shocker. I'm afraid to ask what his dad did. I don't want to enter sensitive territory where Matthew doesn't want to go. "I had no idea." What the heck am I supposed to say? "I'm sorry."

Matthew points up ahead. "You mind if I pull over at the rest stop? I need to use the restroom."

"Of course not."

Matthew leaves the interstate and pulls up to the rest stop. We get out of the car and amble to the building. Inside, I head to the lady's room, and Matthew veers off to the men's room.

While washing my hands, I look in the mirror.

My reflection screams at me, *You killed your mother.*

I flinch and look down, rinsing my hands as fast as I can. The water turns to blood. The blood from killing my mother. I blink harder, my lips parting to scream for Matthew to come help me. Before the words come out, the blood is gone. My head is playing games with me.

A few women saunter in, laughing and talking.

With my head down, I dry my hands, toss the paper towels in the trash, then run out of the restroom.

Matthew is in the lobby, looking over the state map.

Seeing him, my heart calms. Even more so when I stand next to him. "Ready?"

He turns to me and shifts his bangs out of his eyes. "Whenever you are."

We head back to his car.

"I think I'm going to go back and get a snack." Matthew stops. "Do you want anything?"

"Nah. I'm good. I'll wait here for you."

Matthew heads to the open building with vending machines.

Since the warmth of the sun feels so good, I sit on a bench and wait. Just as I sit down, my phone rings. I grab it from my coat and see that it's Shannon. I answer, thinking something is going on with work. "Hey. What's up?"

"I heard Matthew came to pick you up?" she singsongs in a snarly tone.

"Yeah. We're on our way back now. Is something wrong?"

"Seriously? You had to ask *him* to come get you? Don't you have a boyfriend?"

"For your information, Brad isn't my boyfriend," I fire back in the same sassy tone. "Second, what's the big deal with Matthew coming to get me?"

"The big deal is, if he has a girlfriend, you should've told him no and found another way home. How would you feel if your boyfriend put another girl first?"

My eyes close while exhaling so I don't mirror her attitude. "Shannon, you need to calm down. Matthew isn't putting me first. You know we're friends."

"Friends?" she squeals, almost laughing. "How is he supposed to have a girlfriend if you're always butting into his life?"

"Well, if the girlfriend can't accept Matthew has a 'girl' friend, then she's the one with the problem."

"No, *you're* the one with the problem. You know I like Matthew. *A lot.* He's not at your beck and call if you need something. I wanted to do something with him tonight but no," she baby-talks. "He had to come get you."

Matthew is on his way, so I have to end the call. However, this conversation is far from over.

"Look, I'm not doing this with you. Not right now. Not after what I've been through the past few days. Heads up, if Matthew sees this jealousy, he'll dump you so fast you won't see him run away."

"It has *nothing* to do with me being jealous. It's time you back off and let Matthew have a girlfriend. Maybe you're the one who is jealous."

I laugh at her nonsense. "Me?"

She doesn't fire back.

I look at my phone. Sure enough, Shannon hung up on me. What is her problem? There's nothing wrong with Matthew picking me up. What does he see in her?

Matthew stands in front of me. "Something wrong?"

I tuck the phone in my coat pocket and refuse to let her get to me. "No. Just checking my messages." I hate to lie to him, but this isn't the time to tell Matthew about his girlfriend's childish behavior.

"Mind if we sit while I eat this?"

"Of course not."

He sits next to me and opens a pack of crackers and pops one in his mouth, then holds them in front of me. "Want one?

"No."

"Still want to hear my story?"

"If you want to share it with me."

Matthew looks over the parking lot while twisting the cap off his soda. "The first real memory I have of Dad, me and Michelle were about six. We were in the kitchen, coloring while Mom cooked supper." He gulps his soda, then burps. "Dad came in and didn't like what Mom was cooking, so he took the pot from the stove and slung it across the kitchen. Food went everywhere. He threw something else, but the pot is what I remember."

I grimace at the visual. "That had to be scary."

"It was. But then it became our normal."

"That's *not* normal."

He side-eyes me and puts another cracker in his mouth. "You know what I mean."

"Unfortunately, I do."

"The older we got, instead of throwing things, Dad would take his anger out on us. I can't describe what the house was like when he wasn't there, and the second everything changed when he walked through the door when he came home from work."

I tuck a loose tendril of hair behind my ear. "Did your mom not try to stop him?"

He shrugs. "Yeah, she tried. Once. Dad gave her a black eye and a busted lip. After that, she never said anything."

Matthew tells me about this horrible time in his life without sounding bitter, sad, scared, or even angry. But I know inside, there must be an emotional suitcase ready to snap open and fling everything.

"Do you resent your mom for not stopping him?"

He gulps his drink, then scans the parking lot and twists the cap back on. "Not when I was young, I didn't. We all were scared of him. But now that I'm older, yeah, I do. And I let her know it. I get she couldn't stop him, but she could've left him."

"I wondered why you didn't go see her on Thanksgiving."

"That would be why." He eats another cracker while I take in what he's sharing. "I don't hate Mom, but I don't want to see her. For now, anyway." He looks at me and brushes his bangs out of his eyes. "Mom should've done something to protect us. Because she didn't, things got worse, and something horrible happened."

"Is that why he's in prison?"

"Yep." He puts the last cracker in his mouth and tosses the wrapper in the trash can next to the bench. After he finishes eating, he continues. "It was a Saturday. Mom and Michelle went to town like they did every weekend. Dad was in the garage, doing his usual thing. I hung out with my friends. It was like any other weekend. I came home to get a snack. When I walked in, I heard commotion in Michelle's room. I thought it was odd since she was supposed to be with Mom. Michelle screamed this horrible plea to stop. It scared me. I, I thought someone had broken in and was trying to kill her."

I'm sitting on the edge of the bench, sweating from fear, from the anticipation of what happened. "What did you do?"

"I ran to her room to see what was going on. When I opened the door, Dad was in there."

I cover my open mouth, assuming what happened. "Matthew."

"When I saw what he was doing to her, I wanted to kill him."

I swallow hard and, with hesitation, ask, "What did you do?"

"Michelle had a trophy on her desk. I grabbed it and ran towards the bed and yelled for him to get off of her. He turned just in time to block my swing. I swear I was going to hit him until I killed him, but he took the trophy from me and hit me instead. I blacked out."

I curl my fingers, bringing my hand to my mouth. "Oh, no."

"When I came to, Michelle was sitting on the floor with me and telling nine-one-one what happened." He delicately moves his bangs and exposes his forehead. "That scar is from where he hit me with the trophy."

I gasp and lean back, then blink, horrified. "Oh, Matthew. I'm so sorry. You and Michelle didn't deserve that. Our parents were supposed to protect us, but they're the ones who hurt us."

He looks over the parking lot. "Yep. Sucks, doesn't it?"

"That's why you have long bangs? To cover the scar?"

"I don't like the reminder." He gulps his soda.

"It's a reminder how you tried to save your sister."

"I don't want people asking me what happened."

"Matthew, look at me."

And he does.

"You don't have to explain it. Just say it happened when you were young. Maybe people won't ask or even notice it."

With his eyes wide, he points at it and squeals, "You can't miss it, Carlen. And people are going to ask about it. And, yes. That's why I wear my bangs over it."

With caution, I lift my hand to his forehead. "May I?"

Matthew leans away, and his eyes tell me absolutely not. Unfortunately, I know what it's like to do that when someone's hand comes at me with memories of Mom slapping me.

"Why?"

"I want to see it again."

He rolls his eyes and huffs. "Whatever."

Matthew flinches when I gently move his bangs with my fingertips to look at the scar. It's not hideous, but it is obvious. How could a father do this to his child? Like I have the answers. Once I have the bangs to the side, I sit back.

We look at each other.

I smile at Matthew.

"What?" he asks, agitated, shaking his head so the bangs cover the scar.

"Maybe I like seeing both of your eyes."

He looks away.

I nudge his arm. "Yeah, I know. I'm embarrassing you."

His phone rings. "That's Michelle." He quickly reaches into his back pocket and swipes the screen. "Hey." As he listens, he brushes the cracker crumbs off his pants. "Yeah, that's fine. You guys have a safe trip. I'll see you in a few days. Bye." Matthew closes out his phone.

"Someone's going to have the apartment to himself," I tease

and give him a gentle nudge.

"Yeah, that means I have to cook too," he grumbles and finishes his soda.

After Shannon's comment, guess it would be a sin to invite him to eat with me. Then again, when she finds out he's got the apartment to himself, she'll offer to cook for him.

"Ready?" Matthew tosses the empty bottle in the trash container.

"Yep. Let's hit the road."

We take our time and saunter to his car.

"Do you and Brad have plans tonight?"

"He wants to do something. I told him it depends on what time we get back."

Once we get in his car and buckle up, Matthew's phone chirps. He reads the message and replies.

Bet it's Shannon. They're probably making plans for this evening. Guess he'll have someone to cook for him after all.

We leave the rest stop and head to Hendersonville.

Chapter 15: Friends

We're home. Matthew pulls into a parking spot and kills the engine.

I unbuckle and reach for my pocketbook on the floorboard. "Thanks for everything, Matthew. Let me pay you for the gas."

"No. We're friends. You would do the same for me."

I nod and sing, "Yes I would, but let me pay you."

"Nope."

We get out of the car at the same time and meet on the sidewalk to say our goodbyes.

Matthew tucks his keys in his pocket while jerking his hair out of his eyes. "Is something wrong? You've been quiet since we left the rest stop."

I debate telling him. It's my problem, not his.

"Carlen, if I said something—"

"It's not you," I tell him quickly to erase that concerned gaze staring at me. "It's Shannon. She called me while you were at the vending machines."

"What did she say?"

It's wrong to tell him what happened, because it will cause trouble. "Nothing, just, she's drama sometimes."

"Would you tell me if it was something more?"

"Yes." I punch his forearm and smile. "Everything's cool."

"If you don't go out with Brad, want to watch a movie and order pizza?"

I shake my head, confused. "Don't you already have plans?"

Now he looks confused. "No. Why would you think that?"

"When Shannon called, she said she was hoping to see you tonight."

"Do what?" He laughs like I'm joking. "I told you she's not my type."

Now I feel like he's picking with me and laugh. "Then why are you dating her?"

His eyes bulge. "What are you talking about?"

"Um, Shannon told me you two were a couple."

Matthew raises his sprawled hand, then makes a fist and lets out a growl. "Wait until I see her."

She lied to me? It should piss me off, but it makes me smile. "So, you guys aren't dating?"

"Hell no." He scowls and squares his shoulders like he's ready to fight. The sweet guy who wouldn't hurt a fly. "I only went out with her on her birthday, because I felt sorry for her. Then she called me the next day crying and needed someone to talk to. Again, I felt sorry for her, so I met her at McDonald's. She said she wanted to be my girlfriend, and I told her no. I made it clear there's only one girl I want, and that's *you*."

My mouth drops, and my eyes almost pop out.

"Sorry I blurted that out, but it pisses me off Shannon said that. She knows how I feel. I told you she was jealous of you."

My mouth is still open. I'm waiting for Matthew to tell me he's joking or punking me.

He runs his fingers through his bangs. "Please say something."

Still in shock, I slowly close my mouth and swallow the big lump in my throat. "I, I'm the girl you want?"

He rolls his eyes. "Carlen, everyone at work knows how I feel about you."

"Yeah. We're good friends."

"Just good friends?" He shrugs and grunts. "That's it? Nothing more?"

More? As in girlfriend and boyfriend? How can I tell Matthew I don't have those kind of feelings for him without hurting him? I tuck the hair behind my ears and exhale, trying to figure out how to handle this. "Um, Matthew, I had no idea you felt this way. You know I care about you, but—"

His hand goes up. "You don't have to finish that sentence. I get it." Matthew walks backwards and laughs, but I know he's hurting. "That's why I've never said anything. I knew you didn't feel the same. You like this Brad," he mutters with sarcasm.

I'm not losing my best friend to Shannon, but I am losing him. That's what my heart tells me, because it's breaking into tiny pieces. My eyes water with each step he takes. "Matthew, please don't walk away from me," I plead, not sure I can handle this. "*Please*," I beg harder and reach out my hand to him.

"Hey, it's okay. You can't help how you feel. Neither can I."

He jerks his head to move his bangs. "Hope it works out with you and Brad."

Before I can say anything, Matthew runs to his apartment. He's gone. Perhaps forever. I shuffle to my apartment with my head lowered, avoiding people in passing.

Once inside my apartment, I run to my room, drop my things and curl up on my bed. Wasn't coming home with the guilt of killing my mother enough? Stacy isn't home to hear me cry, so I don't hold back and sob as hard as I can. It's like I'm on a roller coaster and can't get off. First, my dad's accident, then finding out I'm the one who killed Mom. And now I've lost my best friend, and it leaves an emptiness inside of me I've never felt before.

"Why? It's not fair." I scream into my pillow until my lungs are empty.

Time becomes a blur, lost in a meltdown. I cry until my body gives out. Until I'm so exhausted, I can't move. I stare, listening to my faint breathing.

The front door opens. "Welcome home," Stacy sings from the living room.

I'm so tired, I can't answer.

Stacy stands in the doorway, looks at me, then frowns. "What's wrong?"

I blink slowly, too tired to speak.

She narrows her brows, coming toward me. "Carlen? What happened?"

That's all it takes for round two of crying. "It's Matthew." That's all I can say, blubbering and sobbing.

"Oh no." Stacy sits on the edge of my bed and places her hand on my forearm. "What happened to him?"

It's hard to tell her, still sobbing. "I, I don't think we're friends anymore."

The frightened concern on her face instantly turns into a grimace, and she laughs. "That's ridiculous." She pops my arm. "I'd bet money you two are talking again before you know it." Her face stills with confusion. "Wait. What happened between you two?"

"Matthew told me he wanted to be more than friends. He was hurt when I told him I didn't feel the same."

"Oh, I'm sure he'll get over the initial rejection. You know it had to hurt. Give him a few days. The guy's not going to give up your friendship over this. Trust me, he needs time to lick his wounds."

163

"You really think so?" I grab her wrist, and my glare warns her. "And don't just say that to make me feel better either."

"I'm not just saying that."

From her tone and the sincerity in her eyes, I believe her. A long, relieved sigh escapes. "I hope you're right."

"So, you really don't feel the same? Like there's maybe just a little something there?"

I shake my head slowly. "No."

"Have you thought or wondered what it would be like to kiss him?"

I scowl at the notion. "Ew, no. He's like a brother. That would be gross."

Stacy shrugs like she doesn't know what to say. "Then I guess it is one-sided."

"How could I miss that?" I fling my hand. "How could I *not* see he liked me more than a friend?"

"The signs were there. I tried to tell you."

"Well, *I* didn't see them."

"Because you weren't looking, but they were there." She slips off her stilettos. "How's your dad?"

"Good. He's going back to work Monday."

"Back to life, eh?"

"Guess so."

"I need to shower and change. Dillon wants to go out to eat." Stacy gets to her feet and points her stiletto at me. "I can tell him we need some girl time if you need me to stay home."

"No, I'm fine."

"Are you sure?"

"Yeah, I'm so tired, I'm numb."

"Okay, then." She strolls to the doorway. "I'll check on you later."

After she leaves, I sit up and reach for my phone to send a text to Brad.

Hey, I wanted to let you know I'm home.

His reply pops up. *Glad to hear that. Meet me in an hour. I promise, you won't be disappointed.*

What do you have in mind?

It's a surprise. I can't tell you. I have to show you.

Brad has me curious enough to take him up on his offer. Even though I'm tired, it would distract me from what happened with Matthew.

Where do you want to meet?
At the Mountain Deli where we ate. I'll be in my truck waiting for you.
Now he's got me more than curious and eager to meet him.
See you in an hour.

~ ~ ~

Brad arrives first. After parking next to him, I exit my car. He meets me and has a new haircut and a fresh-shaven face. He's just the distraction I needed.

"Nice smile," he sings.

I almost cover it out of instinct but tell myself to accept the compliment. "Thank you. You have me curious. What's the surprise?"

"It's not here. I have to take you there."

"How far is this surprise?"

"About ten minutes, and we need to hurry."

"What about my car?"

"We'll be back within the hour, so it'll be fine here."

After getting into his truck, Brad pulls away from the sandwich shop. I can't even guess where he's taking me. We head down I-26. The sky glows with red and orange. It's going to be dark soon.

"Do I get a hint where we're going?"

"Let's see. A hint." Brad has his attention on the road while massaging his jaw. "We're going to a house Dad and I are working on."

That doesn't help me at all. If Brad is going to show me how he installed the electrical work, I'm going to be bored, not wowed. What do I know about wiring?

Brad gets off at the next exit. In no time, we're on a curvy road. My ears pop as we head up the mountain. The winding curves become so sharp we have to travel at a cruising pace. The trees are so close, it's like a path etched into the woods just enough for the road. There's no shoulder. If I stick my hand out the window, I could probably grab branches in passing.

"I bet it's spooky at night on these roads."

"Oh, it is. We had a late night last week, and it was pitch black coming down the mountain."

The thicker it becomes, and the more the two-lane road

165

narrows, and it's creepy. Like the road is taking us into the center of the mountain.

"Almost there."

Brad turns onto a one-lane road. It's so narrow, I draw in as branches tap the truck. It's like we've left civilization. I side-eye Brad, a bit concerned and having horrible thoughts. Enough to send my heart to my stomach. I have no idea where he's taking me, and neither does Stacy. Only that I met Brad at the sandwich shop. What if he brought me out here for a bad surprise? I swallow the lump in my throat and place my hand on the door just in case I need to run. "How much longer?"

"We're here."

It's like we came out of a dark tunnel and back into civilization. The road is a driveway and opens up to a clearing, and we're in someone's front yard. I roll my eyes. How stupid of me to think Brad brought me out here to, well, I can't go there.

"This is it." Brad parks in front of the house under construction. If you want to call it a house. It's only a concrete slab, a frame, and a roof.

"What did you want to show me?"

"It's in the backyard. Let's hurry."

We get out at the same time and meet in front of his truck.

"We don't have a lot of time. Ready to see something amazing?"

I nod, eager. "Yeah. You have me curious."

We walk fast toward the house.

"I'll go in first, for safety reasons."

I follow him up the steps. Brad leads the way through the skeleton of a house and points out this and that and explains the process of wiring a house. He's so smart. And distractingly handsome. What did he say about receptacles?

We exit the house and stand in the backyard with a view of the mountains, and it's absolutely gorgeous. The sun is setting behind them, and the sky reflects a red and orange I've never seen before. In awe and mesmerized, I can't pull my eyes away. Although I've seen a sunset before, this is the first one I watch light up the sky on fire while melting behind the snow-capped mountains.

Brad nudges my arm. "Nice view, eh?"

Staring at it, I mumble, "It's absolutely beautiful."

"Thought you might like it."

"It's breathtaking."

Within minutes, the sun melts behind the mountaintop right before my eyes. It's gone.

"We need to head back. It's going to get *really dark*," he tells me in a fretful tone.

Brad leads me through the house without stopping this time and then we run to his truck. The urgency is there, and I wonder why. What's the big deal about heading back in the dark? Although he's cute when he's nervous.

I pull the buckle over my shoulder and snap it. "That was really nice."

He buckles up and starts the truck. "Glad you liked it."

We head down the curvy mountain roads, and it's like darkness came faster than flipping a switch. Now I get the urgency. Brad wasn't kidding when he said it would get dark. A kind of darkness I've never seen before. The headlights are like flashlights and barely show us the way. I'm ready to get out of here. This road seems longer than when we came here. My anxiety rises at the creepiness.

Once we hit the interstate, my tense body unwinds like getting off the fastest roller coaster after a thrilling ride. "I don't know if I could handle that road at night by myself. That was spooky."

"That's why I wanted to get us out of there. I'm not fond of those kinds of roads either. Deer come out of nowhere, and there's no shoulder."

Within minutes, or so it seems, we're back at the sandwich shop. Brad pulls into the spot next to my car and puts his truck in park.

"That was really nice. Thanks."

"I have a good idea every once in a while." He rests his hand on the back of the bench seat and trails his fingers over my shoulder. "The night is still young." He takes a lock of my hair and twirls it. "Maybe I can come up with another good idea."

If he wants sex, he needs to twirl someone else's hair. The sunset was nice, but a booty call, if that's what this is, is the last thing on my mind after what happened with Matthew.

"Can I talk you into coming to my house? I promise no one will stop by this time."

"Brad, it's been a long day. I'm really tired and should go home."

"If you come to my house," he draws circles on my shoulder

and smiles, "I have a really nice sofa you could relax on, and we could listen to some music. I'll even give you a nice backrub."

There was a time when I would have killed for this moment, but something feels different. "It's a tempting offer, but I have to get up early. Maybe another time."

Brad exhales and removes his arm from the back of the seat. "Then I don't want to hold you up." From his blunt tone, he isn't happy.

We get out of the truck.

Brad meets me at my car. After he opens my door for me, we look at each other. I'm wondering if he'll kiss me, but he doesn't. A part of me is relieved he doesn't, but I'm not sure why. Something really is off. "Goodnight." I get into my car and insert the key. "Thanks again for the sunset."

"You're welcome." Brad shuts my door and heads back to his truck.

I start my car and leave. If he's mad at me, he'll have to get over it. I have enough to worry about.

~ ~ ~

After a bathroom break, I saunter back to the appliance department and glance down the aisles, looking for Matthew. He's here somewhere and clearly avoiding me, not passing my department on purpose. I miss him. His happy spirit. His goofiness.

Shannon comes out of the hardware aisle. Our eyes lock as we walk toward each other. The anger in me rises with each step I take. My hands curl into a fist. There is no one around, so I taunt her. "Well, well, well. If it isn't the biggest liar in Hendersonville."

"Shut up."

We stop and eye each other with a death stare.

"Are you and Matthew still dating?"

"Don't even start with me."

I gasp and place my hand over my chest. "Oh, I wouldn't *dream* of wasting my time on you." Before she can say anything, I leave her standing there. At my desk, it takes a moment to let the anger simmer. I shouldn't have even spoken to Shannon. How could someone lie like that? Surely she knew I'd find out.

"Could you tell me where the light bulbs are for ovens?"

I pull my eyes away from the monitor and smile at the

customer, an older lady all dressed up like she's going to church. She's slightly hunched over and holding a bulb and smiling. I love the older folks. They're always so nice. Well, most of them. And they're not always in a rush like everyone else.

"Yes. They're on aisle five mixed in with the other light bulbs. Just look for the ones that state they are for ovens."

"Oh." She frowns and straightens her back. "I walked the appliance aisle several times. No wonder I couldn't find them." She laughs at herself.

"I know it's confusing. You would think that's where they'd be. Would you like for me to show you where they are?"

She shakes her head and waves me off. "No, dear. I can manage now that I know where they are, but thank you." The energetic woman scurries away with her black, patent leather purse hanging from her crooked arm.

"Hi, Carlen." Janet is old enough to be my grandma. And as sweet as one too.

"Hey. I didn't know you were working today. I thought you had Saturdays off."

"I do." She readjusts her glasses. "Mark asked if I'd trade with him, so I'll be off Monday instead. I wanted to see how your father is doing."

"He's fine. Thanks for asking."

"Matthew said it was quite the scare."

Hearing his name is like having someone grip my heart and stop it from beating. "Yes, it was." As much as I try not to, I ask, "Is he working in the lumber department today?"

"No. He called in sick."

The handheld radio screeches. "Janet, what's your location?"

She holds the radio in front of her and responds. "Home décor. What cha need?"

"Come to customer service for me."

"On my way." She tucks the radio in her pocket and walks away. "See you later."

I can't answer, still in shock Matthew called in sick. He's not sick. He's avoiding me. I take out my phone to send him a message, but something tells me not to, so I don't.

Chapter 16: Peace

Gloria closes the door once we enter her office. I settle in the oversized chair and rest my arms on the sides. I don't know why, but it seems like forever since I've been here. Perhaps because so much has happened. There's not enough time in this session to talk about everything, so I have to be selective. However, there is one subject that is imperative I talk about.

Gloria presses the back of her skirt and sits in her chair in front of me. "So, tell me what's happened since we last talked." She smiles, waiting for me to begin the session.

"My dad had an accident, so I had to go to Charlotte." With time limited, and my important question looming, I give her the short version of what happened and explain that was the reason I had to cancel my last appointment. "He's fine, but it scared me."

"Oh goodness. I'm sure it did." Gloria reaches behind her and takes a legal pad from her desk. "How did you handle staying in the house? I know how you struggle with visits." She thumbs the end of her ink pen and scribbles.

"There wasn't much time to think about her with taking care of Dad and keeping busy."

"Does this mean you didn't hear your mother's voice?"

"Oh, I heard her. There was this one time I felt her in the kitchen. I told her she didn't scare me anymore. To get out of my head and leave me alone."

Gloria stops writing and looks at me with the widest eyes. "Carlen, I'm *so* proud of you."

Her enthusiasm makes me smile so big I'm probably blushing. "Thanks. I couldn't believe I said it."

"So, what happened?" She writes faster than I've ever seen.

"Well, nothing. She left me alone."

Gloria stops writing again, and her eyes meet mine. "You know she's only old messages playing in your head?"

I nod.

"Do you see how you have the power to stop them?"

"Maybe, it's just, things were different this time."

She tugs the end of her skirt over her knee. "Different? How?"

"I've always liked Patty, but I got to know her more personally this week. She's the neighbor who lives next door. We invited her over for lunch before I left. Matthew was there." That moment is now a sweet memory replaying in my head. "We talked. We laughed. We had a real family meal. I mean, not that we're family, but it felt like it. Other than me and Dad, that's never happened in that kitchen before. With them there, it seemed to wash away the bad memories."

Gloria smiles and listens intently, sporadically taking notes.

"With Patty there, she overshadowed Mom's presence. She um." I shrug, trying to find the right words. "I don't know, she added good vibes or something. I don't know how to describe it."

"I'm so glad to hear this. And the fact you accept Patty. That's progress, Carlen. You don't open up to women, but you seem to have connected with her."

I grin and sing, "I know. Shocking, isn't it?"

She nods. "It is. That's a big step for you. I'm curious. What was it about Patty?"

"A lot of things." I reflect over the past week. "When I was in the emergency room waiting for Dad to come back from having his CT scan, she was so nice to me. She didn't have cold eyes. I was so scared, but she really tried to comfort me. I've never had that before. Not to mention, she's so good to my dad."

One eyebrow rises while a curious grin grows. "Are they more than friends?"

I laugh. "You're not the only one who wants to know that answer. Even Matthew asked me. But Dad says they're only friends." I raise a finger and add, "However, if you saw them, you would think they were a couple."

"And you would be okay with that?"

"If Dad is happy, *absolutely*." I steal a glance at the clock. Time is getting away from me. If I'm going to ask my question, I better do it now. Nervous, my fingers tap the arms of the chair. My heart picks up speed. "Um, I need to ask you something."

"Carlen, you can ask me anything."

With the anxiety rising even more, I cross my legs and rock my foot. "While I was there, Dad and I talked about Mom's murder."

"I thought he was resistant to that."

"He is, but I told him I needed to talk about it." Is it me? It's suddenly hot in here. I run my sweaty palms across my thighs.

"How did that go?"

I shift in my chair. "Um, it went okay. But that night, I had a bad dream. Dad saw who killed Mom." It's wrong to lie to Gloria, but there's no other way to ask her. "It was Patty. Mom got into a fight with her for coming over and pulled a kitchen knife on her. Patty tried to take it away from her, but in the scuffle, Mom was stabbed. Dad told Patty he would come up with the story about the teenager breaking in."

Gloria's eyebrows perk up, and she shifts positions in her chair, giving me her full attention.

"I finally fell back to sleep, but then I had another nightmare. This time, it was Patty's husband who stabbed Mom. I know Dad doesn't know who did it, but I've never had nightmares like that before. But the worst one was, the cops found out Dad lied and arrested him." Now comes the question. I have to ask it in a way that doesn't cause suspicion or obligate Gloria to notify the police. "If Dad did see who did it, that means he lied to the police. He could be arrested for that, couldn't he? I mean, even if it was self-defense or maybe someone threatened to kill him too if he told the police."

"Carlen, I'm not the right person to answer that question. However, I would think if your father wasn't truthful with the facts at the time he was questioned, especially concealing the identity of the person, he would face charges."

It's the answer I feared and melt in the chair, trying not to react, because it wasn't a hypothetical question. Dad did see who did it. And he lied about it to the police. So, if I tell them what really happened, I might not be arrested, but he will be.

Paul Dupre, turn around and put your hands behind you. You're under arrest for obstructing a police investigation, tampering with a crime scene, and making false statements.

"Carlen, are you alright?"

I flinch when Gloria leans over and places her fingertips on my knee. No, I'm not, but I can't tell her why.

"Did you remember something?"

"No. Just still rattled at the nightmares." I bring my knees to my chest and curl up in the chair. "They were so real."

"Have you been journaling?"

"No." I exhale and command my body to simmer so Gloria's radar doesn't detect my troublesome heart. "With the accident, I haven't had a chance."

"Carlen, did something else happen while you were at your father's?"

Oh heck. Her radar is going off, and she knows something is up. Think quick Carlen. "Um, no. I was just thinking about everything that happened the past week. The way I told Mom to leave me alone, and she did, maybe I don't need those answers after all."

"But you were so determined you needed to know them."

"That need to know doesn't seem to be there anymore. I don't think I'd confront her if she walked through that door. It doesn't seem to matter anymore."

"Hmm." She eyes me with a perplexed gaze. "This visit really was different, wasn't it?"

Finding out I killed my mother? Uh, yeah. I laugh, not that it's funny and tell her, "You have *no* idea."

"Does this mean you're ready to come out of that cage you talk about?"

My laughter simmers at her question. But then I smile. "After the week I had, maybe."

Gloria studies me harder than she probably ever has. "You definitely seem like you're in a different place. I can't put my finger on it."

"Trust me. I am different. Did you ever think you'd hear me say I don't need those answers anymore?"

"I was hoping one day you might let go, but I didn't expect to see it happen overnight." She raises her finger and smiles. "Not that it's a bad thing."

"Tomorrow might be a different story, but right now, I don't care about those answers. I can move forward without them."

"Carlen." Gloria leans closer and crosses her arms on her thighs. "It looks like you're coming out of that cage, even if you don't realize it. You've taken that first step, and I want to encourage you to continue. You are ready for this."

This scares the heck out of me. Enough that I look away from Gloria. My heart is going full speed. Me, free? I thought that once.

"Did I say something to upset you?"

"No. I was remembering something."

"Can I ask what it is?"

I let myself go back in time. "When I was young, I would look out my bedroom window and stare for hours, but not at the birds, the trees, or the sky. I saw a world out there. Not like the one I lived in, but one without fear. A world where I wouldn't have to hide. It was a world where I could finally spread my wings and soar through the air. I would finally be free and happy. I just had to turn eighteen so I could get away from Mom and go live in that world."

"And now that you're in that world?"

I roll my eyes at the stupid fantasy. "You know how the story goes. It didn't turn out the way I thought it would. I left that house. I'm in that world that waited for me, but I'm not free. I'm still a prisoner."

"Only if you allow that. You can still be free."

I look at her. "Can I? I do feel different after what happened the past week, but can I truly be free from her? From that house? From the memories?"

Gloria doesn't hesitate with her answer. "Yes. You can."

"Then why doesn't it feel like it? Even if I don't need answers, I still feel stuck."

"That's because you grew up in fear and isolation. That's how you were conditioned as a child and all you know. That doesn't magically go away because you turned eighteen or left that house. You have to *un*condition that behavior. And it starts with coming out of that cage. Fear is often the root of panic attacks. That leads to isolation. The lack of motivation to change that can be why you're depressed."

"But I don't know how to be anything other than who I am."

"That doesn't mean you can't learn."

"It's frustrating to know the only thing I did was go from cowering in my bedroom to cowering in my apartment. I'm twenty-one years old and still look out my window at that world like I did when I was a little girl."

Gloria drops the legal pad on the floor, quickly eases to the edge of her seat, and crosses her arms over her knees. She squints with her eyes penetrating mine. "What are you afraid of, Carlen?"

Her deep tone causes me to cower. "I, I honestly don't know."

She eyes me harder. "I want you to look out my window."

I hug myself and do as she asks.

"What do you see in that world you're looking at?"

"Fear."

"Why?"

"I thought people would accept me, but I'm scared they see me the way Mom did and hate me."

"How come you don't see the people who accept you the way your father does?"

That's something I can't answer.

"Carlen, remember those pictures you brought home from your father's?"

I turn to her and nod.

"Picture that little girl with the broken arm. Tell me what she did that was so wrong that it was deserving of her mother to neglect her when she was hurt."

I see that little girl sitting on the couch, compliant, even though she was hurting. My eyes water, and I shrug, unable to name anything. "She didn't do anything wrong."

"No. She didn't. And what about that ten-year-old girl? What did she do wrong?"

I shrug again. "Nothing."

"I want you to put those pictures in a place you see on a regular basis, like your fridge or bathroom mirror." She picks her legal pad off the floor and sits back in her chair. "I want you to talk to that little girl every day. Tell her what she needs to hear."

I press my lips together to keep from crying, because that little girl is so sad. "This fear I have of people not loving me, does it have to do with Mom not loving me?"

She rests her arms on the sides of the chair and tilts her head. "Hmm, that's an interesting question. I'd like you to answer that."

"Guess I don't have to. If my own mother couldn't love me, no wonder I find it hard to believe someone else would."

She waves her finger and shakes her head. "But, that's not true. That's that faulty thinking. People do love you."

I raise an eyebrow. "My dad doesn't count."

"What about Stacy? She knows you and accepts you. And you have this friendship with Matthew."

The mention of him hurts so deep, my eyes mist over. I haven't had time to tell her we're not friends anymore. That will have to be another day. I can't talk about him right now.

"And you told me about this guy you met at work who took you out to the diner."

The thought of never seeing Brad again doesn't sting

nowhere near the loss of Matthew.

"We're so different. I don't see it working between us. He's a nice guy, but right now, my life is a mess. Maybe I'm not ready to be in a relationship."

"There's nothing wrong with taking time to work on yourself."

"Brad's not going to wait for me to do that."

"Be careful of that negative thinking, and don't assume what he will do."

"With everything that's happened the past week, I need life to stop for a minute and give me a break."

Gloria laughs. "Trust me, we all have days like that."

If only I could tell her my kind of day means remembering I murdered my mother. And I still need to decide if I'm going to turn myself in.

~ ~ ~

Stacy, all decked out in a tight dress, strides into the living room. "Are you sure you're going to be alright?" She stands in front of the couch, eyeing me like I'm some invalid. "I can tell Dillon you and me need a girl's night out."

I pause the movie and reach for popcorn in the bowl balanced on my stomach. "No. Go to the birthday party. You've been planning this night all week."

She huffs and places her hands on her hips. "And you've had one hell of a week. I feel bad leaving you here. And I know Matthew's not coming over since you guys aren't talking."

"I'll be fine. Go to the party."

Deep down, I want Stacy to stay. A girl's night with her is long overdue and much needed after my session with Gloria. My burden is heavy, and I don't know what to do. As much as I need my friend, it's selfish to ask her to give up this night. What would Dillon's parents think if she doesn't show up for his mother's birthday party? No, I won't deprive her of this evening.

I flick my hand and motion for her to leave. "Go. Have fun. We can have a girl's night tomorrow."

She studies me, squinting. "Carlen?"

"Stacy, if I really needed you to stay, I'd tell you."

"Are you sure you're going to be alright?"

"Am I in bed?" I shove popcorn in my mouth and raise my eyebrows. "Am I crying?"

"No, but—"

I point to the door. "Go."

She straightens her back, holds her head up high and sings, "If you say so." On her way to the door, she reaches for her purse and coat on the side table. "See you in the morning."

"Bye."

Once she's gone, I continue with the movie. My thoughts drift to Matthew, and I wonder if he's licked his wound, as Stacy put it, and would come over if I invited him. I fill my mouth with popcorn, tempted to send him a message. I have no problem making the first move and reach for my phone next to me. Halfway through my text, I stop. What if I'm wrong and he's still licking his wound?

The minutes pass. I have no clue what's happening with the movie, even though I'm watching it. Life is starting to weigh me down. If I don't get control, the depression will take over, and I can't have that. I need to hear his voice, so I pause the movie and swipe Dad's number.

"Carlen. Hey, sweetheart."

As always, his cheerful voice makes me smile. "Hey, Dad. Are you busy?"

"For my daughter? Never."

"I talked to Gloria about, you know, what I remembered."

His tone drops with concern. "Are you okay?"

No, I'm not and need him. Dad is the only good thing in my life, and I won't risk losing him. I know what I have to do.

"Dad, I've been struggling with doing the right thing."

"I know you have. I haven't mentioned that subject, because I figured you'd talk about it when you're ready."

"I'm ready to talk about it." Gloria has encouraged me to take control of my life, and that's what I am going to do. The guilt is sure to follow me for the rest of my life, but my head is clear and my heart is at peace. "Dad, it's not an easy decision." The guilt already attacks me, telling me what I'm doing is wrong. I fan my face and blink away the tears. They can come later, but for now, I will do this.

"Carlen?"

"Dad, I've been so torn over what to do. Should I go to the police and tell them what happened, or should I let the past rest?

I'm scared we'll go to jail if I go to the police, but if I don't, then I feel guilty."

"I'm so sorry you have this burden."

"My conscience tells me the right thing to do is go to the police. But if I do, they'll arrest you for lying about what happened. I don't care what happens to me, but I refuse to let you go to prison for protecting me." The visual of him being arrested plays in my head. I pound my thigh and cry out, "I can't lose you, Dad. It would break me. It would literally break me. More than carrying the guilt of not confessing would."

"Carlen, if you need to talk to the police, don't worry about me. I'll be fine. I'll deal with the consequences of my choices."

I fling my hand and squeal, "Don't you think it's time for this nightmare to end? For both of us."

"But, sweetheart." He's crying, no matter how much he's trying to hide it.

"Dad, if I go to the police it's going to be all over the news. It might even get national attention. If it does, the media will twist the story for ratings. The town will hate us and feel sorry for Mom, which I get. But she wasn't the victim." I have no idea where this burst of confidence or courage comes from, but I've never felt so strong inside. "You and I know it was self-defense, but no one will see that now. Maybe when it happened, but not now. No one will understand you did what you did to protect me."

He cries harder, and I hear the guilt he's carried.

"So, it's best just to let it go like you said. No good will come from it, only more heartache for us."

"It's just." Dad sobs harder than I've ever heard. "This has haunted me for so long, because I didn't know if I did the right thing. Then I worried you might remember and how you'd handle it."

"Okay, so, now I know, and I'm going to deal with it. Maybe the truth is going to free me."

"Are you sure this is what you want to do?"

"Yes. I need you, Dad. I can't let them arrest you for trying to protect me. After we hang up, let's never talk about that day again."

He sniffles but laughs. "Seems like I've heard that somewhere."

I laugh. "Me too."

"Carlen?"

"Yes?"

"How are you going to deal with this?"

"By finding peace with it. I didn't mean to hurt Mom, but she would've poured that boiling water on me. If I had been younger, I probably would have let her pour it on me." The sadness returns. For me. For Mom. For that sixteen-year-old girl. "I don't hate Mom. Never thought I'd say that, but I don't. And now I get why you don't and why you have that picture of her on the mantel. We can't change what happened, but isn't it time for us to be free?"

"Yes, it is."

"When we had lunch before I left, that kitchen was the way it's supposed to be. We laughed. We enjoyed it. You know it was never like that with Mom."

"Would you believe I was just about to say the same thing?"

"Were you also going to say how much Patty makes you smile?"

"No. I wasn't going to say that."

"But you know she does."

"I won't argue that."

My eyebrows rise. "Oh, so are you going to admit there's something between you two?"

"Not if you didn't approve."

I sit up, wide-eyed. "Dad, is that a yes? Are you and Patty more than friends?"

"It's not official, but we're talking about it."

I cover my mouth to keep from screaming. "Oh my gosh. Really? Dad, I'm *so* happy for you." I can't sit still and pace the living room. "This just makes my day."

"Well, I'm glad you approve. Speaking of Patty, she invited me over for supper, and I need to shower first."

"Then go shower," I tell him all hyper, doing a happy dance.

"Carlen?" His tone is suddenly concerned.

I stop my little dance. "Yeah?"

"Are you sure you're going to be alright? That you can handle, you know?"

With total confidence, I tell him, "Dad, I've never been so sure of something. I know I'm going to have some hard days, but I'll face them. You need to shower. We'll talk later, but not about that. Tell Patty I said 'Hey.'"

"I will. Bye, sweetie. Love you."

"Love you too."

It's the best phone call of my life. Dad finally admitted there's something between him and Patty. A decision was made. One that feels right in my heart. Now it's time for me to find that peace, and I think I know how to do that. After turning off the television, I head to my room.

Chapter 17: A Letter

Where are the words I had only minutes ago? Sitting on my bed, I tap the pencil against my cheek and try to remember. Just write. Maybe it will come to me. My pencil scribbles across my notebook.

Mom, I can't say these things to you, so I'm going to write them in this letter.

Me, write a letter to Mom? I think back to one of my sessions with Gloria. What was it I said? Something about—I'm not sad Mom's dead. Gloria told me one day I might see things differently. My perspective would be different or something like that. She was right.

When I look back on my life, I won't deny there were things you did for me, and for that, I thank you.

Never in a million years could I imagine thanking Mom for anything, but she'll get credit where it's due.

As for the things I cannot thank you for, I forgive you.

That causes my eyes to mist over. If only I could have seen the woman Dad did.

Don't mistake my tears for love.

Would it be wrong to love her after what she's done to me? Not that I do. But the hate seems to have dissipated. If she were here, I don't think I would even spew my anger at her. That desire is gone, and it feels so good.

My phone rings. I glance at it next to my leg. It's Brad. I stare at it, debating whether or not to answer. Something tugs at me, so I reach for it and answer. "Hey."

"Hello, Carlen. I haven't heard from you and wanted to see how you were doing."

"Okay. Trying to get back into my routine."

"Some friends of mine invited me to come over to watch the football game. I'd love for you to go with me. There'll be plenty of pizza, wings, and beer."

"That's nice of you to ask me, but I'm in the middle of

something right now."

"Can you take a break? I'll pick you up if that's something you're comfortable with," he offers in a tempting, sweet voice.

"Me, with your guy friends?"

"Their girlfriends are going to be there too."

"But I don't know them."

"Come with me, and you can get to know them. They were the ones who told me to invite you. What's stopping you?"

I doodle at the top of my notebook. "Brad, that's just..." Haven't we talked about this?

"Just what?"

"You know I have anxiety about people and places. Especially people I don't know."

"Well, I'm not a couch potato. I like to have fun. You would too if you'd give it a chance. Trust me, after a few beers, you'll be the one having all the fun."

Say it Carlen. For once in your life, speak up for yourself. If you don't want to go, don't. If he gets mad, have an 'oh-well' attitude. Come out of that cage and face life. I sit up straight, having a brave moment and tell him, "Right now, I have a lot of things going on in my life. Maybe it's best if I take some time and deal with them. If you don't want to give me that time, I'll understand."

He doesn't say anything.

"Brad? Are you still there?"

"Yeah, I'm here. And I understand. Been there myself. Go do what you need to, and call me when you're ready."

"Thank you. That means a lot."

"Carlen, I meant what I said. You're a nice girl. Take care."

"You too. Bye."

Whether I'll ever see Brad again or not, it seems to be the least of my worries. When the time is right, if he's not there, then that's how it goes.

Back to my letter.

Once I'm comfortable, my hand scribbles what's in my head.

Mom, I'm writing this letter to tell you I forgive you, and I'm asking the same from you, to forgive me. Until a few days ago, I didn't know it was me who hurt you.

Hurt? Carlen, you didn't hurt me, you killed me. There was no teenager who broke in. There was no robbery. It was you. You!

She's here and poking at my guilt. I close my eyes tight and try to ignore her.

It was you who put that knife in my heart.

I cover my ears and scream, "Stop it."

How does it feel to know your mother's blood is on your hands?

I press my palms harder against my ears, but it doesn't silence her voice.

Did you hear me? There was no robbery. It was you.

"I *know* it was me," I yell from the depths of my burdened soul, then burst into heartbreaking tears. "I didn't mean to."

Oh, Carlen, you know deep down you wanted to plunge that knife into my heart.

"No, Mom, I didn't," I babble, shaking my head. "I wasn't trying to stab you. My hand just…" I cover my mouth, not that it'll stop my crying. "I forgot the knife was in my hand when you came at me with that boiling water."

How dare you stab me and not confess. And you call me evil? If I am, then you are your mother's daughter.

Nothing she ever said hurt more than that.

"I'll *never* be like you. Never." I listen, but the only sound is my labored breathing and my chest heaving. Mom might be silent, but her words still echo in my head.

You are your mother's daughter.

"No I'm not," I scream and run out of my room, then through the living room. Without thought, I bolt out of my apartment and into the cold, dark evening. Once on the sidewalk, my feet pound the concrete, running as hard as I can. Running from what Mom said. I will not confess and let them arrest Dad. That doesn't make me evil.

Or does it?

She got into my head, and now I don't know what to do. With tears blurring my vision, I come to a stop. People walking along the sidewalk glance my way, at the woman standing under a tree, crying.

Matthew, I need you.

Shivering, I hug myself and scan the parking lot for his car. It's in the usual spot. He's home. Without hesitating, I run to his apartment building. Even though I'm out of breath, I march up the flight of stairs. "Please, Matthew. I need you." I knock on the door, then place my hand on my chest. My lungs burn from taking in the cold air so fast.

The front door opens. Matthew looks at me.

I bring my hands together at my chin and plead from the bottom of my heart, "Please help me. I don't know what to do."

"What happened?"

"It's, it's Mom. She, I was…"

"Let's go to your apartment so we can talk." Matthew pokes his head inside and yells, "Hey, sis. Going over to Carlen's." He closes the door, and we trek down the steps.

We stride along the sidewalk in silence. Even though it's a bit awkward, having Matthew by my side has doused the meltdown.

Once inside my apartment, I curl up on the couch with a blanket to warm up.

"You want me to make some coffee or hot chocolate?"

I mumble, "No."

"You know what? I have a better idea. Be right back."

Matthew heads to the kitchen. I huddle under the blanket, still shivering and my teeth chattering. With Matthew here, my anxiety lowers. My breathing is less labored. But I'm still a mess, mentally.

"Drink this." Matthew sits on the edge of the couch and offers me a glass with barely any liquid in it.

"Is that alcohol?"

"It is. I'm sure Stacy won't mind if you have some." He nudges the glass closer. "Drink it so it'll keep you calm."

"You know I don't drink. And I'm already calm."

Matthew eyes me, knowing me. "You won't be once you start talking about your mom."

He has a point, so I take the glass. After one swallow, I pull the drink away and cough. "That burns." I gag and offer him the glass. "Now I remember why I don't drink this stuff."

Matthew moves my hand back to me. "Drink all of it. Just because you're fine now don't mean you will be in a few minutes, so head it off."

He's right. Once I start talking about Mom, I'll be a mess again.

"Here goes." I hold my breath and finish the few swallows. It burns my throat. Then my chest. After it's down, I gag and almost throw it back up. "Holy cow. I feel like I swallowed fire." I set the glass on the coffee table, lean back and cover up with the blanket. "That's so gross."

Matthew sits next to me and leans back. We're almost arm-to-arm, but we don't look at each other. There's awkwardness, but my friend is here with me.

"You'll be glad you drank that in a minute."

"Yeah, I know," I mumble, already feeling the warmness course through me like vines running along a fence.

"So, what's going on?"

"My demons are attacking me."

"Memories?"

"It's not so much the memories. More like…" With Matthew, I can be honest, so the words come out easy. "This is going to sound crazy, but Mom lives in my head. I swear we have conversations."

"That doesn't sound crazy. You don't think I hear my dad's voice?"

"I figured you did."

"What did your mom say to upset you?"

Now that my insides are warm, I toss the blanket to the side. "I was trying to write her a letter. I thought it'd give me some closure. Of course, that's an invitation for her to pop up in my head. She had the nerve…to…tell…" That alcohol must be taking effect. My focus diminishes, slipping into a tranquil haze. One I could get used to.

"Tell you what?"

What was I talking about? Focus Carlen. Oh, Mom's letter. "So, I was telling her how I forgive her for not being a mother to me. I was nice and going to thank her for the things she did do for me." Boy, I feel good right now. What a buzz. My body might float away without me.

"And?" Matthew, a bit impatient, motions his hand in a circle. "I know you're probably feeling really good right now, but tell me what happened."

"Yep, I feel pret-ty gooood," I sing, enjoying my euphoric ride away from reality. Say something now, *Mother*.

Matthew nudges me. "Hey, back to earth."

"Where was I?"

"You said you forgave her."

"And I do," I sing again. "And then I asked her to forgive me."

"Forgive *you*? For what?"

I roll my eyes and tell him in a sassy, high-pitched tone, "Because I hurt her. Of course, she reminded me I didn't 'hurt' her. I stabbed her. And because I'm not going to run to the police and confess I was the one who killed her, Mom said that makes me evil like her."

Matthew slowly leans away with his eyes wide as can be. "You? *You're* the one who stabbed her?"

We stare, both in shock but for different reasons. My euphoric moment has been washed away with the realization I just spilled the beans. That's not the only thing about to spill. I cover my mouth. My stomach is on the spin cycle, threatening to eject its contents.

"Carlen, did you?"

Oh my gosh. How could I be so stupid and tell him? I close my eyes and bawl like a baby who had her favorite toy taken away. "Why did you give me that alcohol?"

"Hey, it's okay." Matthew takes my wrist and eases my hand away from my mouth.

"No. It's *not* okay. You shouldn't have given me that drink."

"Carlen." He raises his shoulders and squeals, "I thought it would keep you calm. You were so upset."

"You can't *know* that, Matthew." I leave the couch, cover my face and cry. "How can you look at me after knowing I'm the one who killed my mother?"

"Wow, how quick you forget."

I lower my hands and look at him. "What are you talking about?"

He jerks his head to move the hair from his eyes. "Remember the day I came home and Dad was in Michelle's room?"

"Yeah."

"I was going to kill him, Carlen. If Dad hadn't turned when he did and stopped me, I would have hit him with that trophy until he was dead. Why would I judge you for doing what I wanted to do?"

"But it's not the same. I didn't want to kill her, Matthew. How can I live with myself?"

Matthew leaves the couch and wraps his arms around me. "Because you're not like your mother."

The words I needed to hear without asking. I weep from relief and hold him tighter than I've ever held anyone in my life. "Please don't say anything. Ever." I rest my head on his shoulder. "If you do, Dad will go to prison for lying to the police. He only did it to protect me."

He rubs my back and presses his head against mine. "He's not going to prison. This stays here."

"Promise? You swear on Michelle's life?"

"Yes."

"Matthew." I break down in his arms. "I didn't mean to do it."

"What happened?"

"I'll tell you, but I need to sit down."

Matthew helps me to the couch. "I'm going to get you something to drink." His hand goes up. "Water. I promise."

I nod. "Okay."

When Matthew returns, I tell him what happened that day and how I remembered it when I was at Dad's.

"I need to finish that letter. Tomorrow, I have to do something with it." I gulp some water.

"Like what?"

I lower the glass and wipe the wetness. "Well, if the weather holds out, I have a place I want to take it."

"I don't go in until twelve. Want me to go with you?"

For the first time, I smile. "Thanks. That means a lot, but you don't have to."

Matthew takes my hand. "What if I want to?"

The alcohol couldn't give me this wonderful feeling that fills my heart. "Then I guess we need to get up early. Right now, I need to finish my letter."

After my letter is written, Matthew stays with me until Stacy comes home. I think I have my friend back.

~ ~ ~

Matthew weaves through the winding mountain road. "Are you okay?"

"For the most part."

"You haven't said much since we left the apartment."

"I want to get this over with."

"Do you think this will bring closure?"

"I think so. My letter says everything I need to say to her."

We pull into Jump Off Rock.

Matthew parks and kills the engine. "Do you need a minute?"

"No. That will only prolong it."

He reaches for my hand. I let him hold it.

He smiles to encourage me. "You can do this."

I squeeze his hand and nod. "It's just, scary for some reason."

"I'm always here for you, Carlen."

"I know you are." Before this gets any more emotional than it is, I nod to the overlook. "Ready?"

"Whenever you are."

We exit the car and walk the path to the overlook. A couple sits on the bench, sipping coffee.

"It's cold."

Matthew laughs and nudges my arm. "Said the woman who isn't cold-natured."

"Hey, it got down to eighteen degrees last night. That's cold."

"True."

At the overlook, Matthew leans on the rail. "Nice view."

"It sure is. Each time I come here I appreciate it more. The mountains are beautiful. You can see for miles and miles." I take in the crisp morning air. "Life is weird, you know."

"How so?"

"All summer, these mountains are full of green leaves. Then they die at the end of summer, but that's when they shine their brightest. When they die."

"I don't understand."

"Everyone wears black to a funeral. It represents death. But here, death is colorful. People drive for hours to see the fall colors. I know the leaves are gone, but I know what it looks like when they shine. So, for me, death here is a beautiful thing."

"I've never thought of it like that."

"That's why I wanted to read the letter here. I'm not really into nature, but I fell in love with these mountains. It's freezing, so I'm going to make this fast." I reach into my coat pocket for my letter.

"I'll give you some privacy."

"No." I grab Matthew's hand to stop him from leaving. "Please stay. I need you here."

"If you're sure."

I pull him back to the railing and unfold my letter. "Do you mind if I read it out loud?"

"Not if you don't."

"Sounds silly, but it feels like I'm reading it to her if I do." After taking a deep breath and forcing my emotions down, I begin. "Mom, I can't say these things to you, so I'm going to write them in this letter. With an honest heart, nothing I say will come from hate. I'm finally at a place where I don't feel that anymore, but I hate what you did. When I look back on my life, I won't deny there were things you did for me, and for that, I thank you. You made a birthday cake for me every year and gave me a gift. It would have been nice to have had a party like other kids, but you did celebrate my birthdays. You let me get my ears pierced when I asked. And you let me paint my room blue when I was fourteen. You fed me, washed my clothes, and bought me what I needed. I just wish you would have loved me."

My eyes water, so I pause, refusing to cry.

Matthew places his hand on my back.

"As for the things I cannot thank you for, I forgive you. That's the only way for me to find peace. There has to be a reason why you treated me the way you did. Why you always looked at me with hate and spoke to me with bitterness. Whatever happened to you, I'm truly sorry, but as my mother, you should've broken the cycle. It stops with me, because I'm going to make sure my kids know I love them."

I flip the letter over, catch my breath and continue.

"Don't mistake my tears for love. It's for the loss of a mother I never had. For the things we never did. The things you didn't teach me. A bond that never was. I needed you, Mom, and I'm not ashamed or embarrassed to admit it. So many times, I've wished for the chance to confront you and ask why you treated me the way you did. Guess what, Mom? I don't need the answers anymore."

I stop, remembering Gloria asking me to say those exact words and making me write it one hundred times for homework.

"Mom, I'm writing this letter to tell you I forgive you, and I'm asking the same from you, to forgive me. Until a few days ago, I didn't know it was me who hurt you. I have to believe you understand why I can't go to the police. Dad protected me that day, and now it's my turn to protect him. I'll carry the burden for what I've done, but I also forgive myself. You gave me no choice. You cornered me and was going to pour a pot of boiling water over me. I never thought I would say this, but I love you, Mom. I hope you're at peace, wherever you are. And it's time for me to have peace. This is goodbye. You can't live in my head anymore."

I hold the letter over the railing but don't release it. Part of this process is accepting when I let go of the letter, I also have to let go of the past. And I agree to come out of that cage. It won't be easy, but I'm ready to take those steps.

This is it. I hold my breath and let the letter slip away. I've never mourned the loss of my mother until this moment. I've never shed a tear for her until right now. I can love her, because I'm not like her.

The letter floats aimlessly without any direction. In no time, it's so far away, it's gone.

I cover my mouth with both hands and cry.

"Carlen."

"I'm okay. It's the first time I've ever cried for her."

Matthew wraps his arms around me. "If you didn't have a heart, you wouldn't have tears."

"You always know what to say." I hold him tight and rest my head against him. "Thank you for bringing me here."

"That's what friends are for."

Still holding him, my eyes close while saying one last goodbye before we leave. *Mom, I really am sorry. Forgive me. I do love you, even though you couldn't love me.* I lean back and look at Matthew, taking in a deep breath. "Are you ready to go? Breakfast is on me."

Matthew eyes me but doesn't say anything.

"What's wrong?"

"This might not be the best time to bring up the subject, but this seems like the best place."

"What subject?"

Matthew releases me and looks over the mountains.

"Please tell me what's wrong."

"You know how I feel about you. I have to ask." He looks at me. "How do you feel about me?"

"Matthew, you're my best friend in the world."

He rolls his eyes and walks away.

"No, wait." I grab the sleeve of his coat and pull him back to me. "You didn't let me finish."

"Maybe I don't want to hear I'm just a friend," he tells me with hurt already in his eyes.

"Maybe I wasn't going to say that."

"Okay, finish what you were going to say."

It's not easy, because I'm scared for so many reasons. My heart skips a few beats. Especially staring into his eyes. "Matthew, you are my best friend. Are my feelings the same as yours? I don't know. But what I do know is, I need you in my life. Will you give it time to see what happens?"

He jerks his head to shift his bangs. "What about Brad?"

"Brad is a nice guy, but he's not my best friend. I can't share things with him like I do with you. He's not the one I call when I need someone. He's not the one I want to sit on the couch with and watch movies as mundane as that is. He's not the one I'm comfortable with. He's not the one I miss when I'm alone. Right now, my plate is full. And I'm confused. I'm not making any promises, but will you be patient with me? Give me some time to see what happens?"

There's no expression on his face. Then he smiles. "For you? I'll be patient."

The weight of the world just fell off my shoulders. I can finally breathe and offer him my hand. "Care to walk a girl to your car?"

Matthew takes my hand. "Anything for my best friend."

"I like the sound of that."

Matthew exhales. "Got a question for you."

I look at him as we walk. "What?"

He looks at me. "Will you help me write a letter to my dad?"

"Anything for my best friend."

Hand in hand, we stroll along the walkway. I'm ready to come out of that cage. There's a world out there waiting for me.

The End

Five Years Later

Thank you for reading Carlen's story. As a new author, it would mean a lot if you could take a few minutes and leave a review on Amazon. Reviews are what promote a book.

If you would like to contact the author, she welcomes comments at janecool777@gmail.com. Or, you can look her up on Facebook.

Also, check out Grace E Summer's other books. If you like mystery, romance, and drama, I'm sure you won't be disappointed.

Printed in Dunstable, United Kingdom